Book One of The Order: Vitruvian Man (2nd Edition)

Copyright © 2019 by Brad A. Townsend

ISBN# 978-1-7324574-6-1

Content Notice: This story contains adult situations, language, and consensual sex between adult men.

Cover Design by Brad Townsend

Original Image used for cover licensed from iStock

Edited and Formatted by Brad Townsend

The Order: Vitruvian Man

Ten men, five couples, best friends and brothers in arms.

Genetically modified by Dr. Aaron Thomas, they became the most successful SEAL team the US Government ever had. Forced to fake their own deaths in 1992, the men have lived new lives for over eighteen years.

Ken, their Captain, on the day he discovers a new ability related to his genetic enhancements, is kidnapped. The events of his disappearance and captivity spark additional changes in Ken, his partner Brad, and other members of the team. In the midst of trying to rescue Ken, they begin to discover a deeper meaning to their existence and what Dr. Thomas really did to them back in 1992.

This story is the first Chronicle of their epic journey, of the trials and tribulations they face as they start to awaken and unlock something within them that can never be extinguished. They quickly find that only the love between them as men, partners, and brothers will allow them to survive and face a darkness they never knew existed.

Author's Note/Introduction

First off, if you are reading this either as a preview or if you purchased the book – Thank you!

You might notice this is a 2nd Edition of the book. I re-wrote the series to make some changes, which in my opinion will make it better. The Order is my first foray into writing and was originally a creative outlet I never intended to publish. The story evolved over time into something much longer and far more complex than my original idea. In fact, the original concept was a five-page short story. That's a far cry from six books!

When I started The Order, I posted it on a free gay website in a serialized fashion. Each 'Chapter' was an installment, or mini-story, unto itself that fit into the larger, overall plot, and the web version ended up being 30 Chapters. It was too challenging to reformat it, so each eBook has five chapters and there are six books. **Vitruvian Man** is the shortest book in the series, and each book gets progressively longer. The chapters are lengthy but have plenty of breaks to keep them flowing. I don't apologize for that – it took me nearly five years to complete the rough draft, which was just shy of a million words, and I didn't want to spend another year reformatting it.

Another reason for the new edition is my learning curve as an independent and self-published author. To be blunt, I pretty much did everything wrong the first time around. I still have a lot to learn, but this time I'm taking it slower, and hopefully the story is better and will reach more readers.

There are a few points worth noting before you proceed. **Vitruvian Man** is the only book in the series that can be considered standalone. The end is definitely open, but it is not a cliffhanger. If you enjoy the characters and storyline, you can continue the series, but the remaining five books are one long story broken up into five books. Also, without giving anything away, the story evolves drastically as it progresses. The further in you get, the more spiritual and religious the story becomes. The religious elements are a mix of my own worldview, pulling from several religions, including Christianity, with a good bit of Norse Mythology and mysticism. Ultimately, it is a fantasy novel, and nothing in the story is meant to be offensive or taken literally. My intent is to present an entertaining story that will make you laugh, cry, and enjoy the characters and their relationships through their journey.

The Order is a labor of love, and I genuinely believe in it. I hope you find it enjoyable enough to continue and read all six books. My email is at the end of each book, so feel free to contact me with any questions or comments. My biggest wish is that you would leave a review, which helps me more than anything, or suggest it to a friend. Independent authors live and die by reviews – they are our lifeblood!

One last thing; the entire story was inspired by a song, *The Humbling River*, by Puscifer. I would highly recommend you listen to it after you finish the book.

So, without any further ramblings, please continue and enjoy the first book of **The Order: Vitruvian Man (2nd Edition)**.

Brad

Chapter One – Prologue

Syria - 1992

So, it's finally come down 'ta this. The doc said it would, but I hoped he was wrong.

With a heavy sigh, Captain Bruce Dutcher continued his thought: *Hell, who am I kiddin,' he's never wrong. At least I don't have 'ta face it alone. I don't think I could do this without Alan.*

Bruce glanced back at his team, his best friends and brothers who waited on the helicopter. Pride washed over him as he looked at them, and pain at what they were about to go through. It was a shame events came to where they were, forcing them to give up their lives and disappear.

Ruefully shaking his head, he thought: *The price of bein' too successful.*

Bruce began preparing his team for this inevitability months ago, but now that the moment was upon them, the men felt apprehensive about what path their lives would take and how they would live. However, they were soldiers, Navy

SEALS, the best in the world, and would survive. Each of them had the utmost confidence in the doctor, but starting new lives away from the military and everything they knew was... well, daunting, to say the least. At least none of them had any family to grieve when the world thought them dead.

Bruce pushed aside his concerns to focus on the present; he needed to feel and appear confident to his men. They trusted him, and the doctor, and he knew they would follow him. Their loyalty ran deep, and he loved them for it.

Shouting over the noise of the rotors, Bruce said, "Doc, we're ready! Let's get this show on the road!"

Dr. Thomas knew Bruce could hear him despite the noise and in a normal tone of voice replied, "Very good, my boy. You all know what to do."

Bruce asked, "Doc, are you sure you'll be okay on your own!? I'd feel better if you came with me and Lt. Whetherson!"

Dr. Thomas grinned and said, "Rest assured, Bruce, I will be fine. I think the phrase you would use is, 'This is not my first rodeo.'"

The doctor's uncharacteristic grin was rare for him. He was a very positive man but rarely smiled. As Bruce and the others got closer to the doctor after working with him for a few years, they worried about him. Occasionally, when he let his guard down, a deep thread of sadness surfaced.

The doctor held up a small device, a trigger switch devised for that moment. Toggling the switch, the light turned on, and Bruce knew there was no turning back. Every bit of electronic information regarding each of them vanished with the flick of that button, and the doctor assured him hard-copy paper trails would soon follow. Bruce had no idea how the doctor could manage that, but he was sure it would happen. Oddly enough, Bruce felt relieved; there could be no more doubts and moving forward was the only option.

Bruce knew better than to argue, so he shook the doctor's hand and hollered, "See you in a few months, Sir!"

Turning and ducking his head, Bruce trotted back to the waiting helicopter. He hopped on board the Sikorsky MH-53 and gave the pilot a thumbs-up for takeoff. As large as the craft was, it still bounced slightly from his weight. Bruce would miss the helicopter; it had been modified and designated for their use and held many memories of the past few years of his life. It held a distinct smell to his enhanced olfactory perceptions; a mix of fuel, saltwater, used equipment, and even the musky scent of their sweat from years of running missions. It was oddly comforting, and he was sorry the craft would be another casualty in securing their safety.

Flipping on his Commlink, Bruce said, "Alright, ladies, this is it. Switch 'ta channel 5."

The contemplative looks staring back at him told him everyone had the same thoughts, and an unusual quiet fell among them. Typically, there would be laughter and shit-talking amidst their usual banter.

With everyone on the secure channel, encrypted by one of the doctor's devices, Bruce reviewed the plan one final time. As with any mission, each man had his role down pat and repeated it verbatim. If they were nervous, none of them showed it, and with the mission underway, he saw the same relief on their handsome faces; the fact that there was no turning back gave them a sense of freedom and direction. Jim's mischievous grin was back and he winked to let Bruce know everything was going to be alright. One of them patted his shoulder as he often did to them, expressing their comfort and support.

The wind picked up, and the flight grew bumpy. As the ten men headed out to sea the sky darkened and scattered lightning periodically lit up the thick clouds. Bruce wasn't sure why the thought occurred to him, but he realized stormy weather always seemed to accompany crucial times in their lives. He wasn't a superstitious man and let the thought go, but with his enhanced perceptions, he felt the thunder inside him and sensed there was more going on than he could comprehend.

Snapping back to the present, Bruce asked, "Keith, are you good to go on the pilot?"

Keith responded with a crisp, "Yes, sir, Cap."

In his Captain's voice, Bruce said, "Alright, everybody! Suit up!"

In pairs, the men helped their partners change into scuba gear. Alan had prepped his and Bruce's equipment and was changed and waiting for him. Alan couldn't help but admire Bruce's physique as he stripped off his flight suit. His body was perfect from head to toe, deeply tanned and heavily muscled. The genetic alterations induced in Bruce and the rest of the team transformed all of them into perfect physical specimens. On top of his body, Bruce always seemed so graceful and confident, like a statue in motion. He radiated a natural charisma, but at the same time he was one of the humblest men Alan had ever met. Ruggedly handsome, Bruce's physical traits along with his personality made him perfect to Alan.

After he joined the program, Bruce, along with James, Keith, Paul, and Don, became far stronger than ordinary men, with their bone and muscle density over four times that of a typical fit adult male. All of them weighed in excess of 400 lbs. and were solid muscle, however, entirely proportioned to their height along with a low body-fat ratio. They looked like Greek statues or bulked-up fitness models with their frames covered in thick, lean muscle.

The changes also encompassed augmented physical abilities, including agility, speed, dexterity, and balance, as well as enhanced senses. Alan, Gary, Jim, Dan, and Fred didn't have the increased muscle and bone density of their counterparts, but the doctor enhanced their minds in addition to their bodies, so they were smarter and more intuitive. They became empathic, allowing them to sense and induce emotional responses in ordinary humans. Between the mental and physical attributes of the men, they were the most formidable SEAL team that had ever existed, which is why they were also one of the most highly kept secrets in the US Government. Project Glass Hand was a name only a handful of government officials even heard of, off the books and above Top Secret.

The doctor designed each couple to be dependent on one another, one representing the body and one the mind, and whether it was the doctor or nature taking its course, the couples fell in love with one another shortly after meeting and training together. All of them were gay, which the doctor said was necessary from a genetic standpoint for optimal effectiveness of the procedure, but regardless, they formed intense emotional bonds and fell deeply in love with their partners after the initial changes.

Once everyone changed with their gear prepped and ready, Bruce gave the pilot a new set of coordinates for their drop, and then over the secure channel said, "Alright guys, let's execute this like any other mission. If anyone's got any questions or doubts, this is your last chance 'ta bring 'em up."

No one said a word, and he didn't expect them to.

The pilot flew below radar cover, and an hour later they hovered at the given coordinates. His voice came over the Commlink, "We're here, Captain. In the middle of nowhere, but this is the spot."

Bruce acknowledged, "Roger that," and then nodded to Keith, who moved forward as he pulled out a special syringe prepared by the doctor. Keith caught the unsuspecting pilot off guard when he reached around and pulled off the pilot's flight helmet and oxygen tube, putting him in a chokehold. The pilot panicked, especially from the sting of the needle that entered his neck, flailing his arms and legs as much as he could in the tight confines of the cockpit. Much stronger than the pilot, Keith easily held him until the serum took effect.

The pilot quickly calmed down, and Keith let him go. With a face void of emotion, he put the helicopter on autopilot and changed into a wetsuit Alan had prepped for him. While the pilot changed, Bruce went to the back of the aircraft and lowered the rear panel. The water below looked cold and dark, almost black, and he heard the crashing of the waves along with the thunder and lightning in the sky.

Turning his head back to the men, Bruce shouted, "Schrader! Shogren! You're up! Let's go!"

Bruce dropped the inflatable raft for the pilot to use once they got him down. The doctor said a nearby submarine would pick up the distress beacon, and Bruce had never known the doctor to be wrong, so he felt confident the pilot would be alright.

James and Dan pinched their noses, held their regulators, crossed their legs, and jumped. Bruce watched them splash down and saw James bob up first, giving a thumbs-up as soon as he cleared his mask.

Don and Jim were next, followed by Paul and Gary, and then Keith and Fred. While the others jumped, Alan made his way to the cockpit, connecting another of the doctor's devices to the navigation system of the helicopter. Flipping the switch, the light started flickering, letting Alan know it was transmitting data.

Alan moved back and shouted to Bruce, "It's plugged in and working! We have three minutes! Let's get him down!"

The pilot had drop training and knew what to do, even if he wasn't in control of himself mentally. The serum controlled his actions and prevented him from remembering anything that was currently happening. The pilot jumped, and Jim and Don got him safely onboard the inflated raft. Jim climbed in with him to double-check to make sure he was secure and wouldn't fall out unless the raft capsized.

Bruce and Alan looked at one another and smiled. They had come so far together, neither could imagine a life apart. Placing a hand on Bruce's solid shoulder, Alan squeezed firmly, putting the feelings running through him into the gesture. With his touch, Alan's emotions pushed into his lover, causing Bruce's breath to catch. Alan had the same response from Bruce's reaction.

Bruce chuckled and swiped his eyes, saying, "You fucker."

Alan said, "Well, Bruce, this is it. I'm glad it's you and me."

Bruce responded, "Me too, Alan. As long as we're together, we'll make it work."

Alan steeled himself against the dark, frigid waters he was about to plunge into. He envied Bruce's warmer body temperature but not his extra mass with the swim they were about to make. Even with the higher oxygen content in Bruce's body to help with buoyancy, it would be a long swim.

Bruce said, "On three… one… two…"

The little kid grin Bruce sometimes got appeared as he pushed Alan off the platform one count too soon. He heard the beginning of "You fuckkerrrrrrrrr!!!" before the wind ripped Alan's shout away even from Bruce's exceptional hearing.

Bruce chuckled to himself and jumped after his best friend and lover.

When Bruce surfaced and cleared his mask, the others had gathered and waited, hanging on the edge of the raft containing the unconscious pilot. A few seconds later, the helicopter moved and started to gain altitude. They watched until it was almost out of sight and then saw the ball of fire as it exploded, plummeting into the frigid depths of the Mediterranean.

Just as the ball of fire impacted the water, lightning ripped across the sky accompanied by heavy rain. Jim reached into the raft to activate the S.O.S. beacon, saying, "Sleep tight, fella. Hopefully, that submarine is close."

The raft drifted away, helped by a solid push from Keith and Don. The ten men formed a circle, arms out and around each other's shoulders while their sturdy legs kept them treading water.

Bruce looked at them and said, "Be careful, guys. We'll see each other back in the States in a few months. Stick 'ta the plan, and everythin'll be fine."

Grinning, right before he put his regulator back in his mouth, he said, "Remember, for a bunch of fuck-ups, you're still the best."

The rest of the men, including Alan, grinned back and flipped him off. With that gesture, they started swimming in pairs at slightly different angles, each heading towards the shore and leaving their old lives behind.

The doctor arranged for papers and money to get them out of Syria and back to the United States, and three months later the men arrived in pairs at predetermined rendezvous points. By the time they reached Atlanta, after taking a very scenic tour of the U.S. to ensure no one from the Government saw through their 'accident' and tried to trace them, the doctor had houses, vehicles, and new identities for them complete with background stories and family histories. He also acquired a facility for a new laboratory and had the building modified according to his needs. It was apparent he had been planning the changes for some time.

Sitting in the new lab, Bruce and Alan looked over their new identities. Bruce's name was now Ken Habersham, and Alan's was Brad Wilson.

The doctor had taken care of everything, and they started their new lives together.

Chapter One

18 Years Later – Atlanta, GA

Ken looked forward to getting home. After an intense workout at the lab with Bryan and Kevin, he could use a massage. With their new client, some up and coming rap singer, he expected a long night and wanted to get the kinks out of his back and shoulders before heading to work. Aside from the massage and alignment, Ken wanted to get home to his partner. He and Brad had been together nearly twenty years as best friends and lovers and were tighter than ever.

As Ken pulled into the garage and shut off the engine, Brad's car was already there, and his handsome face broke into a smile. He knew the massage would lead to great sex and put a lid on his libido. His training ingrained the necessity to stay in control and alert at all times, and the only time he let his guard down was when the house was in 'vault' mode, or if he was with the doctor at the lab.

Closing the garage door with the remote, Ken entered the house through the laundry room and went into the kitchen. The first things he saw were Brad's legs and the island covered with grocery bags. The top half of Brad's body remained hidden behind the open refrigerator door while he put everything away. Brad wore shorts and sandals, allowing Ken a good view of his sturdy, muscled legs.

Calling out his usual "Hey, B!" greeting, Ken entered the kitchen and hung his keys by the security panel.

Brad's typical "Hey, sissy!" response was slightly muffled with his head in the refrigerator. "What time do you need to head out tonight?"

Ken said, "Yeah, I don't have 'ta be downtown until 2100, so we have plenty 'a time. In fact, I think we need 'ta have a little fun before dinner. What'cha think?"

Brad's face broke into a smile, and he replied, "Like I just won the lotto! Give me a couple of minutes to finish here, and I'll head back. Is the garage secure?"

Ken nodded, "It is… I'm gonna' flip the switch if you have everythin' out of the car?"

"Yeah, I'm good. Go ahead."

Ken opened a small panel by the door, and immediately after entering his code the air pressure changed as seals activated throughout the house. He felt and heard the slight 'thunk' as titanium bolts went into every exterior door and window sill in the house. Even after eighteen years, Ken still never wholly relaxed until he heard that noise.

While Brad put groceries in the fridge, Ken moved behind him, wrapping his arms around his lover and resting his chin on Brad's shoulder, giving him a full-bodied hug. The warmth and strength of Ken's body, coupled with their stubbled cheeks rubbing together and his hot breath in Brad's ear, had the desired effect.

Brad relaxed into the embrace, inhaling deeply and taking in Ken's scent. Ken had worked out, and even though he didn't sweat much since the program unless he pushed himself, he still had a natural musky smell that Brad found intoxicating. Closing his eyes, Brad put his hands on Ken's forearms wrapped around his waist.

Chuckling, he asked, "You know what you just did to me, right? You fucker."

Grinning, Ken moved one hand down and cupped the front of Brad's shorts, whispering his reply in Brad's ear, "Yeah, I got an idea. Finish up quick."

Ken pulled back and put his hands on Brad's shoulders, giving him an affectionate squeeze and pat on the back. A quick peck on his cheek followed as Ken moved out from behind him, going through the den and down the hall to their bedroom.

When Ken came home, he often thought about how lucky he was to have Brad in his life. Not only was he an amazing man and head over heels in love with Ken, he was also a total stud and everything Ken ever dreamed about in a partner; stunningly handsome with a remarkable body and the soul of an angel.

Brad needed to be physically exceptional to be with Ken and worked hard to keep in shape, but the eye candy was still amazing and never got old. At 6' 2'', with golden blond hair and 245 lbs. of lean muscle, Brad was definitely a looker. Physically, everything about Brad turned Ken on, from his muscular physique to the hair patterns on his body, covered with a light dusting of the same blond hair on his head, and his eyes a crystal blue Ken frequently got lost in.

Beyond his looks, Brad was a remarkable man. He was fun to be around, although he tended to be the more serious of the two, kind, compassionate, good with group dynamics, and sensitive to the needs of people around him, often going out of his way to help others, even to his detriment and sometimes Ken's. Brad was wise for his years, although none of them knew exactly how old they were anymore. Ken wasn't sure if they stopped aging once the doctor changed them or if they just slowed down, but neither one of them looked or felt a day older than when they entered the program.

Ken was a looker, too. With no conceit or cockiness, he was aware of his looks. Dr. Thomas made him that way; he made all of them the way they were. The closest description he could think of was Steve Roger's transformation into Captain America. Ken and the other four men representing the body could bench press half a ton if they pushed themselves. There were other alterations besides strength, and according to Dr. Thomas the changes were ongoing, which is why Ken and the other guys continued working with him in secret. After faking their deaths and acquiring new identities, they were still together as friends and workmates, with Dr. Thomas as their mentor and surrogate father.

Ken thought Dr. Thomas somehow made them all fall in love with one another. With all of them gay, a fact the Navy wasn't aware of at the time, being in the military forced them to suppress their preferences for men, and their outward demeanors were extraordinarily rugged and hyper-masculine.

The Black Ops team they formed was the most successful the Navy had ever seen; ultimately too successful. It was unfair to compare them with ordinary men, even ones as highly trained as other Navy SEALS or Army Rangers… again not out of arrogance or cockiness. With their genetic enhancements, ordinary men, regardless of how much training and conditioning they had, couldn't compete.

There were serious ramifications to the program and the changes they underwent. The need for the partners was one, but with the bonds between them, none of the guys saw any of the reasons as a downside. Their pairings were for their safety and well-being, and the security and welfare of others.

The main reason was Ken, or the other four 'bodies,' could kill another man during sexual intercourse. The fact that he weighed 420 lbs. would be a shock, but he could keep his strength in check and not hurt another guy. The downside was in the case of fluid exchange during sex, as Ken's DNA would overwrite theirs, and without immediate and proper treatment, that person would die a quick and painful death. Part of the alterations in Brad and the partner's representing the mind were specific enzymes to prevent that from happening. In fact, their DNA was designed to be compatible with their partner's so it couldn't be overwritten. Brad and the other four 'minds' also received a temporary physical and metabolic boost from their partners after making out with them... nothing close to Ken's scale, and it only lasted a short time, but it allowed for hours of incredible, fun-filled sex.

Other changes in the 'bodies' included substantially augmented senses, which were one of the more challenging changes to adapt to; eyesight, hearing, smell, and touch the most prominent. The modifications in Brad and his group were mental more than physical, with their changes being increased intelligence, intuition, and empathy. There was no telepathy, which Ken jokingly gave the doc shit about. Dr. Thomas never denied the possibility, saying it was intentional and 'perhaps later.' Ken could never tell if he was serious or joking when he said that.

Ken's thoughts went through his mind as they occasionally did when he walked into the house and saw Brad. He realized how lucky he was to have such a remarkable man in his life, and memories of events that led up to that point in their lives together flashed quickly through his mind. He didn't think of them consciously much anymore, but they were always present in the back of his mind. Their past was a comfort he cherished, and their future something he very much looked forward to. He could no longer imagine his life without Brad in it.

Ken turned his thoughts back to the present as he put his gym bag in the closet. Going to the bathroom, he took a leak and washed his hands but nothing else. He grinned, knowing Brad would want to smell him as he was. Ken always got a kick out of that. Taking off his shoes and socks, he kept his underwear and t-shirt on knowing Brad would want to finish undressing him.

Finished with the groceries, Brad came down the hall and as soon as he walked into their bedroom, he was struck by the sight of Ken standing there, his dream man from head to toe. Everything about Ken, every minute detail, put Brad's libido into overdrive. Along with Ken's extraordinarily handsome face, every aspect of his features and body were desirable. Even more amazing to him, and incredibly humbling, was Ken felt the same way about him. They shared a connection, probably part of their pairing from the program, but it didn't matter. The important thing was he knew Ken felt the same way.

Unfortunately, Brad didn't have the control over his body Ken did and became instantly hard again, which was easy to spot in the shorts he had on.

Brad walked over, and without saying a word, lifted Ken's shirt up and over his head. He loved the motion of Ken's muscles as he raised his arms, watching his chest thicken when his arms came back down. The heat from Ken's body, along with his scent, was intoxicating. Removing his own shirt, Brad dropped it to the floor and closed the gap between them. Bringing his arms up, one around Ken's shoulders and behind his neck and the other around his waist, he pulled them into a tight hug.

With the house in 'vault' mode, Ken let his defenses down and desire loose. He put his arms around Brad the same way, pulling him tight, but instead of kissing they rested their chins in the crux between the other's neck and shoulder, relishing the touch of their bodies. Brad never tired of feeling Ken against him, and his hands started roaming. Ken brought one hand up between them, running it through Brad's chest hair and found a nipple, and chuckled at the resulting shudder. Their erections, hard but still contained, pushed against one another through their shorts.

Snaking a hand down, Brad popped Ken's ass, and Ken's knowing grin indicated he knew what it meant.

"Okay stud, before I get lost in this Calgon moment, I need to put the brakes on and take care of you."

Brad reluctantly pulled back, his arms falling to his sides. Ken's eyebrows rose at the mention of being taken care of. It was an old joke but always made them smile.

The eyebrows didn't go unnoticed, and Brad said, "You know what I mean, big guy. First, I get to rape your body with my hands, and then, when I have you at my mercy, I might decide to let you have a happy ending. If, and I mean, IF, you're a good boy. You know the drill. Take off your underwear, or better yet, let me take it off."

Brad pulled Ken's underwear down and let it fall to the floor, leaving Ken completely naked.

"Arms out, feet apart."

Ken knew the routine well, as they repeated it after every workout, and sometimes just for fun because it always led to great sex. Straightening his posture, he put his feet slightly wider than shoulder-width apart, and held his arms straight out at shoulder height. It was the Vitruvian Man pose the doctor taught them, saying it had a symbolic meaning. Oddly enough, even after years of working with him, he had yet to explain the significance.

Brad retrieved his tablet and calipers and started a thorough visual examination, measuring Ken's body fat and the size of each muscle group. Dr. Thomas was very meticulous about wanting everything recorded, accepting no excuses for lack of data. Brad ran his hands over every inch of Ken's body as if he were examining a thoroughbred horse, poking here and there and pressing on his abdomen and lower back.

On his knees, Brad glanced up with a grin and said, "I love my job. Have I ever told you that?"

Ken smirked and replied, "Only every time we do this."

Touching Ken, even though it was clinical, always excited Brad. Ken enjoyed it as well, evident by the state of his erection. Ken was never a hardcore jock before the program and wasn't used to being touched in such a manner, but after his transformation, it became a regular, almost daily activity.

He was no longer body-shy, but with his body, he didn't have to be. Of course, at the moment, he was letting himself go, but when Dr. Thomas performed the exam or one of Brad's counterparts, Ken didn't have any problem keeping himself in check. However, Brad's hands were the issue at the moment. Through his empathic ability, Brad's love and tender care for him were evident with every touch and squeeze, and that turned him on far more than the physical act of touching.

"You pushed yourself today, didn't you? In particular, your upper back and shoulders."

"Mmm-hmmm."

Brad chuckled as he asked, "Any particular reason? Trying to impress someone?"

With a grin, Ken replied, "Don't be a douche. I did it for your benefit 'ta see if you could figure it out without me spellin' it out for you."

"Well, the douche comment is going to cost you. Get in the chair."

Moving to the massage chair in the corner of their bedroom, Ken draped his body comfortably, placing his face in the hole and his chest and arms on the pads. Brad pulled out a bottle of special oil that the doctor provided and started the massage.

Over the next hour, while Brad worked on Ken's body, they talked as only best friends can, shooting the shit, cracking jokes, and hanging shit on one another. Sharing the same sense of humor, they could laugh at themselves or each other at the drop of a hat.

Ken's muscles were so dense, it took significant effort to attain the deep tissue movement the doctor required, so by the time Brad finished he was breathing hard and sweating.

"Okay, time to get on the bed."

Ken ignored him, acting like he fell asleep until he heard Brad rolling up a towel and knew his ass was about to get popped if he didn't move. He knew Brad was smiling, and with an exaggerated groan, he moved to their king-sized bed. Brad already had the comforter pulled down and the pillows set, and Ken crawled to the middle of the bed, wiggling his butt at Brad before maneuvering onto his back. Brad finished undressing, then climbed on top of Ken, straddling his stomach. The sight and touch of their naked bodies caused a quickening of their breath and a renewed desire in the pit of their stomachs.

Ken put his hands behind his head as Brad gazed down at the physical perfection of the man in his bed —his man, his best friend, and his lover. Brad always went a little off record at that point in the massage and confessed the changes to Dr. Thomas years ago, and the doctor assured him it would make no difference in the outcome of the record-keeping.

Looking down, Brad stared into Ken's piercing green eyes as he sensually continued the massage, starting with Ken's chest and slowly moving up to his neck and shoulders. Closing his eyes with a sigh, Ken, relaxed and put himself in the care of his lover.

Fuck his hands feel good.

Leaning over, Brad kissed Ken's forehead while running his fingers through Ken's hair. Ken still kept his hair short, and Brad loved running his fingers through it. He also loved touching Ken's strong, masculine face. Holding Ken's head gently but firmly, Brad kissed his way across Ken's forehead, down his nose, on each cheek, then moved to his neck and earlobes, moving slowly from side to side. While kissing him, Brad massaged Ken's temples and gently rubbed his thumbs over Ken's forehead. Ken became a little overwhelmed by the sensations Brad stirred in him, not only from the physical tenderness but emotionally from the love behind it. Brad's feelings bled through his touch, and Ken felt them as tangibly as his hands.

With everything Brad stirred in him, Ken teared up, thinking to himself, *"God, I love this man so much."*

After a few minutes Brad pulled back, saying, "Okay, stud, you've worn me out. I need a recharge, courtesy of Ken Jr."

Staring at one another and smiling through their eyes, they sighed in pleasure as Ken slipped into his lover, joining their bodies in the most intimate way two men could connect. Their hands roamed as their passion built, each loving the feel of the other. It wasn't just the touch of their muscled bodies; what they felt for each other went far more in-depth, augmenting the fires of their desire with the emotional intensity between them.

Ken was aware of the trembling in Brad's body and knew it wasn't only from passion. Brad always put more than one hundred percent of himself into the massages, and his arms were fatigued. It was part of his job as a trained physical technician to keep Ken's body in top shape, and much of Brad's own pleasure came from making Ken feel good while at the same time helping to maintain his body.

Everything about Brad turned Ken on, and with Brad on top of him, he had a perfect view of his muscular body. Ken caressed Brad appreciatively, almost worshiping him. Some of his touches were gentle, and others firm, gripping muscles and feeling the tightness of his lover's body.

After a few minutes, Ken's deep voice broke the silence as he said, "Hey B, let's flip over. It's time for me 'ta take care of you."

Sitting up, Ken put his arms around Brad's back, and Brad moved his legs around Ken's waist, locking his ankles together. Ken effortlessly flipped them, twisting in the air, so Brad landed on his back with Ken on top of him. Brad learned early on to brace himself for that maneuver because even though he was strong, Ken's weight could take his breath away if it caught him by surprise. As soon as they stopped bouncing, Ken lifted himself by his arms to ease his weight and focused entirely on his lover.

In the midst of making love, Brad moaned, "Oh God, Ken… if you only knew how you make me feel…"

Brad's comment sparked a memory in Ken. In recent months, he had thought about extending their physical connection, even mentioning his idea to Dr. Thomas. The doctor didn't say much but didn't try to talk him out of it either, so Ken went to the part of his mind where he controlled his physical abilities, visualizing their bodies merging, overlaying one over the other into a single body, holding the image and intent in his mind.

Brad immediately knew something had changed; he felt a brief sense of vertigo and began experiencing odd sensations. Ken realized something happened when a strange look crossed Brad's face, and he stopped moving. Scared he might have hurt his best friend, Ken took Brad's face in his hands, looking into his eyes for some type of reaction.

"B? Are you alright?"

Slightly disoriented, Brad answered, "Yeah... What did you do?"

"I was tryin' somethin' new.... When you said 'if you only knew how you make me feel'... I wanted to see if I could do that."

With a wry grin, Brad said, "Well, shit. How about a little warning next time, you bastard."

Embarrassed, Ken said, "Sorry, B, I didn't mean 'ta ruin the mood. It was a bad idea."

"Hell, no, I think it's awesome, and now I know what you were trying, what I felt makes sense. Try again."

"Are you sure? I'd never forgive myself if I hurt you."

Chuckling, Brad said, "You couldn't hurt me if you tried, Ken... apart from breaking my body in half without breaking a sweat."

"Okay, here goes nothin'..."

Grinning, Ken went back to the place in his mind and started slowly thrusting again. This time, with both of them aware of what was happening, it seemed to work. The connection was weak in the first few seconds, but rapidly increased; it seemed as if their bodies were made to be together.

Their lovemaking took on an intensity that caught them both by surprise, and their movements became more frantic, almost uncontrolled, and Ken had to hold himself back so he wouldn't hurt Brad. Brad always sweated more than Ken, but they were both drenched, and veins became visible across their bodies from their efforts.

With his arms around Ken's shoulders, Brad hugged him as tightly as he could, pressing their cheeks together and whispering in Ken's ear, "God, I love you, Ken... don't stop...." With their new connection, Brad felt his own breath in Ken's ear, and it turned him on even more.

The sensation of sharing each other's pleasure drove them both over the edge. It wasn't like each of them had his own orgasm; they shared the *same* orgasm. Their bodies, unable to withstand the pleasure, reached their climax simultaneously, and it seemed to go on for nearly a minute. Brad felt the heat of Ken's discharge inside him, and as soon as his body absorbed Ken's DNA, he felt invigorated as strength flooded into him.

Ken had never broken out in such a heavy sweat during sex, and the feel of his warm body coupled with his sweaty skin was a huge turn on to Brad. Holding tight to one another, they enjoyed the post-orgasmic euphoria, not wanting the feeling to end. The emotions in both men were more intense and gut-wrenching than ever before, and they didn't want to separate.

After a few minutes both of them said, "Shit, that was incredible."

Their shared comment brought a laugh as they hugged tighter, their bodies stuck together in the aftermath of their lovemaking. Once they stopped laughing, they lay still for a few moments, until Brad broke the silence when he quietly said, "I love you, Ken."

Ken didn't reply with words but rolled them over so Brad was on top, and started a kiss. They continued resting together, each lost in his thoughts, drifting and enjoying the after-sex intimacy.

Minutes later, Brad propped himself up on an elbow and said, "Hey, Ken, hold on tight for a sec. I want to try something."

Wrapping his arms and legs around Ken, Brad flipped them over, copying Ken's earlier maneuver, and the bed creaked loudly as they bounced to a stop.

Ken's eyes widened, and he looked at Brad, asking, "Fuck B, how'd you do that?"

"I'm rushed right now, and a lot stronger. It's never happened this fast or intensely before. I always feel charged up after you get off in me, but this time with that new trick it's almost overwhelming, but in a good way."

Brad re-engaged their lips, and after a long passionate kiss, he looked into Ken's eyes. Remaining still for nearly a minute, they stared at each other, and both of them teared up. That was when Brad noticed a strange gleam in Ken's eyes. Not a glow, but his eyes became lighter for a brief second, almost white, then returned to their usual green.

Ken, never one to let a serious situation go to waste, blurted out, "God, we're pansies. Who ordered the waterworks?"

Brad couldn't help but laugh and collapsed on Ken, holding and hugging him. After a few minutes Brad rolled on his side, and they repositioned themselves, facing one another so they could continue to look at each other. Both men had their heads propped up on one hand while their other hand roamed over the other's body, caressing and taking each other in. They were intimately familiar with each other, and long ago gave carte blanche permission to touch the other as they did.

Breaking the silence, Brad said, "You know, we need to talk to the doc about this, probably sooner than later. I might call him and head to the lab after you leave for work. Speaking of work, I need to get you some dinner before you go, so as much as I want to lay here and have endless repeat performances of this new ability, we need to get moving. Let's jump in the shower quick, and I'll get dinner started while you get ready."

"I don't know about endless repeat performances, but you're right. Damn, I'm hungry… In fact, I'm starvin'. That might 'a taken a bit out of me."

Brad sat up and pulled Ken up too, this time almost effortlessly with his increased strength.

With a concerned expression, Brad said, "Sit here and don't move."

He rarely used that tone of voice, so Ken didn't move.

"What, B? I'm fine! That was the most awesome sex we've ever had, and it just took a little more outta me than usual. It's all good."

Brad grabbed a medical bag from the closet, pulling out a blood pressure cuff and stethoscope, taking Ken's blood pressure and listening to his heart.

"Just humor me, and don't fuck around, alright? What we did is new, and there might be side effects. You should probably get one of the other guys to cover for you tonight and go with me to see the doc."

Pulling the stethoscope off he said, "Your vitals are okay, so if you're just hungry, it's probably fine. Let me check your blood sugar."

Ken's vital signs, unique to him, were normal, but the heavy sweating and his appetite, coupled with the brief lightening of his eye color, had Brad concerned. He didn't mention the eye change to Ken, not wanting to worry him.

"There's no way I'm callin' in sick. I'm already coverin' for Kev tonight, so I'll look like a douche if I do that."

"Well, you are a douche, so you need to come up with a better excuse."

Grinning, Ken said, "Okay, fucker, you're askin' for it."

Ken stood up quickly, catching Brad off guard and throwing him over his shoulder in a fireman's carry, walking him to the bathroom. Laughing, Brad called Ken a variety of names while being manhandled by his best friend and lover. Ken also took the opportunity to cop a feel while Brad's sculpted ass was over his shoulder and exposed.

They showered together, and although they each got hard, there wasn't enough time to fool around, so they dried off and Brad threw on some shorts and headed to the kitchen while Ken got ready for work.

A few minutes later, Ken came down the hall in his black dress slacks and shiny black shoes with no shirt, looking like a stripper halfway through his act. His skin shone with an ultra-healthy glow from the massage oil, and veins on his upper body were still visible, which always turned Brad on. Watching Ken come down the hallway. Brad wished they had time for another round of sex before Ken had to leave for work.

Ken saw Brad staring and with a smirk said, "Don't drool, B; it's unbecomin.' I thought you were a professional."

Laughing, Brad retorted, "Well, I was expecting a fully dressed, drop-dead gorgeous, hi-powered private security agent, not a Chippendale stripper. Sorry, my bad!"

"I didn't want to get any food on my shirt."

"Dig in; there's plenty. I warmed up the rice from last night since you said you were hungry and threw in another chicken breast."

Brad filled his plate but mostly wanted to sit and watch Ken eat. He loved how the muscles in Ken's jaw and temple flexed as he chewed and swallowed, especially after a massage when his skin glowed with health. Ken's muscles danced under his skin even with the smallest movements, and Brad never tired of simply watching his masculine beauty. Ken noticed him staring and stopped mid-chew.

With his mouth full, he tried to say, "Wha' the fuchh," and started laughing.

Brad looked down at his plate as a tide of emotions unexpectedly surged to the surface of his mind, overwhelming him and catching him off guard.

"I don't know, Ken. Fuck! I'm sorry..."

Squeezing his eyes shut, Brad fought back tears as his body trembled with the onset of the powerful emotions.

Seeing Brad's reaction, Ken rushed to his side and knelt beside Brad's chair, putting an arm around his shoulder in concern. Brad rarely lost control of himself, and it scared him.

"B, what's wrong? Talk 'ta me!"

It took a minute for Brad to get himself under control. Putting an arm around Ken, he rested his chin on Ken's shoulder, and the warm solidity coupled with the simple act of being held helped calm him. To Brad, there was no safer feeling in the world than in Ken's arms. Ken's hands gave him comfort, one rubbing the back of his head and neck, while the other soothingly ran up and down his back.

Once he got himself under control, he said, "Damn, I don't know why I'm crying. I was just sitting here looking at you, and these emotions just came up out of nowhere. It was overpowering and a bit jumbled. I'm already feeling better. Thanks, Ken, I didn't mean to go all 'big girl' on you."

Gripping Brad's shoulders, Ken looked into his eyes, seeking an answer to what just happened and brushing the remaining tears away with his thumbs.

"Alright, maybe it was stupid 'ta try. I shoulda' known somethin' like this might happen."

"Don't blame yourself, Ken; the doc all but said to try it."

"Yeah, but it's uncharted territory, and we know how that can lead to unforeseen consequences."

"I think it's just a temporary adjustment… I'm sure the doc can explain it better, but I think our nervous systems temporarily linked, and your hunger and this emotional thing with me are like little aftershocks."

"Oh God, you just sounded intelligent, now I know somethin's wrong."

Brad couldn't help but laugh.

"Fuck you. Alright, finish eating and go get dressed, or you're going to be late."

A few minutes later, while Brad put the plates in the dishwasher and cleaned up, Ken came down the hallway fully dressed.

As he pulled on his aviator sunglasses, Ken asked, "No jokes, how do I look?"

"Like a badass security agent. I pity the fool who wants to mess with your client with you on the job."

"Now that's what I wanted to hear. Why can't you be this supportive all the time?"

Laughing, Ken dodged the wet dish towel that came flying his way.

"Okay, B, I gotta hit the road. I'm not sure when I'll be home. The club our client wants to go to closes at 0400, and if she decides to stay, and then hit Waffle House or IHOP after, who knows how late, or early tomorrow, it could be."

"Alright."

Brad gave Ken a quick parting kiss and straightened his jacket more squarely on his shoulders.

He sniffed and said, "Damn, you smell great. Have a good night, and be careful. If the doc clears it, I want more of the best sex we've ever had tomorrow, so don't wear yourself out."

Ken flashed Brad his sexiest smile along with a double eyebrow raise in response to his comment.

Ken entered his code on the security panel, the air pressure changed, and Brad heard the familiar "thunk" of the door and window seals pulling back. Apparently, his strength wasn't the only thing augmented by Ken's new ability. As soon as the house was out of 'vault' mode, Brad noted the subtle shift in Ken's posture, exuding a serious demeanor with a 'don't fuck with me' attitude.

The kitchen door shut, and Brad was alone in the house.

He heard the garage door open and Ken's Explorer pull out of the driveway.

Brad texted a '711' code to the doctor, which meant 'it's urgent to call back but not life-threatening,' and his phone rang within seconds.

"Doc?"

"Yes, Bradford, what is it?"

Even after almost twenty years, the doctor still called the men by their formal names. It was another of his idiosyncrasies, like never using contractions when he spoke.

"Could we meet at the lab tonight? Something happened we need to discuss, and I think it should be sooner rather than later, if at all possible, sir."

"Of course, my boy, of course. If I leave now, I can be there in half an hour. If you do not mind, could I beg a favor?"

Brad grinned, knowing exactly what the doctor's 'favor' was.

"Yes, sir, of course. A Number Four Platter, add a chicken plank, extra fries, no slaw, and a large sweet tea?"

"You are a remarkable young man, Bradford!"

"It's no problem, sir."

With a smile Brad thought, not for the first time, that one of the reasons the doctor gave Brad and the mental partners perfect memories was to remember his food orders.

"Very good, Bradford. Please do not forget extra ketchup!"

"Never, sir."

Still smiling, Brad grabbed his keys and headed out.

Brad stopped to pick up the doctor's food on his way to the lab. They called it the lab, but it was actually an old healthcare facility the doctor had renovated to suit their needs. The front of the building contained a medical testing business that was inaccessible from their side, so once inside the building there was complete privacy.

No one knew how he pulled it off, but an immense sub-basement comprised most of the facility they called the lab. Their entrance was at the rear of the building via a secure, reinforced steel door. The lab even had a specialized full-sized gymnasium for Ken and the other physically enhanced team members, as well as rooms on the medical side for sleeping or emergencies in case someone got hurt. The doctor could perform full-blown surgery if necessary.

Brad walked in and set the doctor's food on the only open spot on his cluttered desk, then went to his own workstation to download Ken's exam data from his tablet. The lab was networked, but typically wasn't connected to the internet, as the doctor didn't trust some pre-pubescent genius hacker not to break in. There was a hijacked satellite link to several top-secret government computer systems, but the doctor didn't say much about that and only used it when necessary. Other than that, everyone had their own workstations, tablets, and smartphones. The doctor developed nearly all his own applications and databases for his research and was light years ahead of what even the US Military had at its disposal. During Brad's time in the Navy, he had seen some large, sophisticated systems, but nothing to match what the doctor put together.

It wasn't long before Brad heard the doctor come in and call out his name.

"Bradford!?"

Brad got up and went back to the doctor's office.

"Good evening, sir. Thanks for meeting me on such short notice."

"Not at all, Bradford, not at all. If you do not mind, I am famished so you can fill me in on what you wish to discuss while I eat."

The two men settled themselves, and Brad started the conversation.

"Well, sir, Ken told me you two discussed this at some point, and while you didn't encourage him to go through with it, he said you didn't prohibit the attempt either. After his post-workout exam today, which you know usually leads to some extra-curricular activities, something happened."

The edge of the doctor's mouth rose almost imperceptibly in a knowing smile at the reference to his and Ken's 'extra-curricular' activities.

"In the heat of the moment, I made a comment… 'I wish you could feel what you're doing to me.' I felt dizzy, and Ken immediately sensed my disorientation. He stopped whatever he tried, thinking he might have hurt me. When I asked him what he had done, he said he tried a new technique, wanting us to share our physical sensations. Once I knew what he attempted, I realized what I felt and told him to try again. Sir, it was the most fantastic sex either of us has ever had. After we finished, I noticed something odd, and there were a few side effects in both of us; Ken's in his body and emotional in me.

"Ken commented that whatever he did must have taken a lot out of him because he was ravenous, and I don't think he noticed how much he ate before leaving the house. I fixed enough dinner for at least five people, and Ken ate everything I didn't. He also sweated profusely during sex, which he rarely ever does. For myself, as you know, I gain some temporary benefits from intercourse with Ken, but this time it happened almost immediately, the effects were much stronger and longer-lasting, and included my senses. I also experienced a short but intense emotional rush that was disconcerting and extremely unsettling."

During Brad's debriefing the doctor didn't say a word, spending most of his time using his teeth to open packets of ketchup before digging into his fish and chicken.

"You mentioned something else, something odd. What was that?"

The doctor ate, listening with no hint of surprise or concern, which put Brad at ease. If the doctor didn't seem concerned, then he must have been expecting something along the lines of what Brad described.

"Well, sir, after we finished, I noticed Ken's eye color change briefly, turning a light shade of green, almost white. It wasn't a glow like in the movies or on TV, just a change in color."

"So, we can strike possession by a Goa'uld off our list?"

Brad looked at the doctor, stunned for a second. He had no idea the doctor was a Stargate SG-1 fan!

Brad held in a chuckle but couldn't help a brief smile at the doctor's joke. The doctor had a very dry sense of humor, and half the time no one got his jokes or didn't know if he was joking or serious.

"Um... Yes, sir, I believe we can."

"This is all very interesting, Bradford. Not unexpected, but interesting. It seems Kenneth has taken a huge step on his own and is unlocking another part of himself, inside both of you in fact, which you must learn to adapt to just as you dealt with the initial changes in the past. There is no need to be concerned, but there are precautions. The next time Kenneth can come in with you, I would like to have a discussion with you both. Until then, explore this new technique as you see fit, as long as it is under the protection of your home or here in the laboratory."

"Thank you, sir. It's a relief to know this isn't unexpected. What about the side effects on me? I'm still pretty charged up, and usually my benefits would have dissipated by now."

"In the future, after coupling with Kenneth and employing this ability, the benefits to you will strengthen even more and last longer. The negative side effects were most likely a one-time occurrence. Additional training might be necessary for you to cope with the changes. There is a reason for the increase in strength and duration in you as part of your pairing with Kenneth and your role in supporting him physically and emotionally. I will explain more when we sit down together. The only thing I ask is please do not mention this to the others just yet. They may not be ready for this step, and I do not wish to cause them undue alarm or anxiety."

"Of course, sir. I understand. I'll make sure Ken doesn't inadvertently spill the beans."

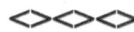

Pulling out of the driveway, Ken headed to the office where he and his buddies ran a private security firm. Initially, they all wanted to go their separate ways thinking it would be safer, but Dr. Thomas insisted they stay together, telling them as long as they maintained a low profile everything should be fine. The few members of the US

Government that ever knew their team existed thought them dead, and after eighteen years, most of them were likely retired or passed away.

The doctor worked some technological voodoo erasing all records of them, even pictures and paper files, making them virtually disappear, and none of the men had any family they were aware of, which was a requirement of the program as part of the selection process.

Calling the office to check in for the night's job, Ken pushed the phone button on the steering wheel of his Explorer and said, "Call Sally." A few seconds later the phone rang through the cabin speakers, and Sally picked up on the second ring.

"TGH Securities, how may I help you?"

"Hey, Sally, it's Ken. I'm headin' downtown now. Do I need 'ta stop by the office for anythin' before I head 'ta the hotel'?"

"Hi, Ken! I forgot you were filling in for Kevin tonight. How are you, honey?"

"I'm actually doin' pretty fuckin' fantastic."

"Well, we both know what that means. Is Brad home recovering?"

Laughing loudly, Ken said, "Yeah, I think I wore him out. We tried somethin' new, and it was over the top. Best. Sex. Ever."

"Well, it's nice to know someone's having a good time. I wish I could say that."

"Never fear, sweetie, your prince charmin's out there somewhere!"

"Well, tell him to get a move on! I'm tired of waiting. Don't you have any straight friends as good looking as you and Brad you could hook me up with?"

"Sorry, sugar."

"Story of my life. Oh well, back to tonight's job. There's no reason to come by unless you want to stop in and see me. I'll email you everything you need for tonight."

"As much as I'd love 'ta come by, I'm runnin' on a tight schedule, so I'd better not push it."

"I think the only thing tight about you right now are those fine black slacks I know you're wearing to cover that sweet tush. I'm getting flushed just thinking about that hot derrière of yours."

An image of Sally fanning her face popped in his head and Ken smiled to himself. All the guys loved Sally; she was a godsend and kept the company running while they were out in the field. She knew they were gay but flirted with them in fun. Ken's phone buzzed as he received her email.

"I know I've said this a thousand times Sally, but thanks for puttin' up with all our shit, and keepin' us straight... well, you know what I mean. I just got your email and should be set. I'll call if I need 'ta clarify anythin'."

"Alright, Ken. Take care of yourself tonight. I know the type of crowd you'll be in, and there just might be some stray hands trying to cop a feel. These types of events can turn violent when it gets late after everyone is either drunk or high."

"I will. Don't worry about me, hun. I'll check in tomorrow 'ta go over the billin' information."

"Alright, Ken. Have a good night."

Twenty minutes later, Ken pulled up at the valet parking of the downtown Atlanta Hilton. Checking in with security he got everything situated, and set his earpiece to monitor the hotel frequency.

His client that evening was a young up-and-coming rapper Ken had never heard of named Lil'B, who managed nearly overnight success. Ken was born in the 1960s and preferred music from the '70s and '80s. Rap and Hip Hop weren't a part of his generation, and he personally didn't care for those styles of music. He also didn't care for the culture of violence present where most rappers performed. Someone always managed to sneak a gun past hotel security, and once the drinking and drugs started, managed to get insulted and feel the need to demand respect at gunpoint.

While waiting for his client to arrive, Ken went to find a bathroom and check his appearance.

Looking in the mirror, he had to admit he looked intimidating. Black suit, white shirt, classic tie, and the aviator sunglasses topping it all off. He couldn't look more like a G-Man if he tried, which suited his purposes just fine.

Smelling his cologne, Brad's favorite, made him miss his partner. He wished Brad was on assignment with him, but the client designated only one security person for the night's job.

His client was an hour late, but Ken's duties didn't start until the limo pulled up to the front door, so he milled about the lobby and gift shop while he waited. While in the gift shop, on a whim, he bought a card for Brad to let him know how much he loved him. It was sappy and out of character for him, but for some reason he was missing Brad more than usual.

Once the limo arrived, Ken moved to the door and introduced himself to the driver, showing his ID. The limo driver opened the rear door and stood aside, letting Ken help the young woman out. Leaning over, Ken took her hand and introduced himself.

"Good evenin', Ma'am. My name's Ken Habersham, and I'll be your security escort this evenin'. Please try 'ta stay close to me at all times for your protection."

The young woman lowered her glasses to the end of her nose and looked Ken up and down, saying, "Mmmm mmmm mmmm dayumm, you are fine! I won't have any trouble stayin' close to that ass."

After working for many performers over the years, some quite famous, Ken saw through her bravado, reading her body language. The front she put on for her fans he found annoying, but underneath it all was a nice young lady Ken quickly took a liking to.

Her entourage was huge, and with so many people there was no way everyone could go clubbing, so the after-concert party stayed in the Hotel. With the number of people, the Event Manager ended up opening three additional suites adjacent to the main party, and the evening went smoothly until 0100 when a commotion in the hallway outside the main suite indicated trouble. He hoped hotel security could handle whatever was happening but was prepared to intervene. He would only have to deal with the problem if it came into the room and involved his client.

Chatter over his earpiece told Ken the situation was rapidly escalating, and just as he heard, "I'm gonna need some help....!" Someone in the hallway shouted, "Lil'B, get 'yo bitch ass out here!"

Ken leaned over and asked his client, "Ma'am, do you know that man yellin' out in the hallway?"

Her body language told Ken she was terrified even before she answered his question.

"He's my ex. Thinks he owns me and says I owe him money from my music."

"Okay, Ma'am. There's nothin' 'ta worry about. I'm gonna take care of this before he even gets close 'ta you. What's his name?"

"Musab. But if you want to piss him off, his real name is Tyrone."

Just then, the unconscious body of a hotel security guard flew into the room, hitting a large group of people and knocking them down. There was blood on the man's face, and drinks flew everywhere. Lil'B squealed loudly, scrambling up on the back of the big overstuffed chair she sat in. People started screaming, and a general panic ensued.

Ken watched Tyrone move into the room, along with a few friends. He was a big man, at least 6' 5" if not taller, reasonably muscular, and his friends were of a similar size. Planting himself squarely in front of Lil'B, Ken raised his deep voice to be heard over the commotion.

"I'm sorry, Sir, but you aren't steppin' any closer to my client. You need 'ta leave. Now. Consider this your only warnin'."

"Get outta my bizness! I'm here to get what I got comin' to me! Outta my face or…"

Ken wasn't sure if it was a knife or a gun Tyrone went for, but it didn't matter. Faster than anyone could see Ken's fist connected with Tyrone's solar plexus, forcing all the air in his lungs to vacate in the space of a few heartbeats and sending him flying across the room to land on his ass. The guys backing up Tyrone comically looked at each other and then leaped for Ken at the same time. They were quick, Ken gave them that, and moderately strong, but Ken... well, Ken was a genetically enhanced Navy SEAL, and there wasn't a man on the planet outside his unit that could stand up to him, even all three of Tyrone's friends together.

Two had knives, and one had a gun. Ken disarmed the one holding the gun first, shattering most, if not all, of the bones in the guy's hand while doing so. The two with knives were on him before the gun hit the floor. To them, it felt like hitting a brick wall. Ken smirked at the surprised looks on their faces before they lost consciousness. Unfortunately, one of them ripped the sleeve of Ken's jacket as he fell to the ground, and the other one grabbed his shirt, tearing it open and popping off most of the buttons. At least they didn't break his aviator glasses, which would have really pissed him off.

Immediately, Ken turned to Lil'B, asking, "Ma'am, are you alright?"

She was shaking, and her eyes looked like they were about to pop out of her head, but she managed to nod a quick 'yes.' Ken quickly checked the unconscious security guard, who seemed to have a broken nose and some missing teeth.

That's definitely gonna' hurt.

He was breathing though, and that was a good thing. Activating his mic, Ken said, "Hotel security this is Ken Habersham, the security agent workin' for the rapper in Suite 11B. You need 'ta get some people up here, pronto. There's been a fight, and there are four unconscious people; one of them is yours and in need of medical attention. There's one additional perp who's about 'ta be unconscious."

Tyrone still sat on the floor wheezing, trying to suck air back into his lungs. Pulling off his tie, Ken bound Tyrone's hands securely together, and once the big man got his breath back he started shouting again.

"What the fuck?! Let me up, or I'm gonna kick 'yo ass!"

A long string of F-bombs proceeded from his mouth, telling Ken exactly what he was going to do to him.

Ken glanced at Lil'B, who was still shaken but managed to say, "Now you see why I dumped his ass."

Smirking, Ken gave Tyrone a solid thump, knocking him out cold. Picking up Lil'B like a baby and shielding her with his body, Ken moved them out of the room. He held her against his chest, and when she put her arms around his neck, the heat and strength of his body made her feel safe. Her shaking subsided, and by the time they arrived at the elevators, she wanted to walk on her own. When she spoke, she seemed to have lost some of her attitude.

"Damn, Ken, that was some major *GI-Joe, Kung-Fu Panda* shit you pulled on Tyrone and his boyz. Thanks, white boy."

She leaned up and kissed his cheek, giving him a fiercely strong hug for such a little body. On the way down in the elevator, Ken instructed security to send her limo around, and by the time they made it to the front door of the hotel, her driver was waiting.

"Ma'am, I think you should call it a night. Tyrone might have a few other friends hangin' around."

"Thanks again, Ken. Sorry about your suit. At least they didn't break those cool-ass glasses."

Ken helped her into the limo and watched it drive off. As the limo pulled away, he noticed his reflection in the windows lining the front of the hotel. His suit was in tatters, one sleeve missing and his shirt ripped open. He realized people were staring, at first because of the torn clothing, but then to try and get a better look at his incredible body showing through. Ken was about to have the valet retrieve his Explorer and head home when he received a call over his earpiece.

"Mr. Habersham, this is hotel security. We need a statement about tonight's incident for insurance. The police are taking statements at the side entrance by the loading dock. Please make your way there as soon as you can."

"Alright, I'm on my way."

"Thank you, sir."

Ken knew he sounded irritated, but it was necessary. He was a consummate professional, but he *really* wanted to get home and crawl in bed with

Brad. The adrenaline from the fight was still in his system, and a good fight always made him horny.

Being familiar with the hotel, Ken knew where the loading dock was located and headed that way. It was late, and the side street dark. He thought it odd the police would use that entrance, but figured they probably wanted to keep the excitement out of the lobby.

As soon as Ken turned the corner, his combat instincts told him something was wrong. The loading dock was dark, and there were no police cars. His soldier's intuition screamed '*ambush!*' and even as he flattened himself against the wall to lessen his exposure, three sharp points of pain hit his body, one on his arm and two on his back. Looking down, he saw a large dart sticking out of his bicep.

He tried to move back around the corner of the building, but his body wasn't reacting fast enough, and he realized he was in trouble. His vision blurred, and he dropped to one knee, almost passing out. His mind growing fuzzier by the second, he was having trouble thinking and reacting.

A nearby voice said, "Shit, there was enough juice in those darts to drop an elephant, and he's still awake."

"Yeah, they said he was badass. This should finish him off so we can get him into the van."

Pain wracked Ken's body as multiple tasers hit him, and the last thing he heard was, "Damn, this guy weighs a fucking ton."

He heard his aviator glasses fall off and hit the pavement, and then blackness…

Chapter Two

Brad woke seconds before the alarm went off at 0600. He never slept well when Ken wasn't in bed with him, and that night was no exception.

Man, he's going to be in a bad mood when he gets home... He hates the all-nighters.

Crawling out of bed, Brad proceeded with his morning routine of running, working out, showering, and eating. He hoped Ken would be back by the time he finished, but when he opened the garage door, Ken's Explorer was still gone.

Brad started to worry after lunch when he still hadn't heard anything. Brad wasn't one to be a mother hen; he didn't like anyone treating him that way, and Ken was the same. However, Brad was pissed he hadn't even received a text. Brad called Ken a few times, but his phone went straight to voicemail. He didn't leave messages, figuring Ken would see the missed calls and get back to him.

Ken's silence was uncharacteristic, and Brad started to feel something was wrong. By 1300 he decided to call Kevin since Ken filled in for him on the schedule, thinking they might have talked. Kevin didn't pick up either, so Brad left him a voice message.

"Hey Kev, this is Brad. Have you heard from Ken? He's still not back from last night's job, and I haven't heard a word from him. Give me a call as soon as you can."

Brad lay by the pool to take his mind off worrying, listening to music on his iPod, but he couldn't relax and his anxiety worsened. After a while, he pulled out a net and started cleaning the pool as a distraction, even though it didn't need it. With his earbuds in, Brad didn't hear Kevin opening the gate.

<>

Just as Kevin opened the gate, a series of events ensued nearly simultaneously. Three sharp points of pain hit Brad, one on his arm and two on his back. His arm jerked up, and he dropped the pole as his back arched in pain, causing him to stumble and fall to one knee.

Brad looked up, attempting to get his bearings and identify safe cover when he saw Kevin running towards him. Kevin's mouth was moving but Brad couldn't hear him, and it dawned on him he no longer heard his iPod either. Blinding pain exploded through his body, and he convulsed as if hit by multiple Tasers, and then blackness…

Something was wrong. Brad's awareness was slowly returning, and his eyes were open but it was dark, and so quiet he could hear his heartbeat pounding in his chest. He tried to talk but couldn't move his mouth. He was breathing, so his autonomous systems were functioning, but somatic control was absent.

As Brad returned to full consciousness, an overpowering sense of disconnectedness hit him. Intense loneliness and isolation, unlike anything he ever experienced, permeated his mind. His enhanced intellect connected the dots, and he realized Ken was gone. He had never been so overtly aware of their connection until it was suddenly absent, leaving a gaping hole in him.

Pushing down panic, Brad assessed his situation. A sheet against his back and a pillow beneath his head told him he was in a bed. Air moved over the bare skin on his legs, arms, and chest, and he felt his swimming trunks. He recalled being worried about Ken, seeing Kevin, massive pain, and now he was in a bed in some sort of sensory deprived state.

He was awake and aware, but everything felt wrong, and his frustration and anxiety, mixed with fear for Ken, caused a hot tear to drip down his cheek.

Standing beside the bed, Kevin saw the tear and exclaimed, "Doc! Something's happening!"

Standing by his friend, Kevin watched helplessly, wanting to comfort him, to hold his hand or rest a hand on his shoulder, but the doctor insisted on no skin contact.

◇◇

Kevin was confused by what occurred when he went through the gate. He was just finishing an assignment when he received Brad's message, and since he and Bill lived so close, he figured he'd run by their house to see what was up.

When he arrived the garage door was closed, and no one answered the front door, so he figured Brad was back by the pool. Heading around the side of the house and practically being family, he didn't hesitate to use his code and open the gate. If he was lucky maybe Brad was working on his tan au naturel. Although Kevin was genuinely in love with Bill, he loved the sight of a good-looking naked man with a body like Brad's. As soon as Kevin saw Brad cleaning the pool in his shorts, he was disappointed and chuckled to himself.

I'm such a whore.

At that moment Brad's arm jerked, and he arched his back, crying out in pain. Out of nowhere, three dark pronounced bruises appeared; one on his arm and two on his back. To Kevin's wartime experience, Brad reacted like he had been shot. Surprise crossed Brad's face, and with his enhanced vision, for a split second, Kevin saw Brad's bright blue eyes turn white before rolling up. Moving as fast as he could, Kevin dashed towards Brad, but just before he reached him, Brad's body convulsed and he collapsed to the pavement, unconscious.

<>

At Kevin's exclamation, Dr. Thomas quickly moved to Brad's bedside.

In a quiet voice, his face sad and filled with concern, the doctor leaned down close to Brad's ear and said, "Ah, my poor boy. I know you cannot hear me yet, but I am so sorry. It will be better soon."

Dr. Thomas inserted a syringe in the catheter attached to the back of Brad's hand and pressed the plunger.

"Kevin, help me strap him down. He will wake in a moment and might panic, and we need to restrain him so he cannot hurt himself. He may be confused and not make sense, so do not be alarmed."

<><>

The agonizing loneliness and isolation were more than he could take, and Brad was at the limit of his control. The depth of his love for Ken hit him like a Mack truck, and Ken's absence created a hole that was about to kill him. As much as he cared for his military brothers and Dr. Thomas, life without Ken wasn't worth living. Brad's mind raced, spinning with dark, negative thoughts and emotions, and with his sense of time skewed, his loneliness seemed unending.

A sound so faint he wasn't even sure he heard it jolted him, and Brad forced his thoughts still to listen, straining to feel or hear anything that might tell him what was happening or where he was. It came again but was too unclear to make out, and he started to sweat from the strain of listening, and proof he wasn't alone.

Dr. Thomas looked at Brad's straining form, his eyes expressing compassion for his young charge. He knew what Brad experienced and deeply regretted being the source of such emotional distress. He wondered at the unexpected turn of events, of Ken's abduction the day after unlocking another ability, especially one that should be dormant for several years yet. He wanted to believe it was coincidence but suspected otherwise. Even without all the facts, his impressive intellect began piecing together parts of the puzzle, and he didn't like the picture forming in the slightest.

"Kevin, I need you to gather everyone as quickly as possible. While you take care of that, I will see what information Bradford might have that can shed some light on what is happening."

"Yes, sir. Right away."

Dr. Thomas regretted concealing information from Kevin but needed to talk to Brad alone. He was still unsure about revealing the new development between Ken and Brad to the others. It was a significant and essential step in their evolution but could be dangerous if Kevin and the others weren't ready. Brad and Ken had always been slightly more advanced than the rest of the team physically, emotionally, and mentally. The others would reach the same stage eventually, but on the path he set his remarkable young charges on, his philosophy was to let nature take its course and not interfere more than he already had.

With Kevin gone, the doctor took Brad's hand and said, "Bradford. Come back, my boy. It is time to wake up."

The whispers became louder, and Brad was on the verge of making out words. He sensed motion and felt seasick. Someone squeezed his hand, and his heart leapt inside his chest.

Ken!?

The touch was like an anchor, and he fought with every ounce of his will to grab hold and pull himself towards it.

The feeling of movement strengthened as the darkness receded, and a pinpoint of light appeared in the darkness. As the light expanded he heard a voice, but it was still too faint to make it out.

Suddenly, Brad woke up. In an instant, his vision, hearing, and other senses became active again. The sudden shift was jarring, and his breath caught in surprise.

Dr. Thomas, looking into Brad's eyes, immediately noted when there was recognition.

"Hello, Bradford, welcome back."

Brad wasn't able to speak right away. He felt immense relief at being out of the darkness, but the void, the absence of Ken, was still there.

More tears fell, and all he could bring himself to say was, "Doc, he's gone."

Squeezing the doctor's hand, Brad closed his eyes, his body shaking in quiet grief.

Releasing Brad's hand, the doctor firmly gripped his shoulders and said, "Bradford, look at me, son."

Brad looked up, his blue eyes red and glassy from the intense emotions running through him. When they made eye contact, Brad saw many things; compassion first and foremost, and concern, but also uncertainty and fear. In all his years with the doctor, Brad had never seen him that way.

"We do not know that. I will not lie to you. Kenneth is not with us, and I assume he is in great danger, but you are our best chance of finding him. You must focus on that."

"Why can't I feel him, doc? Our connection must have grown so gradually I never realized it was there until it was gone. I've never felt so alone."

"That is my fault, Bradford, and I am deeply sorry. Typically, after the trauma you experienced, I would handle things differently. In this instance, because of what you experienced, I have temporarily suppressed your connection with Kenneth. It is necessary for multiple reasons. First and foremost, it probably saved your life. Your link to Kenneth is still developing, and you experienced whatever happened to him. I had to stop it before it killed you."

Brad sounded desperate, almost hysterical, and tried to grab the doctor's arms, but the restraints kept him from doing so.

"Please, doc," he pleaded, "You have to undo whatever you did! I need him back!"

"I will, son, I will, but we must proceed with some level of caution. I do not believe Kenneth is dead. You have to remember how hard it would be to kill any of the bodies, but you, while very tough in your own right, could be killed by what would merely incapacitate one of them.

"What is happening to you is new, and I have no wish to cause you or Kenneth any permanent damage by rushing in blindly. Kevin is gathering everyone, and in a few moments you and I will meet with them and begin formulating a plan. Let us get you cleaned up and into some clothes."

Brad took a quick shower and put on some spare jeans, a t-shirt, and sandals from his locker. The doctor came in and gave him another shot to continue the suppression of his connection to Ken. He didn't like it but understood.

Not long after, everyone arrived and was seated at the conference room table. The guys were stunned at Brad's haggard appearance when they first came in, and every one of them gave him an encouraging hug or pat on the back, asking him how he was holding up. It was immediately apparent how emotionally distraught he was, and their natural instinct was to close ranks around him in support.

When Dr. Thomas came in, the room fell silent, and the men became laser-focused. Their best friend and Captain was missing, and both Brad and Ken needed them.

"As you all know, Kenneth is missing. I believe he has been abducted. No one has attempted to contact us, so we must assume it is not a ransom, which means they want something from him, and we have limited time to rescue him before they are successful.

"Bradford, please go over events starting from yesterday afternoon to present."

Brad glanced at him, "Everything, Sir?"

"Yes, Bradford. I have reassessed my reasons. I wish to protect you all, but events are accelerating my plans for you far ahead of schedule.

The timing of this is terrible, but secrets only serve to cause suspicion and doubt."

Brad's hands gripped the lectern tightly enough that his triceps and forearms flexed, tightening his t-shirt. Fresh anxiety hit him as he recalled how often Ken stood where he was, addressing everyone as a team. Taking a deep breath to settle himself, he started recounting events.

"Okay… well, Ken got home about 1700 yesterday from his workout with Bry and Kev. I was putting groceries away when he got home, and after I finished, I gave him his post-workout exam, which led to…"

Trying to lighten the mood, a few of the guys chimed in with a "Boom Chicka Bow Wow," which caused Brad to blush and even crack a smile.

"Alright, you fuckers. Yes, we made out."

Glancing at the doctor, who didn't like them cursing, Brad said, "Sorry about the F-Bomb, doc."

Brad recounted the events, telling his buddies everything.

"...And what happened next was the most amazing, mind-blowing, over the top sex we've ever had. The physical charge I got was unbelievable, and my senses were also enhanced which has never happened before. I flipped us over on the bed without any effort."

Raised eyebrows and "Oh, shit" looks passed among them as what Brad said sank in.

Kevin interjected, "Brad, wait a second. When I got to your place, and I saw you experience whatever that was, your eyes changed color just like you said Ken's did."

The doctor explained, saying, "What Kenneth succeeded in doing was linking his nervous system with Bradford's, allowing them to feel and share each other's sensations. It is a remarkable ability, and when fully under control by both parties, what is currently happening will not be an issue. The timing of Kenneth uncovering this new ability is terrible, however, it might be the key to rescuing him if our other attempts fail.

"Although I do not know who is behind Kenneth's abduction, I believe I have pieced together some of what happened based on evidence exhibited by Bradford's injuries.

"Whoever abducted Kenneth is aware that he and most likely you four," the doctor glanced at Bryan, Rick, Pat, and Kevin, "are physically exceptional. The kidnappers knew they needed to ambush Kenneth to incapacitate him, and carefully planned their assault, orchestrating his isolation and shooting him with three heavy tranquilizer darts followed by multiple Tasers.

"The neural pairing between Kenneth and Bradford is still active, but suspended. This is dangerous, and in the future, once this ability is fully understood and controlled, it should not be kept active as it is now. As soon as I stop the suppression in Bradford, the connection will resume, but it puts Bradford at risk depending on Kenneth's current condition. There is no way whoever has taken him will know of this, so we might be able to use it to our advantage.

"I believe the tranquilizers used to incapacitate Kenneth were nearly potent enough to kill him. Fortunately, this did not happen, and his heightened metabolism burned through them earlier today. Once that occurred, the link reestablished with Bradford, coinciding with Kevin's arrival at their house. It was a delayed reaction, and Kenneth's nervous system inadvertently broadcast his experiences to Bradford as his mind regained consciousness. It was as if the attack happened to both of them simultaneously but with a time delay buffered by the tranquilizers.

"If Kenneth were in control of his faculties, he would realize what is happening and stop it. I do not think he would risk Bradford's well-being even if it meant his own demise, so we must assume he is still incapacitated in some way, which is the reason I am reluctant to stop the suppression.

"Before I consider taking that route, we need to exhaust all other, more conventional means of investigation. Richard and Loy, you will lead the on-site investigation at the hotel where Kenneth was taken. You all have your areas of expertise. Bradford, if he is up to it, will stay here and run the operation. If he is unable for any reason to continue, William can take over. Gentlemen, you are the most elite group of men in the world. We know whoever captured Kenneth had the knowledge and skill to take him out unaware. We are not unaware, and from now on, none of you goes anywhere alone. Stay sharp and alert, and we will prevail. We will bring Kenneth home."

Rick and Loy, accompanied by Pat and Darren, immediately left for the hotel. Kevin wanted to go to the office and look over the phone and appointment records with Sally, and Bryan and Lane stayed in the lab ready to do whatever was needed as more information became available.

Bryan and Lane stayed close to Brad, trying to keep him distracted while keeping an eye on him. Bryan's steadfast presence was comforting, and Lane's chatter prevented Brad from withdrawing further into himself.

Dr. Boris Cromwell stared intently at his new test subject, sitting restrained in a holding cell. Ken was the most magnificent male specimen Dr. Cromwell had ever seen; whoever created him had outdone themselves. The name on his driver's license and credit cards read Kenneth Habersham, but Dr. Cromwell knew that was false. However, despite his best efforts, he could not discover Ken's true identity, and it vexed him. Someone had gone to incredible lengths to make sure Ken's past remained hidden.

The preliminary blood and tissue samples showed his captive to be in perfect health; too perfect, in fact. The DNA results were phenomenal and obviously not natural, showing genetic markers and additional helices Dr. Cromwell had never seen before. The full MRI and CT Scans revealed an uncanny muscle and bone density, along with countless physiological modifications, many subtle and at the cellular level, to compensate for the changes. The sheer number of mitochondria in his cells was astounding, and Ken had at least one additional nerve trunk off his spine, possibly more. Dr. Cromwell considered himself a genius, but he quickly became lost as he looked at Ken's test results.

Based on the information furnished by General Burgess the results were not unexpected, but he was skeptical of the General's claims. The General was a military man and not a scientist, and

Dr. Cromwell thought his descriptions of Ken too far-fetched to believe.

An alert from one of the monitors attached to Ken pulled his eyes away from the test results; they were so intriguing he could not stop staring at them. His eyes widened in surprise at Ken's level of brain activity. For the level of sedatives administered, what was happening should be impossible!

Ken's body was burning through the tranquilizers much faster than expected, so Dr. Cromwell switched to something less lethal but more mentally disabling. The new mixture was more potent and should keep Ken's brain in a fog and make him extremely susceptible to suggestion.

As Ken came to, his first realization was how awful he felt. The bruises and lacerations on his arm and back hurt like hell, his entire body was sore, and he felt like he needed to throw up. Instinctively he tried to still himself but couldn't find his center. The place in his mind where he controlled his abilities was present but unavailable, surrounded by a chemical barrier he could not penetrate. Surprisingly, he wasn't upset, even though he knew he should be worried.

He couldn't see and quickly realized he was blindfolded. Air against his skin told him he was naked except for some underwear or shorts, and he was sitting upright in a sturdy metal chair. Multiple leather straps secured his arms, wrists, legs, and neck, keeping him immobile.

Aside from his pain and discomfort, Ken's only other thought before losing consciousness again was, *"Man, Brad's gonna be pissed I'm late..."*

<>

Dr. Cromwell gasped in surprise as Ken's DNA overwrote the cultures, destroying them in seconds and ruining his initial tissue samples. The ramifications of that were not lost on him, and he needed to test the limits of the reaction before he could move forward. Without hesitation he called

Robert, one of his junior assistants, to the command center.

Every person in the facility had extensive background checks as part of their security clearances, but unbeknownst to them, deeper personal surveillance to use as leverage and control if necessary. Robert's private browsing history showed his preference for men; men like Ken. With a little chemical assistance, Robert should fall into a trap that would tell Dr. Cromwell precisely what he needed to know.

"Dr. Cromwell, Sir? You called?"

Robert sounded nervous. He rarely interacted with Dr. Cromwell directly and was scared and intimidated by the man.

"Yes, Robert. I require your assistance."

"Of course, Sir, whatever you need, I'll be more than happy to help."

"I'm sure you are aware of our newest guest, the center of my current research project. We are running a series of tests, and I need a second set of samples. There are anomalies we did not predict in his genetic makeup, and the first set of samples were contaminated."

Robert was confused, "What type of samples do you need, Sir?"

"A full blood panel, urine, and DNA swabs. He might be lethargic and unresponsive, but you should be able to manage. Robert, this is extremely important, and your discretion paramount. I will disable the security cameras in the holding cell for the duration of your visit."

Robert was about to question the need for secrecy but kept silent.

He stammered slightly as he replied, "Um. Uh, of course, Sir. I'll do my best."

<>

Dr. Cromwell kept the cameras active but disabled the lights on them. Before Robert entered the room, Dr. Cromwell flipped a switch, and an odorless gas filled the chamber. He wasn't sure if it would affect Ken, but it would definitely affect Robert, reducing his inhibitions and inciting his libido. With no hint of regret or remorse, Dr. Cromwell was sending Robert to a death sentence. In his mind, Robert's demise was an acceptable loss for the sake of his research.

<>

When Robert arrived, the glass walls of the holding cell were already polarized to an opaque state. He was surprised at the weaponry the guards carried; whoever the test subject was must be important or possibly dangerous. Robert showed his I.D. to the security guard, who swiped his smart card, and immediately a solid *thunk* resounded as the door bolts pulled back, followed by a slight hiss as the seals opened.

Stepping into the room Robert stopped in his tracks, awestruck. The most perfect man on the planet sat in front of him, practically naked, blindfolded, and strapped to a chair. Ken's physique was beyond words, like a comic book superhero; like the men on the internet he fantasized over.

Robert noticed the security camera lights turn off when the room sealed. As soon as the door closed, Ken's head whipped around in his direction, and with the *thunk* and *hiss* of the door some of the tension drained out of his posture. Robert was mesmerized, his arousal evident as he stared at the man in front of him.

His breathing deepened, and he flushed as his eyes slowly moved over every inch of Ken's tanned, muscular body. As his eyes continued to roam, he noticed more and more detail about Ken that elevated his excitement. Ken had just the right amount of hair on his chest, and while Robert couldn't see the color of his eyes because of the blindfold, in his fantasy, Ken's eyes were dark brown, almost black. His hair was dark brown and short, cut close on the back and sides and longer on top, making him look military. He hadn't shaved in a few days, and the scruff on his face added to his ruggedly handsome features.

Ken's deep voice resonated through his chest, but his words were slurred like he was drunk.

"B, is that you?"

Robert seized the opportunity and replied, "Yeah, it's me."

"Oh God, B. I was worried you'd be pissed 'cause I was late. I can't see you, man. I can hear you, but I can't see you. Can you let me up?"

"No, I can't... Not yet. It's part of the game."

"Game?"

"Oh yeah... I think you're going to like it."

Robert set the sample containers and equipment on the small table in front of Ken. Robert circled Ken slowly, taking off his lab coat and loosening his tie as he moved. The heat radiating off Ken's body hit him, along with his scent, and Robert trembled with excitement.

"B..."

Robert couldn't help himself and reached out, putting a hand on the ball of Ken's shoulder. Dr. Cromwell's serum was in full effect, and any sense of professionalism or propriety in Robert was quickly breaking down. As soon as he touched

Ken's shoulder, Robert turned into a wild man, wanting to feel each and every muscle at the same time. Robert ran his hands through the sparse hair on Ken's chest, squeezing his biceps, shoulders, and pecs, touching every part of Ken's body he could reach from his vantage point behind the chair.

He stopped suddenly when he noticed the substantial tent in Ken's shorts.

"Oh God, B… Your hands feel good."

Sweating in excitement, Robert practically tore his clothes off as he moved around to Ken's front.

Ken smelled Robert's excitement in his sweat, but something wasn't right. His brain wanted to tell him it wasn't Brad, but the suggestive state of his mind from the sedatives overrode reason, reinforcing the idea it was Brad in front of him.

Robert continued touching Ken, fulfilling a fantasy of being with such an incredible man, and he was in awe at the heat and solidity of Ken's body.

The illusion of Brad's hands sent signals to Ken's libido he couldn't resist, and he became aroused. He wanted to feel Brad's hands on him, but even more, Ken wanted to touch him back.

Ken's reaction fueled Robert's fantasy, and his mind clouded even more as the influence of the gas overpowered rational thought and behavior. He moved in front of Ken and dropped to his knees, staring at the object of his desire.

His eyes glazed over and his hands reached out, freeing Ken from his shorts. Touching Ken shattered any remaining resolve he had, and he lowered his head, taking Ken into his mouth...

<>

... it was over in a few minutes, and Robert stood up, unsteady on his feet and wiping his chin from the results of Ken's orgasm. Robert was a smart young man, and as reason came back to him, he realized Dr. Cromwell set him up. He specifically sent Robert on this task, knowing what would happen, but Robert still wondered why. He knew he had been drugged and was angry at the manipulation.

Ken's chest heaved, and he moaned, "Oh fuck…." under his breath.

Dr. Cromwell observed everything on a monitor in his office, and the scene played out exactly as he wished. As soon as Robert worked Ken to release, Cromwell flipped a switch, sending additional sedatives into the catheter on the back of Ken's hand, causing him to lose consciousness again. Dr. Cromwell sat back in his chair, continuing to watch.

By the time Robert caught his breath, Ken had gone still, breathing slow and deep.

"Damn, he fell asleep."

Standing up, Robert put his hands on Ken's shoulders, trying to shake him awake, but Ken barely budged.

"Holy crap, this guy is solid."

In a panic, Robert noticed almost half of the leather straps holding Ken immobile were shredded and useless, ripped apart by his body's reaction to his orgasm.

Robert started putting his clothes back on to finish his task but suddenly felt light-headed. He straightened up as excruciating pain so intense he couldn't even scream wracked his entire body. Robert's back arched as he fell to the floor, overcome by a massive seizure, and in seconds he stopped breathing, his body lifeless, and his face expressing horrible pain.

Dr. Cromwell observed Robert's death dispassionately. He wasn't sure how the genetic markers in Ken's DNA worked, how they got there, or what purpose they served, but he was determined to discover Ken's secrets and duplicate them. Dr. Cromwell was confident Robert's autopsy would reveal significant data. General Burgess was paying a high price for his research and expected results, and Dr. Cromwell was not one to disappoint powerful allies.

Later that afternoon, the autopsy showed massive cellular breakdown in Robert's body as if his DNA unraveled and all the proteins and cells in his body denatured and lysed, spewing their contents into the interstitial fluid in his body. Even more intriguing was evidence of genetic remodeling with the disruption. If the process had been slower,

Robert most likely would have become a giant puddle of plasma. As it was, the progression happened blindingly fast and Robert's body could not stand the assault on his cellular structure, and he died almost instantly.

Dr. Cromwell knew he would have to accelerate matters to achieve results. He thought it a pity he could not spare Ken.

"Let us see what you can do, my friend, before that magnificent body of yours gives out."

<>

Ken regained consciousness, blindfolded, naked, and spread eagle on a cold metal table. Steel bindings replaced the shredded leather straps from earlier, and a padded leather brace held his head mostly immobile, allowing for some slight motion.

Hearing movement and identifying several distinct smells, he attempted to focus, but the place in his mind where he controlled his abilities remained unavailable. He gave no outward sign of his frustration or worry but knew he was in trouble.

Ken's memory was foggy, but he recalled being shot with three tranquilizer darts and multiple tasers, and vaguely remembered a make-out session with Brad which confused him - maybe it was a dream, but damn it seemed real - and now he was strapped to a table. He usually had an excellent sense of time, but his internal clock was confused after being unconscious and drugged. He had no idea how long it had been since his capture, but it was long enough for him to be ravenously hungry, and the thought of food made his stomach rumble loudly.

Dr. Cromwell stared at Ken obsessively, as if he could discern the vast, world-changing secrets of his existence merely by watching him. Aside from the sound of Ken's stomach, Dr. Cromwell noted the signs and knew immediately when Ken awoke.

"Ahhh... You are awake. And famished! Let me see what I can do about that."

With the test results so far, Dr. Cromwell produced more effective serums to use against Ken's advanced physiology and metabolism. He flipped a switch, and a concentrated protein solution flowed into Ken's body through various catheters. Additional liquids to prevent dehydration and restore electrolytes also fed into his body, giving him an immediate boost in energy. It did little to appease his hunger, but he felt much better.

Ken's Mental faculties were unavailable, but his physical senses were unaffected, and he counted 52 points of discomfort on his body. Some were catheters, but others felt like needles or electrodes.

"We are finalizing your preparation for the next phase, and will begin shortly."

After years of working with the doctor, Ken recognized the familiar smells and sounds of lab equipment, and applying his senses, he tried to visualize the man talking to him, picking up on the stiff cloth of a starched lab coat and the slight, practically inaudible squeak of a stool rotating as the man moved. He smelled pipe tobacco. The man's English was fluent, but Ken detected a trace accent. It seemed Slavic, but he wasn't sure.

Ken's training was instinctual and he started forming a profile, building and processing information to identify where he was, who held him captive, and what they wanted. He had a good idea already, and it didn't bode well for his future.

A faint *Beep* followed by rapid typing on a keyboard ensued, and after a slight delay the back of his hand burned as more chemicals entered his system. A warm sensation quickly spread over his body, his skin flushed, and he immediately became erect. Ken tried as hard as possible to will his erection down but couldn't do it, and in seconds he was hard to the point of discomfort.

Ken heard Dr. Cromwell stand and move over to him, and decided to break his stoic silence, asking, "What the fuck do you want from me?"

"Nothing you can give me voluntarily. I'm sure you could tell me quite a bit about yourself if you were so inclined, but I could never be certain of the truthfulness of your information. Therefore, I have no choice but to gather the information I need through... other means."

Ken didn't like the sound of that, and if the situation weren't so serious he would have scoffed at the melodramatic pause.

"We have already gathered much information, although I'm a bit upset about losing one of my promising young researchers. At least Robert died happy."

Right away, Ken knew Dr. Cromwell referred to his dream of making out with Brad. It was a hallucination, and Ken killed some poor guy without meaning to. He was already angry at being taken, but Robert's death added to his list of paybacks once his buddies rescued him.

"We are going to chart your neurological pathways. To do this, we will stimulate your sympathetic and parasympathetic nervous systems simultaneously, as well as the tertiary system you possess. The human orgasm is one of the few times when both systems are active, and we can gather more data that way. The next phase, I believe you will find most pleasurable, at least initially. Later, perhaps not so much, however, there is nothing you can do about it. Fight all you wish, but it will not matter. I've learned enough to shut down your brain activity. I intend to learn everything I can from your body while you are alive, and the rest after you have expired."

Ken was seriously pissed off yet completely helpless, at least for the time being. If his captors wanted a fight, they would get one. Ken knew Brad and the guys would already be searching for him, and he had to give them time and hold out as long as he could. Just thinking of Brad boosted his resolve, and he couldn't help thinking how much he loved the man who was his best friend and partner. He sucked in a deep breath to steady himself.

Come on, guys, get a move on and get me outta here.

"Okay, fucker, quit starin' at my dick and get on with it."

Dr. Cromwell blushed, embarrassed because he was staring at Ken's impressive organ, standing at attention.

Recovering his composure, he quickly said, "Bravo, my boy. That's the spirit! Fight as long as you can... The longer you last, the more information I can gather."

Cromwell moved away to type, and another *Beep* soon followed.

Within seconds Ken broke out in a heavy sweat. Nearby fans started up, and a soft breeze brushed over his sweaty skin, inducing a pleasant, soothing sensation. Ken wasn't prepared for the strength or intensity of the sensations that hit him. Every muscle in his body tightened, and he would have come off the table if he hadn't been strapped down. He could barely breathe, and his whole body turned beet red.

Dr. Cromwell's eyes widened in surprise at Ken's reaction. His musculature was incredible, and Dr. Cromwell found himself getting excited despite his clinical detachment, and made a mental note to review the recordings later in private.

Ken couldn't help himself and exclaimed, "Oohhhhh Fuck!"

Breathing heavy, his chest heaved as he sucked in air, and his abs tightened with each breath. A powerful orgasm hit him but didn't stop and quickly became painful. Fire ripped through his body as Dr. Cromwell altered the signals to his nervous system. The pain was relentless, and there was no reprieve. Ken tensed his body to fight off the pain, but his normal defenses were unavailable and he could only endure it.

Except for his initial outburst, Ken kept silent through it all, and after minutes the signals stopped. Soaked in sweat, his muscles were pumped, with veins showing everywhere. What he experienced would have killed a normal human, but Ken was far from reaching his pain threshold. As he recuperated, he felt the sting of more fluids entering his body to help with his recovery. He wasn't sure why, but his thoughts turned to the last time he and Brad made love when he discovered the new bonding technique.

Unexpectedly, another orgasm hit, more intense than the first, and the pain that followed more extreme. Ken wasn't sure how long he could hold out if the pain levels continued to elevate. Fire shot through all the nerve receptors in his body, inducing every sensation imaginable, the effects magnified because of his enhanced senses. Massive disorientation hit as well when his proprioceptors became confused, and he lost all awareness of the position of his limbs and orientation. His empty stomach heaved, trying to expel its contents in reaction to what was happening. Pressure and stretch receptors in various organs fired off corrective hormone cascades trying to compensate, and his vitals were all over the map.

Beep.

Ken lost track of time, enduring the torture in stoic silence, not wanting to give in to his captors. His body was on fire, with only seconds between each round of stimulation. In those brief seconds, while they pumped him full of fluids and protein, his body did what it was designed to do; recover as quickly as possible. After an hour Ken lost consciousness, his body continuing to twitch and spasm after he passed out.

Dr. Cromwell was more than impressed. In the next phase, he would stop the fluid and protein intake to see how long Ken could last and how his body recovered without aid. He was interested to see how Ken's physiology would prioritize its recovery.

After a few minutes, Dr. Cromwell forced Ken back to consciousness. When Ken came to, the strong smell of his sweat and semen hit him, and even through the fog of pain, he thought:

Brad would so love this.

Ken lost consciousness after twenty minutes without the replenishing fluids and proteins. He stopped sweating halfway through, and his movements diminished to the point where he was merely twitching. Grimly, Ken never made a sound, not wanting to give them any satisfaction.

Dr. Cromwell was in awe of Ken's physiology. The manner in which his body controlled and monitored itself without conscious control, the way it redirected resources and repaired itself was something he never thought possible. Whoever created his subject was a biological Einstein. Dr. Cromwell was barely scratching the surface, and it would take him years to process the data he had already collected. Excited, he was ready to move on to the next stage.

They gave Ken thirty minutes before starting the flow of liquids and proteins again to help his body regenerate. A technician wiped him down with some type of antiseptic, cleaning off the fluids covering his body. His skin was still hypersensitive, and the evaporation of the alcohol coupled with the abrasive wipes was uncomfortable.

Exhausted, Ken felt like he could sleep for days to recover. He kept thinking of Brad and the guys looking for him, willing them to move faster. His instincts told him his captors had barely scratched the surface with what they were doing to him, and the worst was yet to come.

Ken was a trained Navy SEAL, and normally it would take far more than his current situation to break his resolve, but the chemical attack on his mind that impaired his control over his abilities also affected his will. The emotional and mental struggle raging in his mind was grueling, and his determination began to falter, vacillating between holding on and feeling guilty for not being strong enough.

Smelling pipe tobacco, Ken knew his captor was back.

"Well, my boy, you are exceeding anything I could have imagined. Whoever made you is a genius. I am jealous of his intellect and vision, and I am going to make it my life's work to duplicate and even improve upon what he has done."

Ken knew he shouldn't say anything, but his gut was telling him he was not going to survive.

Instead of prolonging the pain, he would rather have it over sooner.

I'm sorry Brad, I think I've failed you'n the guys. I guess I'm bein' a coward, but I don't know if I'm up 'ta this. I love you so much, I hope you know that.

"You stupid fucker. Compared 'ta him you're in diapers suckin' on your mom's hind tit and shittin' guacamole into your Huggies. You'll never figure this out. Just get it over with."

Dr. Cromwell's expression turned stony, his lips pursed, and his voice went cold.

"We shall see."

The change in Cromwell's tone was clear. Ken's plan was working, but he was going to pay for it. More typing on the keyboard ensued, and Cromwell's attitude was apparent in his typing as he pounded the keyboard.

With the last keystroke, Ken started counting down.

Three. Two. One. *Beep.*

A faint hydraulic hiss followed, and the shackle holding Ken's right wrist raised up a quarter of an inch then slammed down hard, catching him by surprise. Ken didn't know it, but it came down with enough force to break an ordinary man's wrist.

Ken steeled himself, and other than letting out an "Oomph" of surprise, he remained stoically silent.

Beep.

The shackle rose and slammed down again, much harder. Ken tensed his body, getting ready for the next one, and started sweating.

Beep.

His wrist splintered. It took everything he had not to yell, and his breath was coming in harsh gasps from fighting off the pain.

Beep.

Ken's wrist snapped, and he screamed.

Beep.

The shackle on his left wrist rose.

Oh, Fuck!

Dr. Cromwell ignored Ken's screams as he watched his test subject react to the inflicted pain and damage. Glancing at the monitors, he smiled as the data flowed. The neurological information was unlike anything he imagined, and he was almost giddy at what he saw.

By the time his left wrist snapped, Ken was hoarse from screaming. His body strained, bowing from the pain and pushing his chest up. He struggled so hard the metal band across his chest bent, breaking a few ribs in the process. His body raised enough for the blindfold to catch on the corner of the leather headpiece, and Ken saw Dr. Cromwell's long thin face staring back at him. They made eye contact for a brief second before the pain pushed Ken over the edge into unconsciousness.

Dr. Cromwell increased the flow of nutrients, adding a highly-concentrated mix of vitamins and antibiotics. He would have included painkillers if Ken had kept his mouth shut. He kept Ken unconscious for a short time while he set the bones, wanting them to heal correctly so he could break them again.

Next time it will be his thighs, something more substantial and traumatic to his body.

Almost before he could set the bones, they started knitting back together. At the rate he witnessed they would fully heal within a matter of hours.

Next time he would hold back on the nutrients and see how long it took.

Rick, Loy, Pat, and Darren drove to the Hilton where Ken worked the previous night, talked with Hotel security, and reviewed the available camera footage. The Atlanta Police were holding Tyrone and his friends, and Lil'B was pressing charges as well as the Hilton, but Ken was in trouble because he never showed to give them his incident report. Pat and Darren checked, and Ken's Explorer still sat in the Parking Garage in the valet section.

None of the information uncovered so far was good news, and there was even some confusion after reviewing the security footage and audio recordings. The head of hotel security didn't recognize the voice that instructed Ken to head to the loading dock. It didn't make sense because the Atlanta PD used a small conference room off the lobby to take everyone's statements. Rick convinced the manager to give him a copy of the audio file but doubted they could identify the voice that led Ken into the ambush.

Rick and Loy traced the route Ken should have taken from the front of the building to the loading dock, and when they reached the corner, scanned the area. Rick immediately noted a pair of broken aviator sunglasses against the curb. Loy knew them on sight, and Rick smelled a faint trace of Ken's cologne on them.

Their frustration level was high over the lack of information. The thought of Ken, not only their Captain but their brother being taken from them, tore them up and the pressure to find him consumed them. Why or how, after all the years they had been safe and anonymous in their new lives, could something like this happen? God only knew what was being done to him while they ran into dead end after dead end. The lack of evidence proved whoever was behind Ken's abduction knew precisely what they were doing.

With his hands on his hips Rick exclaimed, "Fuck! If it happened, it had to be right here! This spot is out of sight of any security cameras, and there are at least two vantage points where someone could have gotten off an easy shot."

He pointed to the two side streets half a block down in either direction.

Loy didn't look any happier, but trying to stay positive said, "Well, let's check them out. Surely one of them will turn up something."

Rick led the way to the first location with Loy right behind him. They spent minutes going over the area, but the side street didn't turn up anything. The second vantage point was more of an alley, containing a dumpster and a bunch of trash cans. A little further in was a large pile of cardboard boxes, a few of which were big, like something an appliance might come in. Loy noticed movement in one of them and signaled Rick.

Both men immediately went into 'SEAL' mode, moving quietly into position close to the boxes with their guns ready. As soon as Rick got a little closer, he nearly gagged at the smell coming from the box. Whoever was in it hadn't bathed in a long time, and the stench of alcohol and sweat was almost overpowering to his enhanced sense of smell. Even Loy wrinkled his nose once close enough.

Rick put his gun away but was still alert in case whoever it was tried to run.

Tapping the box with his foot he said, "Hey, buddy, come out. We need to talk to you."

There was no answer, just a slight movement followed by snoring. Rick smacked the box with the flat of his hand, making a loud pop, and the man inside let out a startled scream, shouting, "I.E.D! I.E.D! Take cover!"

Frantic movement followed as the man inside scrambled down to one corner.

Loy looked at Rick with a smirk and said, "Nice move, dickhead."

Rick gave him a 'how the fuck should I have known' look.

Loy leaned down at the open end of the box, saying, "Hey man, it's cool. You're safe. What's your name?"

"Who da fuck are you!?"

"Lt. Loy Barton, retired Navy. The dickhead here making all the noise is Lt. Rick Crawford, also retired Navy. Can you come out? We want to talk to you."

The man was clearly a veteran, so Loy used their old rank in hopes of getting him to cooperate. His exit from the box was awkward, which became more apparent once they saw his prosthetic leg, followed by a large pile of crumpled newspapers. The prosthesis was an older design, made of wood, and didn't fit properly.

When he stood up, he teetered, trying to get his balance but waived off any help. When he seemed stable, Loy held out his hand in greeting.

"So, what's your name, soldier?"

The man looked leery but shook Loy's hand, and Rick's.

"Specialist Taggart Keenan, Army; 197th Infantry. Tag for short."

Tag looked horrible. He was African-American and dark-skinned, but his complexion was gray and chalky. His eyes were bloodshot, his teeth yellow, his breath ungodly, and his body odor even worse. It was hard to tell how old he was in his current condition, but they guessed maybe early to mid-fifties. It looked like he had a rough life aside from whatever he went through during his time in the military.

"Tag, were you here a few nights ago?"

"Why? Am I in some kinda trouble?"

"No, not at all. You see, a buddy of ours, another Navy guy, went missing two nights ago. We think someone jumped him right over there," Loy pointed half a block down to the street corner.

"If you were here, did you see or hear anything strange that night?"

"Maybe."

Based on Tag's response Rick let out an impatient sigh, knowing where the conversation was headed. Before Rick exploded, Loy quickly followed up.

"Look, Tag. This is important, and you'll be doing us a huge favor if you can give us any information. I'm not giving you money because I know what you'll do with it. I'll be happy to buy you something to eat in exchange for your help. Are you hungry?"

Tag nodded his head.

"There's a McDonald's a few blocks down. Does that sound okay?"

Tag nodded again and mumbled, "Gimme a sec."

Leaning over, he started fiddling with the harness holding on the prosthesis, but his hands were shaking so bad he was having trouble. Loy guessed he probably lost so much weight after his original fitting that it no longer gripped adequately.

Not wanting to embarrass Tag or make a big deal of it, Loy squatted down and said, "Here, Tag, let me do it."

Tag stood awkwardly while Loy tightened the harness, making it more stable.

"Good to go now."

Tag's 'thanks' was barely a murmur. He was confused as to who these guys were and what they wanted. Some bullshit story about a friend in trouble, but for some reason he didn't understand he trusted both of them, especially Rick, the dickhead who banged on his box! For the first time in months, Tag seemed to have some mental clarity as the fog over his brain began unraveling, and at their mention of food, he realized how hungry he was.

They walked to McDonald's, and Loy let Tag order what he wanted. The shift manager came out from behind the counter when someone complained that a homeless guy had come in. Rick and Loy were intimidating towards the manager, saying they would sit in a corner and not disturb anyone, but needed to talk with their friend. Loy went full-on mental with the manager, scaring him so bad he almost pissed his pants. In hindsight, he might have gone a little overboard, but he felt defensive on behalf of Tag in addition to their urgency to find Ken.

While Tag ate, Loy maintained casual conversation, trying to draw at least part of Tag's story out of him. Rick was getting impatient, but Loy squeezed his leg under the table, giving him a 'calm down' look. While they spoke Loy focused on Tag, eliciting a feeling of cooperation and contentment.

Once Tag was full and drinking his shake, Loy broached the subject of Ken again.

"So, Tag, did you see or hear anything the other night?"

"Mmmm-hmmm."

Slurp.

"I'll be straight wit 'ya... I was majorly fucked up that night, but I heard someone talkin'. I was tryin' ta sleep when I felt cold all of 'a sudden. It scared me, so I was bein' quiet, but I took a peep out and saw a few guys. They was big, like you two, dressed in black and wearin' night vision gear. Two of 'em had nasty lookin' rifles. They was drivin' a black van and had it backed up right off da street. I thought I was trippin', so I shut up and closed my eyes.

"A few minutes later I heard 'em bitchin' 'bout how heavy some dude was. They threw him in the back of the van and took off. Didn't think no more about it 'til you two showed up. Figured it must 'a been a dream, or some sucker got what was comin' to him. Now I ain't so sure."

"Thanks, Tag, that's a huge help. Will you be okay if we take off now?"

"Yeah. Thanks for 'da chow."

As they stood to leave, Loy handed Tag one of his business cards.

"Look, Tag. I'm not sure if you're in a place right now where you want any help. I have no idea what your story is brother, but if you want help getting out of that box, call this number and ask for me or Rick. No pressure, just think it over."

Tag stuffed the card in his pocket with a slight nod and slurped the last of his shake, his eyes downcast in embarrassment. Loy patted Tag's shoulder as they left, and his sincere concern for a fellow soldier who had fallen on hard times bled through with his touch. Rick's attitude softened when he saw Tag's eyes mist over at Loy's touch.

With at least some intel under their belts, Rick and Loy headed back to the lab.

<><>

While Rick and Loy questioned Tag, Darren checked with banks in the vicinity of Ken's abduction on the off chance their ATM cameras might have caught anything useful.

When Rick and Loy arrived, Kevin and Bill were back from the office. Kevin and Sally went over the schedule notes and realized Kevin got double booked, which led to Ken covering for him the night of the abduction. Sally didn't remember making the double entry, and she was meticulous about details. Bryan was the best at cybersecurity, and after examining the network logs he found evidence of tampering. Someone manually entered Ken's name to cover for Kevin. Sally assumed Ken or Kevin made the change; all the guys had permissions in the application and occasionally juggled their own schedules, so it was only in hindsight that they realized the changes were not made by any of them. Whoever did it wanted Ken at the hotel that night, and there were no tracks Bryan could trace.

Brad looked rough but was holding himself together, and each of them immediately went to see him when they got back. Brad was just as much a part of their lives as Ken, and their concern for him just as great. All of the men were physically affectionate with one another, and they ruffled his hair, squeezed an arm or shoulder, patted him on the back, or gave him a hug.

Pat and Darren called on their way back with news. The banks were cooperative, and two ATM cameras acquired images of a black van within the time frame corroborated by Tag. They didn't capture the license plate or anything significant, not even the make or model, but at least they knew the when, where, and how of Ken's capture.

Finally, they were making at least some headway, but after the initial information things dried up again, and the next few days were frustrating for everyone. Brad needed to stay in the lab with Dr. Thomas, and the rest of the guys only left when absolutely necessary. Sally subbed out as many of their appointments as possible to another Security Agency to give them time to focus on Ken.

On the fifth day after Ken's abduction, Brad called everyone into the conference room. Due to the suppression serum, he couldn't take sedatives to help him sleep, and his eyes were bloodshot with dark circles under them. He hadn't shaved, and his beard growing in was scraggly and unkempt.

Once everyone was seated an uncomfortable silence fell, with most eyes downcast in frustration. All of them, especially Brad, felt like they were failing Ken.

In a flat voice Brad said, "Before I start, I want to tell you how much I appreciate what's been uncovered so far. Does anyone have any other ideas?"

No one spoke, and in the silence Brad felt Ken slipping further away.

"Doc, you said you'd consider stopping the suppression only after we exhausted normal means of investigation. I think it's time, don't you?"

"Bradford, I know the answer to this already, but my conscience dictates that I must ask anyway.

What you ask is dangerous and could prove fatal. You know Kenneth would not want your death. Are you sure you wish to do this?"

"Doc, I'm sorry, but my life isn't worth shit if Ken's not in it. He means everything to me. I'll gladly lay down my life to save his. Please do this, for both of us."

The doctor's face was solemn when he said, "Very well. Follow me. Everyone stay in the lab until further notice."

As Brad and the doctor left the room, all the guys stood up, and Kevin called out, "Brad!"

Brad stopped and looked back.

"No one is dying here, you got that? Not you. Not Ken. Do you understand?"

Everyone stood by Kevin, making it evident his words were from all of them. Brad looked at the love and support on their faces, along with their fear. His eyes brightened at the emotional intensity of what he saw, and he managed a nod as he followed the doctor to an exam room.

"Disrobe completely and lie on the table. I need to see as much of your body as possible in case further bruising or marks appear. That will give us an indication of Kenneth's physical condition. I am going to strap you down so you will not be able to hurt yourself if something goes wrong."

The doctor connected an IV to his catheter and connected ECG leads once Brad was settled. Brad watched the doctor draw a syringe and inject the contents into a port below the IV, and the serum started to flow. Knowing the serum was going to restore his connection to Ken, he tried to will it to move faster. As difficult as it was, he kept his emotions in check.

"How long, doc?"

"Just a few more seconds. Bradford, with the physical distance Kenneth will not feel your presence or have any awareness of you. It is different for you, as the mental partner. Of course, if you were together, it would be completely different."

It started as a slight tickle in the back of his brain, and a few seconds later Brad's eyes went wide as Ken's presence was once again a part of him, and he couldn't help the sob of relief that escaped him.

"Doc! It's working!"

Ken's physical sensations immediately became apparent, and Brad was aware of the wires and electrodes connected to Ken's body. His mind felt funny, not foggy but strange, and his vision went dark. In a brief moment of panic, he thought he was back in the empty void, but he quickly assimilated the ability to separate his own sensations from Ken's, and as he settled into the connection, he realized Ken was blindfolded.

Tears of relief filled Brad's eyes.

Thank God, Ken, you're alive!

"He's blindfolded and strapped down to a table."

Dr. Thomas let out a sigh of relief as well, knowing confirmation Ken was still alive would rekindle the drive to find and rescue him.

Mimicking Ken's words, Brad blurted out, "Okay, fucker, quit starin' at my dick and get on with it."

Dr. Thomas observed Brad's body, watching as little red spots appeared where electrodes and catheters were attached to Ken.

He felt flushed, and his body broke out in a light sweat. Nearby fans started up, and a soft breeze brushed over his sweaty skin, causing a pleasant, soothing sensation.

Suddenly Brad tensed and flushed, and he broke out in a sweat. He was immediately erect, and his body contracted as powerful, intense sensations unexpectedly hit him. It caught both him and Dr. Thomas by surprise. His body mimicked Ken's reaction, and he would have come off the table if he hadn't been strapped down. He could barely breathe, and his whole body turned beet red.

Breathing heavy, his chest heaved as he sucked in air, and his abs tightened with each breath. A powerful orgasm hit him but didn't stop and quickly became painful. Fire ripped through his body as Dr. Cromwell altered the signals to his nervous systems. The pain was relentless, and there was no reprieve. Ken tensed his body to fight off the pain, but his normal defenses were unavailable and he could only endure it.

If Brad had been present with Ken, what was happening would have killed him, but the distance dampened the effects. It was still almost more than he could take, but he mirrored Ken's silence, enduring what was happening. He had to hold out and discover something that would help them find Ken!

Drenched in sweat, with veins showing across his physique, Brad was finally able to breathe when fluids entered Ken's body to help him recover.

Brad realized Dr. Thomas was talking to him, but it was hard to hear him. He was with Ken, inside his lover and himself at the same time, and it was difficult being in both bodies at once.

"Bradford! Listen! Can you hear me?"

Through gritted teeth, Brad managed to say, "I… I… can hear… you. It's hard to focus. When I'm there, I'm not here… not so much."

"Good. Bradford, listen to me carefully. I am not sure how long it will be safe to continue this. If you focus, you should be able to hear through Kenneth's ears as well, not just what he is feeling.

The tactile sense is always the strongest, but you should be able to hear and smell everything Kenneth does. Try to focus and see if you can find a clue as to where he is or who he is with."

"Oohhhhh Fuck."

"Sorry, doc, that wasn't me!"

Whatever was happening to Ken continued for minutes before it stopped.

"Bradford, I do not like this... Maybe I should stop this before you are injured."

"Doc, no!"

Someone wiping him off and cleaning him up brought Brad's perception back to his own body, and as the blackness of Ken's vision receded, he saw Bill holding a towel with a concerned look on his face.

"Jeez, doc, what are they doing to him?"

"They are testing him, finding his limits."

The doctor realized what Dr. Cromwell was doing to Ken and why. Stimulating Ken's three nervous systems simultaneously would cause his physiology to work overtime on multiple levels, and his captor was gathering vast amounts of neurological and physiological data during that time.

It was a small victory when Dr. Thomas realized the data Dr. Cromwell gathered was invalid because of Ken's connection to Brad. The neurological data originated from their combined nervous systems, and Ken's captor had no way of knowing that.

A burning sensation in his hand told Brad something entered Ken through the catheters, and within seconds Ken felt better.

"Ken just got a surge of energy from something. I'm not sure what they're giving him, but he feels better."

Before Brad could recover, it started again. Massive pain hit him as all the nerve receptors in his body were stimulated simultaneously. Every muscle in his body contracted again, but he didn't have the benefit of Ken's enhanced physiology to fight the pain or recover during the slight reprieve.

"Bradford, I am not breaking the link completely, but I need to weaken the connection. You cannot keep this up!"

Brad was too weak to argue and felt Bill cleaning him up again with a warm damp towel. When he finished, Bill put a hand on Brad's shoulder, squeezing firmly. Bill's concern bled through his touch, but his support was also evident and it gave Brad strength. Brad knew Bill supported him one hundred percent and would do the same for Kevin if their roles were reversed.

As Dr. Thomas altered the solution, Ken's presence lessened but didn't disappear entirely. Ken was still there, but the sensations were filtered, like viewing Ken from a distance rather than being in his body.

The torture continued for an hour, and tears filled Brad's eyes, not from the shared pain but because of what Ken was going through. Finally, mercifully, Ken lost consciousness.

"Doc, he passed out."

Dr. Thomas's voice radiated anger and contempt for whoever was responsible.

"Thank God! That was barbaric!"

"Doc, please let me stay connected. I hate what they're doing to him, but if I share it, at least in part, I feel like I'm supporting him."

Five minutes passed before Ken regained consciousness, and his first sensation was the strong scent of sweat and semen coming from his body. The smells hit Brad, and he breathed them in, relishing the scent of his partner. Normally it would be a turn on, but in this case it was an affirmation that Ken was still alive and it made him miss Ken even more.

The stimulation started again, but this time there was no surge of energy or relief, and Ken endured the torture nearly fifteen minutes before losing consciousness again.

Brad lay on the bed, grateful for the connection but in agony over what Ken was going through, raging against his helplessness and inability to comfort Ken in any way. Ken had no awareness of him but had to know that Brad and the others wouldn't stop until they found him! He had to!

Half an hour went by before Ken regained consciousness, exhausted and aching all over.

Hold on, Ken!

"Doc, he's awake. Can you amp up the connection for a few minutes? I need to try and get something that will help us."

"I will, Bradford, but at the first sign of anything extreme, let me know. Remember, it takes a short time to reverse the serum if something horrific happens."

The doctor did as Brad asked and fully re-established the connection. Brad sank into Ken, closing his eyes and immersing himself in his lover, attempting to sense anything that could help them discover where Ken was or who held him.

"I smell pipe tobacco."

It started out fuzzy, but Brad began tuning in to Ken's other senses and heard movement as someone moved closer.

"Someone's talking."

"Well, my boy, you are exceeding anything I could have imagined. Whoever made you is a genius. I am jealous of his intellect and vision. I am going to make it my life's work to duplicate and even improve upon what he has done."

"You stupid fucker. Compared 'ta him you're in diapers, suckin' on your mom's hind tit and shittin' guacamole into your Huggies. You'll never figure this out. Just get it over with."

"We shall see my boy."

Brad noted the change in Cromwell's tone and knew Ken pissed his captor off. Brad grinned in his mind, knowing Ken had a knack for getting under people's skin when he wanted to. Brad knew Ken chose his words intentionally but didn't know his plan. More typing ensued, and Brad picked up on Dr. Cromwell's attitude as he pounded the keyboard. After a slight pause, a *Beep* followed.

The slight hiss of something hydraulic was audible, and the shackle holding Ken's right wrist raised slightly and then slammed down hard. It hurt a little but not bad.

Brad's body reflected Ken's tension as he steeled himself for another blow. Tapping into Ken's inner resolve, Brad remained silent, knowing the doctor would sever the connection if he reacted. He had to hold on for Ken and find out something that would help!

Beep.

Again, the shackle slammed down, this time much harder. Brad started to sweat from the pain and the effort of holding back what was happening.

The doctor noted Brad's reaction and asked, "Bradford, what is going on?"

Beep.

Brad's wrist splintered, and his breath was coming in gasps from dealing with the pain.

"Bradford!"

Beep.

The audible snap of Brad's wrist filled the room, and he echoed Ken's scream of pain. His body strained against the straps holding him down, trying to arch up from the pain, mimicking Ken's movements.

Beep.

The shackle holding Ken's left wrist rose.

Fuck!

Dr. Thomas plunged the syringe down as soon as Brad's wrist broke, and the seconds before the serum took effect seemed like an eternity. Brad's other wrist snapped, and he screamed uncontrollably. Everyone heard and ran to the room with Brad, the doctor, and Bill. Dr. Thomas heard another pop and looked down to see blood on Brad's chest, where a broken rib protruded through his skin, mirroring Ken's injury.

Brad's voice was raw from screaming, but just before he lost consciousness, Bryan, Pat, Ricky, and Kevin heard him whisper, "Gotcha, you fucker...."

It had been hundreds of years since the doctor had been so scared. However, it had also been centuries since he cared so much for anyone besides his partner, Albrecht. The young men whose lives he changed were like sons to him. With The Order on the brink of losing the war over mankind against their age-old Enemy, he never realized his path would lead him where he was. He nearly lost two of his children that night, and still might lose one. Brad would live, but the danger he put himself in was far more severe than anyone but the doctor realized. At the same time, though, he could not be prouder. Brad, still unawakened, exhibited a willingness to hold on through extreme agony, even at the cost of his own life, for another human being he loved.

As gently as he could, Dr. Thomas set the bones in Brad's wrists and ribs, wrapping his wounds and doing everything possible to ease his pain and make him comfortable. The doctor would soon have a conversation with Bill and the others, knowing they would be confused and disturbed by recent events and what it could mean for them. He did not want their first exposure in another stage of their evolving nature to mar what should be a wondrous part of their lives. He might have to break a rule and take them on their next step rather than letting them reach it on their own.

Based on his knowledge of Ken and what he should be able to deal with, even though it was tearing at his soul knowing what Ken would have to endure, he had a close estimate of how much time they had to find Ken before he would most likely be dead.

Brad remained unconscious for nearly five hours, and each minute was one step closer to Ken's death. Through his actions Brad drained himself beyond any measure of safety, slipping into a coma for a short time before showing some small improvement. The doctor did everything he could to assist Brad's body without endangering him further.

Brad was having the strangest dream. He remembered excruciating pain, blacking out, and was now in a strange place surrounded by darkness. He saw himself clearly, and glancing down, he wore workout shorts, a sleeveless t-shirt, tennis shoes, and his favorite hoodie, which Ken had given him as a gift. He felt like he was on the set of a cheap sci-fi movie that didn't have much of a budget.

Brad called out, "Hello!?"

There was no response, not even an echo, just an eerie silence.

Cautiously, he moved from where he appeared, uncertain of the direction without any point of reference. The floor seemed smooth and solid even though he couldn't see it, and after a while he trusted it would stay that way, so he picked up his pace.

What's the worst that can happen besides I fall and bust my ass?

Keeping track of time was difficult. In fact, he had an intuitive sense that time wasn't moving, and there was so little to the place that his senses had no bearings. An indeterminate amount of time passed, although it seemed quite a while, and Brad noticed a light in the distance. Slowing down, he moved forward guardedly. As he got closer, it looked like a table with a bright light shining down on a man lying spread-eagled, and a sudden sense of urgency hit Brad in the pit of his stomach.

Something was wrong.

When he got within a few feet of the table, Brad hit an invisible barrier and was shocked at what he saw. The man on the table was in horrible shape, covered in blood and sweat, with many open wounds, some obviously burns, and multiple fractures in his arms and legs.

With the amount of damage and blood, Brad wondered how he could still be alive. As he looked more closely, the man was held down by thick metal bands. The face that slowly turned towards him was bruised and swollen, but as soon as they made eye contact, recognition hit Brad like a bolt of lightning.

"KEN! OH FUCK! KEN!"

For a brief second Brad was too stunned to react, then he launched himself against the barrier, pounding his fists against it, desperate to reach Ken.

Ken stared back, his gaze foggy, with no recognition in his eyes, and tears of fear, anger, and frustration spilled as Brad attacked the barrier. It finally started to give, and as it weakened, Ken gained more awareness. His eyes, nearly swollen shut, held a glimmer of recognition.

In the real world, the computer monitoring Ken's brain activity registered the change, as Brad's attack weakened the effects of the serum Dr. Cromwell used to keep Ken from accessing his abilities.

Ken's lips moved, but Brad couldn't hear through the barrier. Pushing his broken and tortured body, Ken struggled to move. It was agonizing, but with his wrist broken and slick with blood, he managed to pull his hand through the shackle.

Ken continued struggling, veins visible across his body from the strain, and Brad had no idea how he endured the pain. His face, under the blood, was beet red. Inch by inch he raised his arm, fighting to straighten the angle of the fractures, straining to reach Brad. Their desperation to reach each other was clear and seemed to be taking forever, even though it was only a few seconds.

When Ken's arm pulled free, blood and spit flew from his mouth as he screamed, his teeth stained with blood and his nostrils flaring with every breath, fighting off overwhelming agony.

Brad wondered how Ken could still be conscious through the damage and torture, and his heart ached at his suffering.

The progress was slow and excruciating, but Brad was closer. His hand felt broken from punching the barrier, but he couldn't stop. He was about to black out from the pain when his fist broke through.

Ken's outstretched hand trembled, and he couldn't straighten his broken arm, but despite the shaking from his efforts he kept pushing.

Finally, their fingertips touched, and Ken's voice filled Brad's mind.

Brad! Oh God, B! Get me outta here! I can't hold on anymore... I. I... I tried man, but I c...c...can't take this anymore!

Ken broke down and started sobbing.

"Ken! Oh fuck, oh fuck!"

Looking at his best friend, his lover, and what they had done to him, hearing the agony in his voice, set fire to Brad. Terrified for his partner, he didn't know what to do to save him. When their fingertips touched, Ken's emotions became a part of Brad. The extent of his torture became evident, and Brad realized Ken was breaking.

Unaware of how he did it, acting on pure instinct, Brad took everything he saw into himself, desperately trying to share or at least lessen Ken's suffering in any way he could. Through the connection of their fingertips, Brad took the fire, the pain, the guilt, all the anger and hatred directed at whoever was responsible, into himself.

Then, he pushed his love into Ken like a hot brand, searing through the pain with his own fire. Brad let his love for Ken wash over him and fill his lover up, stoking his emotions for the man in front of him. Everything within him grew until what he felt was palpable, and he pushed it into Ken, trying to give him hope and strength.

Ken was in too much pain to notice the blaze of white in Brad's eyes when their fingertips touched. This time Brad's eyes glowed bright enough to light the area for a brief second.

Brad sobbed so hard he could hardly talk, crying out, "You have to hold on, Ken! You have to! I can't lose you! We know how to find you! We're coming!"

Brad woke with a start, confused and disoriented. Powerful emotions lingered from the dream, but he couldn't remember what it was about. He was still strapped down to the bed in the lab, exhausted.

<><>

Dr. Thomas noticed Brad move and quickly went to his bedside.

"Bradford? How are you feeling?"

Brad tried to smile, and his reply was raspy and barely audible.

"Like shit."

Brad's throat was raw from the screaming, and even the small whisperer chafed his throat, making him cough and sending renewed pain across his broken ribs. The doctor still wasn't able to give him any sedatives or painkillers due to the lingering effects of the suppression serum.

A rare smile appeared on the doctor's face, and he cupped his hand in the curve of Brad's neck and shoulder, gently squeezing. To anyone who knew the doctor, it was a surprisingly overt show of affection.

"You were incredibly brave tonight, Bradford. Foolish, but brave beyond words, my boy. I am very proud of you."

"Doc," Brad whispered, "I saw him... I saw the bastard that has Ken."

Chapter Three

At Brad's words, the doctor called for Lane straightaway. Not only was Lane an excellent musician, he was also an exceptional sketch artist, often working with law enforcement agencies around Atlanta. Lane popped out of his chair like he was on a spring and rushed into the room, his expression apprehensive and expectant. The doctor explained what was needed, and Lane ran to his locker to retrieve his sketchbook and pencils. Returning quickly, he pulled a stool to Brad's bedside. The doctor left the room, giving Lane strict instructions to call him if needed. Sitting beside his buddy, Lane looked him over carefully. It hurt to see Brad in the condition he was in, but Lane managed his mischievous grin, wanting to act as if everything was alright.

"Hey, Brad, how are you?"

Brad replied with a weak, "Never better."

"Damn, bud, you about gave us all a heart attack. Now you pull this hero shit. You set the bar pretty high for us peons. We all know you just don't want to miss out on that hot package of Ken's. You aren't fooling anyone."

Brad smiled, grateful at Lane's attempt to lighten his spirits. What gave Lane away were the tears in his eyes, which he sought to hide by lowering his head.

Lane's voice caught in his throat, and his words were thick with emotion as he said, "Fuck Brad, please don't do that again. We couldn't stand to lose you… or Ken."

Lane pulled himself together, and once he expressed to Brad how much he meant to him, he swiped the tears from his eyes and got down to business.

"Okay, tell me what this fuckhead looks like."

After the program, Brad, like Lane and the other 'minds,' had perfect recall, and he described the man he saw through Ken's eyes. Long thin face, salt and pepper hair, more salt than pepper, pulled back into a long ponytail. Goatee. Dark eyes. Wrinkles. Pointy chin, high forehead, thin lips. Thin build. Lane worked quickly and before long had a portrait of the man Brad saw, and it was spot on.

Lane was a huge Tolkien fan, and looking intently at the picture, he mumbled to himself, "Fuck me, this guy looks like Saruman."

Standing, Lane gripped Brad's shoulder, giving him a squeeze of comfort and saying, "Okay, buddy, your job's done for now. Let us take over and bring Ken home. Once we get him back, you'll both be as good as new in no time."

Lane excitedly left Brad's room, holding up his sketch and hollering, "Alright, doc, we're good to go!"

Bill was waiting, and as soon as Lane came in he started flipping switches, saying, "Connections to all key government databases are now established; no secrets today, kiddos! We should have at least three to four hours before any intrusion is detected. I've got the kill switch ready in case we get any surprises. Lane, scan that sketch, and we'll start with facial recognition.

"Brad also mentioned the smell of pipe tobacco. I need someone to pull up a record of all the stores in Metro Atlanta that sell tobacco and run with that search. Find the stores, customer lists, who those people bank with, and pull purchasing and credit card billing info. I know it's a big list, but it's a start. We might get lucky and get a hit."

Darren called out, "On it!" and started furiously typing at the terminal he was using.

Partial hits on facial recognition started coming in after twenty minutes, but the initial pings were false-positives. After an hour and a half Bill excitedly yelled out, "We got a hit!!"

The large screen in the Operations room lit up, and a black and white photo from a newspaper appeared on the screen. The quality was horrible, but before anyone said anything, he hollered, "Yeah, yeah, I know it sucks! Working on it!"

He ran the photo through a digital enhancement algorithm, and after a few seconds the picture sharpened. The caption text under the image appeared Slavic.

"This is from the Kyiv Post online archives through the Ukrainian Embassy. The photo is from 1974. According to the caption, it's a congratulatory piece in the paper for a Bohuslav Oleksander for earning his third Ph.D. from the University of Moscow. His degrees are in Microbiology, Chemistry, and Physics. Now we have a name, let's see what else we can find."

Bill paused while he continued typing, and in less than a minute continued his monologue.

"It looks like he dropped out of sight for quite a few years. Ah, sneaky devil, he moved to the United States and changed his name. Next, we see him in 1994 going by Boris Cromwell. He seems camera shy, but we have multiple hits with positive ID from encrypted DOD records.

Darren piped in, "I have records on both Visa and MasterCard under the name Boris Cromwell. He makes regular purchases of tobacco from a shop at Little Five Points."

Bill continued, "Okay, fuc...., um gentlemen....," as soon as Bill remembered the doctor was in the room and listening, he caught himself.

"We know the man's name, his home address, and one distinct purchasing habit. His employment status in the Social Security database shows he's a dog groomer at Pet World. Yeah, right.

"Usually, in a case like this, lack of evidence is evidence in and of itself. Thank goodness our remarkable government likes to repeat their mistakes. Ahhh…. Here we go. Following the money, Dr. Cromwell receives deposits from the Department of Defense into an offshore account from which he very unwisely transfers money to his Wells Fargo checking account. Following the rabbit trail, the Department of Defense leases a few top-secret properties in Atlanta. Doc, by the way, your new search engine rocks."

A map of Atlanta appeared on the second wall screen with the properties highlighted.

"It looks like we're in luck. We have current satellite imagery of all three addresses within the last fifteen minutes."

High altitude images appeared and quickly zoomed-in to within a few hundred feet above the rooftops. There weren't many cars in any of the parking lots, but one in particular had a black van.

"Okay, there's a high probability we just found Ken."

With a confirmed lead and direction, each man became laser-focused. Adrenaline kicked in, and everyone quickly and efficiently gathered their gear and suited up. Chatter was kept to a minimum as each of them were wrapped in their thoughts, forcing themselves to believe they would arrive in time to save Ken.

Loy drove the van, and Bill, Darren, and Lane stayed behind to run Operations remotely since Brad couldn't be left alone. To their surprise, Dr. Thomas insisted on accompanying them, something he had never done before.

"This is not the type of war you trained for in the Navy, and my presence might be required. I will stay in the van and not venture out until you are satisfied it is safe for me to do so."

The drive seemed to take forever, and the men sat still as stone, immersed in the mindset of the mission. There could be no mistakes, and failure was not an option.

Bill managed to pull the original blueprints of the facility before the Department of Defense repurposed it and marked the known entrances and exits, calculating the vantage points they needed to cover. The tactical information appeared on their HUDs, barely discernable to normal eyesight but clearly visible to them.

"Okay, gentlemen, since it's already dark we won't have to wait. Based on satellite imagery, there are eleven cars parked at the facility. I'm uploading a list of names with photos from the tag registrations. All of these people have Top-Secret security clearance, so I doubt anyone in that building is unaware of what's going on.

"It looks like they only use the front entrance, so the other exits might be sealed off. We'll need to cover them just in case.

"Bry, you'll override the security codes and door locks. We need absolute silence even after we're in the building. Chances are they have a kill switch hooked up to Ken in case of a rescue attempt. We need to be invisible and precise.

"Doc, is there anything you want to say? We have a few minutes before we'll be on site."

"Yes, William, thank you. As I stated before, this is not a conventional war of the type you are familiar with. I wish no bloodshed tonight. Injuries are permissible to ensure control, but unless it is unavoidable, I do not want any man or woman to lose their life this evening. The type of war waged here is an atrocity and is the first step towards something far more sinister, and something I wished to protect you from for many years yet.

"The most powerful ally we have is secrecy, and that must remain so. If our Enemy finds this facility filled with bodies, it will only draw further attention to us. I wish to send them a message that is subtler and will, at the very least, make them think twice before attempting something like this again. To use a phrase you all so often employ, I wish those who are behind this to know who they are fucking with. I want them to feel the consequences of their actions and feel fear. Once you have everyone secured, I will need a few minutes alone with them."

None of them had ever heard the doctor curse, and his f-bomb raised a few eyebrows. The bodies heard the quiver of underlying anger in his voice, and Loy, the only empath among them, felt waves of controlled but intense emotion emanating off him.

After a brief, awkward silence, Bill continued over the Commlink, "Okayyy... You're one click away from the facility. Loy, there's a building to your left you can park behind."

Loy pulled off and parked behind the indicated building. The area was pitch black, and when the back door of the van opened, Kevin, Bryan, Rick, and Pat slipped into the night, silent and invisible. They wore full assault gear; black Kevlar bodysuits, covered from head to toe. Their heads and faces were shielded with headsets for communications, HUDs, and modified night vision designed to work with their highly enhanced eyesight. Small pockets covered their suits, filled with various gadgets; ammunition, C4, detonators, emergency medical supplies, and numerous useful items. The suits were wired to monitor their vital signs and included filters to protect against gas and chemicals, and the lining masked their thermal signatures against infrared detection. The newest version of the suits even included remote activated defibrillators

It felt strange not having Ken as their leader, but aside from their anxiety over Ken and what they would find once inside, everyone felt the exhilaration of being on a mission again. Even after eighteen years, none of them had lost their edge. Almost at the same time, each man had the same thought:

These people have no idea what is about to come down on their heads. Nobody fucks with one of our own.

Utterly silent, each of them took positions to await Bryan's signal.

It took Bryan a few minutes to avoid security cameras and get into position. Not wanting to take the time to pick the locks on the junction box, he bent the steel plate with his fingers until it opened. As soon as he spliced into the fiber optic lines from the junction box, the monitors in the van lit up and Loy's voice came over the intercom.

"Good job, Bry. We're in. Stay back and cover the rear entrance in case anyone tries to sneak out on us."

Blending into the shadows, Bryan knelt down to wait.

The security cameras and door locks were now under their control. Back in the van, the doctor started hacking into and taking over their computer system.

Kevin, Rick, and Pat appeared like ghosts at the front entrance to the building. There was a biometric panel requiring a thumbprint in addition to a card, but the panel remained dark as Kevin swiped his smartcard. A barely audible click indicated the release of the magnetic locks.

Kevin swung the door open and moved forward cautiously. Bright fluorescent lights lit up the short hallway in front of them. Their night vision headsets instantly turned off, and the HUDs switched display format to compensate for the sudden change in brightness. Based on the blueprints, Kevin knew there was a small cubby immediately to the left around the corner, housing a desk with at least one security guard. Pat shut the door silently behind them, making sure the magnetic locks re-engaged.

Loy's voice came over the Commlink, "The building is now sealed and under our control. Unless there's a manual override or panic device, no one can get in or out."

Kevin pulled out a small fiber-optic camera that looked like a short length of wire from one of his many pockets, extending it just past the corner of the hallway. A small picture-in-picture window on their HUDs showed an image of a single security guard sitting at a desk with a row of monitors in front of him, oblivious to their presence. The guard was working a Sudoku puzzle with only occasional glances at the monitors.

The guard never saw or heard anything. Kevin moved blindingly fast, knocking the man out and catching him before he started to drop. He sprayed a small aerosol can into the guard's face to make sure he stayed unconscious.

With the first security guard out of the way, they quickly moved down the hallway. There were two women and a man in the first room who froze when Rick and Pat appeared, dressed in all black and pointing weapons at them.

Kevin stayed on lookout, just inside the door. The man fainted when Rick moved towards him, and the two women huddled together, terrified. Rick and Pat sprayed them and pulled their bodies behind the island in the middle of the room to keep them out of sight.

There was one more lab, smaller than the first, and in seconds two more technicians were unconscious and out of sight.

Kevin saw movement ahead and heard general activity. The hallway opened to a large room, which took up most of the floor plan of the building. A large glass chamber occupied the middle of the brightly lit room, and Kevin's gut wrenched at the sight before him.

Ken was spread eagle on the table, held down by multiple large metal bands. He was naked, covered in blood and sweat, and his body twitched intermittently. Wounds covered nearly every inch of him; blackened areas that were obviously burns, pieces of skin removed, and his limbs were bent at odd angles. A tall, thin man in a white lab coat stood inside the chamber with his back to Kevin. The ponytail told Kevin it was probably Dr. Cromwell, and it took every ounce of Kevin's self-control not to lift his rifle and end the man's miserable existence.

Loy, the doctor, and everyone saw the scene through Kevin's headset, including Brad and the guys in the lab.

Dr. Cromwell was taking skin grafts from Ken's legs to freeze for future study, keeping Ken awake partially out of scientific curiosity, but mostly out of cruelty. Ken continually insulted his intelligence at every opportunity.

One of the technicians screamed when Kevin stepped out of the hallway, and fear hit Dr. Cromwell fast and hard. He realized right away what was happening and bolted towards the back of the building, pausing only long enough to lift a small acrylic casing and press the now deactivated kill switch. The armed guards started to react but lifted their rifles when they saw multiple red dots on their torsos.

In a tight voice, Kevin said, "Bry, he's headed towards you."

While Dr. Cromwell fled, Rick and Pat incapacitated the remaining lab technicians and guards in a matter of seconds.

<>

How dare they!

Dr. Cromwell was furious as he ran down the hallway, throwing his body against the panic bar stretched across the back door. The door flew open, and he slammed right into Bryan's 6', 425 lb. frame, which felt much harder than the door. Bryan grabbed the doctor by the front of his lab coat, lifting him off his feet like a rag doll.

Bryan, gentlest of all the men, was usually quiet and stoic, but one thing he would not tolerate was a friend or loved one being threatened or hurt. Pulling off his headset, Bryan drew the doctor close until their faces were inches apart, so the only part of Bryan's face visible were his piercing green eyes.

The image of Ken burned in his mind, and his rage towards the man in his grasp was nearly incapacitating. Despite his training, Bryan wanted to slowly and painfully squeeze the life out of the monster in his hands. Dr. Cromwell looked into Bryan's eyes and saw his death, and was so terrified he lost control of his bladder and passed out. Cromwell went limp in his grasp, and a strong odor of urine followed. With a frustrated grunt, Bryan head-butted Cromwell, careful not to break his nose.

Bryan's deep gravelly voice came across the Commlink, "I got him, Kev."

Kevin practically shouted, "Doc, we need you! NOW!"

As soon as the image of Ken came across the video feed, the doctor told Loy to move out, and Loy was pulling up even as Kevin shouted his order.

Kevin looked down at his friend, his Captain, whose face was almost unrecognizable from the swelling and blood. Kevin had no idea how Ken could still be conscious, but he was. Patrick found the release mechanism for the shackles, and as soon as they retracted, Ken's body began pulling into a fetal position from the pain. Kevin started removing electrodes and catheters as quickly as he could, trying to be gentle.

Tears shone in all their eyes, and they kept muttering, "Fuck," or "Fuck me," under their breath.

Ken's body spasmed and twitched uncontrollably, and he kept trying to say something, but even with Kevin's heightened hearing he couldn't make out Ken's words. Kevin bent over, desperately wanting to comfort his friend but afraid to touch him; bruises, lacerations, burns, lack of skin, or broken bones covered nearly every square inch of Ken's body. None of them, in all their history of running covert missions in the Navy, had ever witnessed such a level of torture.

Kevin leaned over and said, "Ken, buddy, we're here. You're safe. The doc will be here any second, and we're taking you home. You have to hang on, man, you have to!"

Ken was still trying to say something, and Kevin put his ear up to Ken's mouth, finally grasping his words.

"K... k... kill me, Kev. Please... m... mm... make... it... stop."

Hot tears fell down Kevin's cheeks at Ken's plea.

Where was the doc?!

It seemed like forever before the doctor rushed into the room, followed by Loy, who carried a collapsible stretcher and the doctor's medical case.

The doctor saw Ken over the monitor, but seeing him in person was almost too much to bear.

"Oh, my poor boy, what have they done to you?"

The doctor's voice choked with grief, and he only paused long enough to whisper those words before rushing to the table.

Opening his medical case, the doctor took out a syringe and plunged it into Ken's neck. While reaching for another, Ken's trembling stopped, and he went still.

"Kevin!"

The desperation in the doctor's voice was evident, shouting Kevin's name like a command and a cry for help. Kevin moved to the doctor's side, forcing himself to stay focused for Ken's sake.

The doctor pulled out a long black case and unzipped it. Kevin saw the label, a mix of Atropine and Epinephrine used for Cardiac Arrest. Kevin realized Ken's heart had stopped, and he was no longer breathing.

"Kevin, I am not strong enough to get this through his chest plate. I will hold it in position, but you must push it through. On three… one… two… three!"

Gripping the syringe, Kevin pushed the needle through the dense muscle, cartilage, and connective tissues of Ken's chest. The doctor quickly pressed the plunger, forcing the mixture directly into Ken's heart.

Ken reacted immediately, his back arching as air sucked into his lungs, then he collapsed, unconscious but thankfully breathing once again. Forcing his hands to remain steady, the doctor administered the other syringes.

Relief flooded through them when they realized Ken was breathing again. None of them could imagine what Brad was going through, watching events over the video feed at the lab.

"Kenneth is not out of the woods yet. The serums I administered should keep him alive until we get back to the lab."

The doctor pulled three small vials from his bag, giving one each to Kevin, Rick, and Pat.

"Take these and place an eyedropper full of the liquid under the tongue of everyone here, and be sure to leave everyone in the rooms where you found them."

Activating his Commlink, the doctor said, "Bryan, please bring Dr. Cromwell to me."

Bryan came down the hallway with Cromwell over his shoulder and flopped him hard on the floor. It was clear to everyone Cromwell pissed his pants and had a bloody nose.

They all looked at Cromwell and then Bryan, who shrugged, and with an innocent look on his face, said, "What?! HE ran into ME!"

Turning to Loy, the doctor asked, "Is the code uploaded to their system?"

"Yes, sir."

The doctor sat at one of the terminals in the room and started quickly typing. A moment later the lights flickered, and the entire facility rebooted.

"Bryan, please put that monster in the first room with the others."

Bryan grabbed Cromwell by one foot, dragging him into the other room, not caring if his head happened to knock into a few chairs or doorframes on the way.

The doctor went quickly to each room where unconscious scientists or technicians were piled on the floor. He was alone, and no one knew what he did to them.

<>

His eyes turning white, Aaron looked down on the unconscious form of Boris Cromwell, looking into his mind. He had to know if Ken's abduction was simply someone in the government who managed to trace them, or if The Enemy was involved. He would justify his actions to his superiors if questioned, but his personal mission of saving The Order might be in jeopardy based on the source of Ken's kidnapping.

He read Boris Cromwell's memories, and General Burgess from Project Glass Hand was responsible. He felt no direct presence of The Enemy within Cromwell, although Aaron was sure the 'unknown benefactor' was from Them. There was no direct proof other than his intuition, but his instincts where The Enemy was concerned had never failed him.

How, after all these years?

He knew his age-old Enemy was responsible and wanted no direct trails back to him or his young charges. His response had to be as subtle as their interference, to protect his sons, and give them time to grow into what he needed; what the world and mankind needed.

The man before him was responsible for the horrific torture Kenneth endured, and while misguided, he wasn't truly evil, at least not yet. Through his actions, Cromwell was teetering on the edge and near the point of no return, but he wasn't there yet. As deep as Aaron's anger burned over what Boris Cromwell did to Ken, and as difficult as it was, he refrained from wiping his mind.

Moving on to the others, he altered their memories and planted new ones. Once finished, he hurried back to his sons, ready to take Ken home.

<>

Hurrying back to the others, he said, "That should do the trick. Now, let us get Kenneth out of his horrible place."

Loy extended the stretcher, and Kevin and Rick carefully transferred Ken onto it. They were as gentle as possible, knowing every movement could cause more damage to Ken, and even though he was unconscious, more pain.

After securing Ken in the van, they quickly cleaned up any evidence of their presence and gathered all the tissue samples from Ken, and left. The doctor already erased the data, along with the backups, and replaced everything with a surprise of his own.

Terror unlike anything Brad had ever known ran through him at the sight of Ken on the monitor. Brad's heart, linked to Ken's, stopped beating when Ken's did, but Ken's death severed their connection, and Brad's heart resumed beating.

Bill, Darren, and Lane were with him, holding and supporting him, but Ken's temporary demise was the straw that broke the camel's back. Even after Ken started breathing again, Brad's face remained slack and emotionless. The breaking of their connection set Brad adrift again, and his vision spiraled as he passed out. Darren gently picked him up and moved him into one of the beds.

It took nearly half an hour in traffic to get to the lab, and the drive back was silent as everyone sat staring at Ken with tears running down their faces, their thoughts spinning at the sight of his maimed and tortured body.

At one point, the doctor asked Bill over the Commlink, "William, how is Bradford?"

"Doc, he's unconscious. Right after you gave Ken the adrenaline shot he passed out, and we put him in a bed."

The doctor squeezed his eyes closed and let out a heavy sigh.

"William, keep him under observation. Do NOT let him hurt himself, do you understand?"

Bill and the others panicked when they realized what the doctor meant.

"Yes, sir!"

Bill looked at Darren and Lane, and they rushed to the room where Brad lay on the bed. He was awake, his eyes open and staring at the ceiling, but completely despondent, not hearing or registering their presence.

Nervous glances passed between them. Their concern for their two buddies ran deep, and they were rattled by events. How could this be happening?

Brad was still despondent when they arrived with Ken, moving him into the critical unit, their version of an ICU. The doctor quickly attached Ken to his computers and equipment, working swiftly and efficiently, asking whoever was closest for assistance when he needed certain things from other areas of the lab. All of the men were trained EMTs and aided him as required.

It was nearly an hour before the doctor slowed down, and when he finally emerged from Ken's room, he faced the stares of eight anxious men desperate to know if Ken was going to be alright.

Staring back at his charges, his adoptive sons, and seeing the looks on their faces, he almost faltered. Regardless of the outcome with Ken and Brad, they were now embarking in a new direction in their lives, one he wanted to spare them from taking for many years yet. He would wait until matters were settled with Ken and Brad before deciding how best to proceed.

"What Kenneth experienced was horrific beyond words. That any human could treat another in such a way… it reminds me of darker times. I wished to spare you all exposure to such atrocities for many years to come. Kenneth is not out of the woods yet. His injuries are severe… If he survives the next twenty-four hours, his chances will improve immensely. Once we get past his physical injuries, I am concerned about his mental state. I have no idea what condition his mind will be in after his torture. I have temporarily induced a coma to let his body recover as it was designed to do, and we will have to wait and monitor his progress and cross whatever bridges we find as they arise."

Kevin felt he had to tell the doctor about Ken's request.

"Doc?"

"Yes, Kevin?"

"Doc, with what you just said about Ken's mental state… When we got to him… He…"

Ken's plea was still fresh in his mind, and Kevin started to lose it.

"He begged me to kill him."

Bill moved to Kevin, wrapping his arms around his partner from behind, and Kevin drew strength from the embrace, taking a deep breath to pull himself together.

"I pray we were not too late, and Bradford's sacrifice not in vain. You witnessed the depth of his torture, but Kenneth is resilient, as is Bradford, and they both have all of us to help them. We are family and must be supportive and understanding during their recovery. However, I am as fearful for Bradford as I am Kenneth. He proved far more resourceful than I imagined and put himself in extreme danger by helping Kenneth. I am not sure he is aware of what he did, or how, but he is wounded and severely drained, perhaps beyond our help."

Everyone stood in stunned silence as the doctor's words sank in. They all felt like they just got kicked in the nuts – twice!

"Bryan, would you and Lane clean Kenneth up while I see to Bradford? Be as gentle as you can, and let me know if you need any assistance."

As Bryan and Lane moved by the doctor, he reached out and gripped their arms in a reassuring squeeze. Each of them covered his hand in a show of gratitude and went to Ken's room to carry out their task. The doctor seemed older, his shoulders slumped, and his face expressed a sadness they had never seen before. On top of Ken and Brad, they were worried about him as well.

The doctor entered Brad's room and observed him lying in bed, his eyes open but seeing nothing. The sheets were pulled up to his waist, exposing the wrap around his ribcage that covered most of his bare torso. His hands were in braces from mid-palm to mid-forearm, and his face looked haggard with dark circles under his eyes. His usually tanned complexion was almost gray, and the unkempt beard forming on his face made him look years older.

The doctor leaned over him, placing his hands on Brad's shoulders, looking intently into his vacant eyes.

"Bradford, I know you can hear me even if it is only your unconscious mind. My boy, what you managed to do was incredibly heroic. The others do not understand yet just what it is you did. I am still not sure how you managed it on your own. You have progressed so far beyond what I expected at this time. We cannot afford to lose you, son; I cannot afford to lose you. Kenneth, especially, needs you more than ever even after all you have done for him.

"I am giving you a beacon to follow, but you must make the journey back on your own. I wish I were permitted to help you more, but for the sake of the others, I cannot. Not yet."

The doctor's eyes flashed white for a brief second as he looked at Brad, then he squeezed them shut with a heavy sigh. When he opened them again they were back to their normal color but reflected the sadness and pain he felt for his young charge, as well as his frustration. The only indication Brad heard any of what the doctor said was a single tear leaking from the corner of his eye.

◇◇

Lane gathered clean towels, cotton balls, Q-tips, rubbing alcohol, and hot water.

Bryan still wore his Kevlar, and Lane quietly told him, "Bry, go ditch the suit. I'll get started."

Grateful, Bryan quickly changed, returning in a few moments, and they began the arduous task of cleaning up their brother. Even though Ken was in a coma, his body still felt pain, and they did their best to keep their touches light.

Dr. Cromwell's cruelty became more apparent as they worked. The cuts were deeper than necessary for grafts, and jagged edges intentionally exposed raw nerves. Dozens of round cigar-shaped burns covered Ken's body, but one area on his shoulder was burned down to the bone as if exposed to an intense flame.

It took Lane and Bryan hours to clean him up, and they couldn't believe how many towels they used and the amount of blood. Both men cried on and off while they worked, periodically stopping to brace themselves so they could continue.

<><>

Ken made it through the first twenty-four hours, sending a sigh of relief through everyone, but remained in a coma. His unconscious mind guided and prioritized his recovery as it was designed to do, and his body quickly started showing outward signs of improvement. As long as the doctor kept his body supplied with nutrients, proteins, vitamins, and hydration, Ken would return to full physical health. The swelling in his face was gone, although some bruising was still present; outwardly, at least, he was starting to look like his ruggedly handsome self. Scars would be the last to heal, so he would continue to look rough for a while. Like Brad, Ken hadn't shaved since his abduction and had more than a week's worth of beard growth.

Brad, on the other hand, looked worse than ever. He hadn't had anything substantial to eat in days, and while the doctor pumped fluids into him to prevent dehydration, he was visibly losing weight. The doctor decided to induce a coma to try and reduce his brain activity; something was going on in his mind, but the doctor was making no headway in reaching him through conventional means. There were a few times he came close to breaking his Oath and using unconventional methods, but for the sake of the other men in his care, he always backed down from that decision.

With both men in a coma, the doctor sent everyone home for the first night since Ken's rescue.

"You have all been through your own ordeal since this started, and need to spend time with one another to take care of yourselves. I will stay with Kenneth and Bradford, and rest assured, I will contact you all immediately if there is any change."

Reluctantly the guys agreed and left the doctor alone, going home to eat a solid meal and take comfort in each other. The realization hit them that what happened to their friends could happen to any of them, and that night when their bodies were intertwined as they made love, their love grew deeper and stronger, replenishing their hearts and minds.

<><>

Shortly after midnight, in the dark of the lab, Brad sat up. Glancing around, his face pale, he slowly divested himself of all the wires and electrodes attached to his body.

Naked, he walked to Ken's bedside in the room adjacent to his. He stood silently, looking at his lover before placing a hand on Ken's bare chest, taking comfort in the heat and solidity of his body. Minutes passed, and when he finally moved, he crawled into Ken's bed.

It was difficult to get situated because the bed wasn't designed for two big men, but he finally settled with his head on Ken's chest, while gently stroking Ken's body wherever he could reach. The braces restricted his hands, and he could only use his fingertips, but it was enough to make a connection. Ken was warmer than usual because of the healing process, and Brad started to sweat where their skin touched. Quietly crying, he lay with his lover while his tears fell on Ken's chest, pooling and running across his ribs. If the doctor or any of his friends saw him, it would be unclear if Brad were comforting Ken or seeking comfort from him.

Sally was frantic, and the company was at risk of losing clients if they didn't cover a few jobs, so Pat, Darren, Rick, Loy, Kevin, and Bill headed to the office for at least part of the day. None of them wanted to do it, but with Ken on the mend and Brad at least stable, some of the urgency let up.

Lane and Bryan didn't have any clients until late morning, so they went to the lab first thing, picking up an assortment of breakfast items for themselves and the doc on the way in. Being optimistic, they picked up extra for Ken and Brad. The doctor wasn't known to be an early riser, and when they walked in the lights were off and the lab quiet, so Lane went to check on Brad and Bryan to wake up the doc.

Seconds later, Lane let out an excited shout, "Doc! Bry! Come quick! Check this out!"

The doctor shot out of bed at Lane's outburst, which sounded more surprised than panicked, but urgent, and rushed to Ken's room where Lane stood at the door with a shocked but happy look on his face. The sight of Brad asleep, draped across Ken, amazed and baffled the three of them.

Still half asleep, the doctor mumbled, "Oh my!"

How Brad could have gotten there on his own was a mystery. He was in an induced coma and should not have been able to move, let alone walk. Bryan moved to the bedside and immediately smelled a faint odor of sweat and wondered at it. A smirk came to his face at the thought that popped into his head.

It would be just like these studs to figure out how to have sex even in a coma.

Looking closer, he noticed the changes on Ken's body and exclaimed, "Oh shit, doc, look!"

Bryan gently lifted Brad's arm off Ken's chest, and where their skin had been touching, Ken's body seemed completely healed.

"Quickly, Bryan, take Bradford back to his bed."

Bryan lifted Brad like a baby, cradled in his arms, and took him back to the other room. Lane and the doctor looked at the outline of Brad's body on Ken, outwardly healthy and without scars. On closer observation, they even noted the tear trails across Ken's chest and ribs.

"This is entirely unexpected... and fascinating!"

Whatever happened between them, Ken's healing accelerated significantly, and the doctor stopped the induced coma, letting Ken enter a natural sleep.

Brad, however, continued to decline both physically and mentally. Whatever he managed to do, consciously or not, took its toll on him. He was now awake but extremely weak and groggy.

Brad's voice was barely discernible, but he managed a weak, "Hi doc," when the doctor came in.

"Bradford, thank goodness you are awake."

The tears in the doctor's eyes were something Brad had never seen before.

Lane and Bryan came into the room, one on either side of his bed, both grabbing him and pulling him into a tight hug.

Lane was the first to speak, and with relief in his voice, asked, "Hey, bud, you finally decided to join us?"

The doctor left to get some vials to draw blood and give them a private moment.

Bryan couldn't hold back and said, "Fuck me, Brad, so help me God if you ever do anything like this again, I will kill you myself, you crazy bastard!"

Brad saw the smile on Bryan's face and the wetness in his eyes and tried to smile back. Brad's voice was thin and raspy, and Bryan and Lane were shocked at how weak he was.

"I'm hungry. Do you ladies have anything in the kitchen?"

Lane replied, "Yeah, we got extra biscuits, but I think you need something a little healthier. I'll be back!"

Bryan gave Lane the 'be careful' look, and Lane nodded. They were still not supposed to travel alone, but neither one of them wanted to leave Brad by himself, and Lane would be cautious and alert.

As Lane left the room, Bryan sat on the edge of the bed and put a hand on Brad's shoulder, giving him a squeeze.

"Hey, bud, Ken's doing much better. I bet the doc will let us move you two into the same room if we ask. Whatever mojo you picked up worked wonders on him."

Brad gave him a curious look but didn't respond to his comment.

"Do you think I can see him? Can you help me in there?"

"Sure, buddy."

Again, Bryan was shocked at how weak Brad was and practically carried him into Ken's room.

"I need to sit down, Bry. Sorry… I guess I'm more tired than I thought."

Bryan pulled a chair to the bedside and got Brad situated.

"Brad, you've got nothing to be sorry about. You're a fuckin hero in all our eyes."

Thinking about everything his buddies had gone through, Bryan teared up again and with a sniff pulled Brad against him, crossing his arms over Brad's chest in a hug from behind, holding him for a minute and ruffling his hair as he let go.

Brad squeezed Bryan's forearms, returning the hug and reclining his head against Bryan's chest, but didn't say anything. When Bryan released him, Brad leaned forward and took one of Ken's hands between both of his. The braces made it awkward but as soon as their skin touched, Ken inhaled deeply and his eyes opened. For a split-second, Bryan saw terror in his eyes, and Ken tried to sit up, thinking he was still a prisoner.

Bryan quickly grabbed Ken's shoulders, holding him down so he wouldn't pull any wires loose.

"Whoa, Ken... You're safe! You're at the lab! We got you!"

Ken's vision came into focus, and he started shaking, whispering, "Oh fuck…" as tears of relief filled his eyes.

Bryan began crying too and pulled Ken into a tight hug.

Smiling, he thought to himself: *Damn, I should buy stock in Kleenex with all the crying going on around here.*

Brad struggled to stand, and as soon as Ken realized he was there, grabbed him and pulled him into a fierce embrace. Brad sucked his breath in pain as Ken squeezed his broken ribs, and Ken immediately loosened his grip when he realized Brad was hurt. When he looked, Ken noted the wrappings covering most of Brad's bare torso and the braces on his hands and wrists.

Ken was shocked at how horrible Brad looked. Just last week he was tanning up nice, but now he looked pale and pasty, with dark circles under his bloodshot eyes, and he looked like he had lost weight.

"B? What happened? Who did this to you?"

Even though Ken was weak from his own recovery, Brad felt light as a feather in his arms as he pulled Brad into his lap, facing away, hugging him from behind and being careful of his ribs. Resting his chin on Brad's shoulder, Ken nuzzled him affectionately and held him, wanting to feel as much skin contact between them as he could manage. Neither man had shaved in over a week, and the sound and sensation of their beards rubbing together was pure bliss. Brad covered Ken's hands with his own and pressed against him, feeling the heat from his body. They both cried while Ken rocked them back and forth, holding his lover and soaking in his presence.

At that point Bryan felt like he was intruding, and as he turned to go, he noticed even though Brad was crying, his eyes had a flat, faraway look entirely out of character.

Well, the doc said it was going to take a while. They've been through hell and back for each other.

Bryan prayed both his brothers would get back to their old selves as soon as possible, and went to report to the doc what just happened. The doctor was anxious but gave Ken and Brad some privacy, and by the time he went in, they were asleep with Ken spooning Brad. Ken had one arm over Brad's chest, with their hands intertwined as much as the braces would allow, and Brad clutched their hands against his chest.

Simply being near Ken accelerated Brad's healing. The doctor kept them in the lab a few more days for observation, and the rest of the team returned to their regular schedules at the security firm. They took turns swinging by the lab a few times a day to drop off food and check on Ken and Brad. The doc felt it was safe to return to his own home in the evenings beginning that night, pleased with the physical progress in both his charges.

That evening when the doctor left, Ken secured the lab. The same as when he was home, any remaining tension from the day flowed out of him when the seals engaged and the air pressure changed.

He went to Brad's desk, where Brad sat on a stool working on his tablet. Putting a hand on Brad's back, Ken leaned over and kissed his cheek.

"You know B... I love the doc and the guys, but I'm glad we're finally alone. I want you all to myself."

The funk Brad was in when he first woke up had lifted some, but he still wasn't back to his old self.

"Yeah, I know what you mean. When I was little, my mom always said the best part about company is when they leave." After a slight pause, he continued so faintly even Ken had a hard time hearing him, "It's one of the few things I remember her saying."

Ken stood behind Brad, rubbing his neck and shoulders and enjoying the feel of his body. Brad stopped typing and lowered his head, losing himself in the touch of Ken's strong hands.

Such big strong hands.

Ken kept it up, knowing Brad needed his love more than ever, instinctively knowing something was still wrong. That evening was the first time since Ken's rescue the two of them had any committed alone time, and Ken didn't want to ruin the mood with a serious conversation. It had been nearly two weeks since they had sex, and they needed each other badly.

Brad had always been the caretaker in their relationship, but now it was Ken's turn to take on that role, and he was more than happy to do so. What scared him was Brad had never needed to be taken care of, not like now. He was always the emotional rock of their relationship, wiser and more mature and always knowing the right thing to say, which was why Ken was worried about him. Brad seemed lost, and Ken needed to help him find his way back. He didn't know how, but he would figure it out. He had too.

For minutes Ken rubbed Brad's back and shoulders, kneading his stiff muscles. Sighing, Brad leaned forward so Ken could move further down his back. Reaching down, Ken grabbed the hem of Brad's t-shirt, and Brad raised his arms as Ken lifted it off.

Ken looked down at the man he loved more than anything. He loved Brad's back. *Hell, I love everything about this man.* He could tell Brad had lost weight, but his body was still solid muscle.

Once Brad's shirt was off, Ken became aroused. The feel of Brad's body, his smooth skin, hard muscles, and unique scent kick-started Ken's libido. Before he lost himself in the feeling of comforting his lover, Ken reminded himself what he was doing was for Brad, so he continued his massage, gentle but firm, wanting Brad to feel how much he loved him through his touch.

He leaned over and every so often kissed the top of Brad's head or the back of his neck and shoulders. Increasing his range, Ken ran his hands down Brad's arms, squeezing his biceps, shoulders, and lats. Brad's head hung forward, and he let out almost constant moans of pleasure, letting Ken know how much he enjoyed the sensations.

Touching Brad after everything they experienced tested Ken's control, his excitement evident in the tightness of his shorts. Keeping one hand on Brad's back, with his other hand Ken pulled down his own shorts. He wanted Brad to know how much merely touching his lover turned him on.

Brad was overwhelmed with the sensation and feeling of Ken's presence. For a time, he had been afraid he would never feel Ken's touch again.

The anguish of feeling so isolated and alone, freezing him down to his soul, was still in him. Ken's touch helped to fight it off, right then at that moment. Ken's touch, the touch that could light him up like nothing else in the world. Ken's warm hands on his bare skin, rubbing away the loneliness and filling him back up, were a balm to his injured soul.

Ken moved forward and pressed himself against Brad's back.

"This is what you do to me, B. This is for you. I love you."

Brad felt Ken against his back. Ken knelt behind him, pulling Brad back by his shoulders, molding their bodies together with his powerful arms. The culmination of being so lovingly cared for and feeling Ken's love for him through his touch sent Brad over the edge. Ken's emotions were raw and powerful and on the surface, along with his desire, and in reaction, Brad's body shook in a powerful orgasm.

Ken felt the sudden tension in Brad when his head slumped forward, and his shoulders shook like he was crying.

Afraid something was wrong, Ken softly asked, "B? What's wrong? Talk 'ta me."

It took a couple of seconds for Brad to catch his breath. He was crying, but also laughing.

"Nothing's wrong, you douche, I'm laughing. You just made me shoot a two-week load in my shorts without even touching myself!"

Brad slowly spun around on the stool to face Ken. The wetness on his cheeks, coupled with the smile on his face, confused Ken. They both stood and Brad threw his arms around Ken, squeezing with every ounce of strength he could muster. Resting his chin in the crook of Ken's neck and shoulder, he stood still, holding them together. The heat and urgency of Ken pressing against Brad's stomach could not be denied any longer. Brad knew Ken was on the edge and didn't want to leave him hanging, so he pulled back. They could cuddle after.

Brad turned them both around and put his hands on Ken's shoulders, pushing him down onto the stool. Ken's shorts were still around his ankles, but other than that he was naked. Brad ran his eyes quickly from head to toe, his eyes filled with lust for the Greek god sitting in front of him, his arousal pointing right at him and clearly in need of attention.

Resting his hands on Ken's thighs, Brad lowered himself to his knees, so Ken's crotch was at eye level. The vision of Ken from that angle, his thick chest, deep cut abs, and powerful arms, was intoxicating. Brad inhaled deeply, smelling the heat and scent of his lover, and that sensation was just as compelling as the visual.

Ken watched Brad's eyes rake over his body and saw the lust in them. That alone was enough to send him over the edge, but when Brad touched him, every muscle in Ken's body contracted. Just as it was a few minutes ago, everything in Brad, all the pent-up emotion and need, his love and connection to Ken, entered Ken through his touch.

Ken couldn't say anything, and other than his heavy breathing, his chest heaving from the power of his orgasm, he didn't make any noise. Ken's mouth was open, his eyes shut tight, his handsome face contorted in a mask of intense pleasure. His orgasm lasted nearly a minute, and Brad did everything possible to prolong his pleasure.

Strength and fortitude rushed into Brad more powerfully than ever before when he took Ken's load down his throat.

When his breathing returned to normal, Ken said, "Fuck, that was intense. I love you, B. Come here."

Ken lifted him up, pulling Brad into another hug, only keeping enough distance to look into Brad's eyes. Ken had tears in his eyes, too, and they both brushed the tears out of each other's eyes.

With a grin, Ken said, "Man, here go the waterworks again."

Brad smiled back and nodded. It was a good moment and started a long kiss between them.

Brad broke their kiss long enough to say, "Now that we have your hair-trigger out of the way, it's time for some serious action. Let's go to bed."

Smiling at one another, their foreheads pressed together, they started bantering like their old selves.

Ken retorted, "My hair trigger? What the hell do you call shooting in your shorts without me even touching your dick?"

"That was all part of my plan. I have mad seduction skills, and you completely fell for them. You, big guy, are a pussy."

"So, you think in that pea brain of yours, you just seduced me?"

Brad laughed and said, "Shut the fuck up, and let's get into bed!"

Hand in hand, they moved to one of the exam rooms with a hospital bed and hopped in. Once in bed, Ken held himself up with his arms on either side of Brad's head. Lowering his face, they kissed while Brad ran his hands over Ken's chest and arms, feeling the strength and power in his body, and in seconds they were both hard again.

Ken broke the kiss, staring into his lover's eyes, and with the grin he knew Brad couldn't resist, he asked, "Hey B… do you wanna…?"

Before Ken got any further Brad said, "Yes."

Their eyes, Ken's emerald green and Brad's crystal blue, turned almost white for a brief second, and they sensed the change immediately as their nervous systems linked. With huge grins on their faces, they spent the entire night making love in every conceivable position and place in the lab.

When Bryan and Lane stopped by the next morning with breakfast, the lab was an absolute wreck and reeked of sex. Immediately they knew what happened, and Lane let out a loud, "Holy Fuck! Hahahahahaha!"

Bryan took the food to the kitchen and saw two empty gallons of milk, a big jar of protein powder, and multiple empty bottles of Gator-Ade on the counter.

Looks like someone needed a recharge last night!

He laughed to himself, happy for his two buddies, and knowing what he saw meant they were on the road to recovery.

Ken and Brad woke with a start at the sound of the security system disengaging. Still naked, they quickly threw on shorts and breathed a sigh of relief when they realized it was Lane and Bryan and not the doctor. Stepping out of their room shirtless and barefoot, they were stunned at the condition of the lab. Papers were everywhere, tables cleared off, and chairs knocked over.

Wide-eyed, Ken raised his eyebrows, and Brad muttered, "Holy shit, did we do that?"

Bryan held his nose as he came back from the kitchen, squirting a can of air freshener everywhere.

"Okay, I'm officially impressed by you two fuckers. Now I know what that earthquake I felt last night was! You two managed to trash and stink up an entire building!"

Lane noticed the massive stain on Brad's shorts and laughed again, exclaiming, "Damn, Ken, I'm disappointed! To let a load like that go to waste is criminal."

Brad blushed a deep red, and then he and Ken burst out laughing.

Looking at his watch, Lane said, "Alright, ladies, the doc is on his way, and I figure you have about fifteen minutes before he shows up, so you'd better hurry and clean this place up. Bry, we need to hit the road if we're going to make it to the office on time."

As he walked by, Bryan gave Brad's crotch a big shot of air freshener, and he and Lane were still laughing as they shut the door on their way out.

In a panic, Ken and Brad ran around like madmen trying to get the lab straightened up before the doctor arrived.

<>

As Bryan and Lane got in their Explorer, their eyes were a little glassy. Bryan reached over and pulled Lane into a hug, saying, "I feel the same way, Little Buddy. It's good to see them both that way. For a while…"

Lane covered Bryan's mouth with a quick kiss and then said, "Don't say it, Bry. They're still with us, and that's all that matters."

Both of them were grateful Brad and Ken were recovering and still in their lives, and their heartfelt relief was strong as Lane pulled out of the parking lot to head to the office.

Lane whispered, almost to himself, "The band is still together."

Bryan's usually stoic face broke into a grin at Lane's reference.

"Fuck, yeah."

By the end of the week, between his enhanced physiology and the doctor's exemplary care, Ken was physically as good as new. The strange incident on the night Brad slept in his room took weeks off of his recovery. The doctor knew what happened, but not how. It had to be an unconscious reaction on Brad's part, but what he accomplished bordered on the metaphysical. Science alone couldn't explain what happened, and the closest explanation the doctor had was that Brad exchanged something with Ken along the lines of his life energy, his soul. The doctor vowed to look into it, with great urgency. None of the men should be able to do that yet. Eventually, yes, but not for many years yet.

There was obviously more going on between the two men than the doctor fully realized. Ken exhibited remarkable resilience, and aside from healing faster, his mental state was much better than anticipated.

For the time being Brad seemed to be recovering as well, and the doctor knew what would happen when he started leaving them alone at night. If the smell of air freshener wasn't enough to clue him in, they kept rearranging his papers when they cleaned up every morning.

The doctor determined he would just have to keep an eye on Brad. The long-term effects of what he did were unknown, and the doctor was apprehensive.

At the end of that week the doctor cleared Ken and Brad to go home, with the stipulation that if they left their house they went together, even if it was a quick trip to the grocery store or to get gas. The same rule was in effect for all the guys, for their protection. He did not want Brad or Ken returning to work yet, allowing more time for a full recovery.

Ken exclaimed, "That's great, doc!"

"Yes, Kenneth, not only do I think it is time, but I am not sure the lab can take much more of your 'recovery.'"

Ken and Brad looked at each other for a second, blushing before they broke out laughing.

It had been weeks since they were home last and would have to throw out most of the food in the pantry and fridge, so they went grocery shopping on the way.

On arriving home, they discovered someone had cleaned out their refrigerator and thrown away any spoiled food and found two steaks marinating for their dinner that night, along with a sealed bag of Bryan's yeast rolls. The house was spotless, and Ken smelled how clean it was. The grass was mowed, the hedges trimmed, and the pool crystal clear and free of leaves. It was an unexpected but pleasant surprise and showed how much their brothers cared for them.

The couple settled back into their routines at the house, and since they couldn't officially work, there was plenty of time to work on their tans and work out. Not only did Brad gain back the weight he lost but packed on more muscle.

For the first few weeks Ken and Brad were more physically affectionate with each other, often holding hands or making excuses to touch one another. The sex was better than ever, and Ken's control over their link improved immensely, becoming instinctual in his efforts to start and stop it. The only precaution the doctor emphasized was not to leave it active unless they were together at their house or the lab.

A month later they were cleared to go back to work, and the final piece of the puzzle fell in place to get the entire team back and firing on all cylinders.

A few weeks later, Ken and Brad were on the couch watching a movie after dinner. It was summer, so they wore only shorts, reclining together with Ken's arm draped over and across Brad's chest. Absent-mindedly, his hand moved through Brad's chest hair while watching the movie. Periodically his hand roamed, gripping a pec more firmly, rubbing Brad's abs, or gently tweaking a nipple. Ken was very physical in their relationship, often expressing his affections through touch, and he was almost unconscious of what he was doing; he just loved touching his partner. Not far into the movie, Ken mentioned he was hungry, so Brad got up to make them a snack. Ken paused the movie, and channel surfed while Brad was in the kitchen.

Earlier in the day Brad made a large fruit salad and brought the bowl over with a couple of forks so they could just eat out of it. Ken un-paused the movie as soon as Brad was back on the couch and they sat, shoulder to shoulder, devouring the entire bowl. When Brad resumed his earlier position, Ken noticed a slight tremble in his body.

"Are you cold, B?"

"Yeah, kind of. All that cold fruit, I guess."

Brad snuggled back, and Ken wrapped his arms around him. Ken brought his legs around, scissoring Brad between them, wrapping his whole body up.

"Damn, you are cold."

Unexpectedly Brad shivered hard, and Ken ran his hands up and down Brad's arms, chafing his skin to warm him up.

Ken's body, always warm from his increased body temperature, seemed hot, and Brad closed his eyes, snuggling against Ken and soaking up his warmth.

Grinning, Ken paused the movie and said, "I know how to warm you up."

Brad senses heightened, and he knew Ken activated their link. He turned over, and their arms went around each other as they started a passionate kiss. Ken wrapped his legs around Brad's waist and kept his warm hands moving up and down his back until Brad stopped trembling. They continued to kiss, occasionally pulling away to nibble on each other's necks or ears, their excitement evident as they pressed against one another. Ken managed to pull their shorts down and muffled laughter ensued as they continued kissing while kicking their legs enough for their shorts to slide off their feet.

When they were finally naked, Ken pulled back, a little breathless but managed to say, "Now I got you where I want you, naked, and at my mercy."

Ken was an expert at pleasuring his lover and using his hands, he went to work. With their link active, he experienced the same sensation and started thrust his hips slightly in reaction.

Brad noticed and laughed, saying, "Ken, you perv! You just wanted to get yourself off, didn't you? You are so busted!"

Ken blushed and chuckled because he knew that's what it looked like.

Grinning like a Cheshire cat, Ken said, "Well, that wasn't my intent, but you gotta admit it's kinda hot, and it kills two birds with one stone... or fist in this case."

Brad returned the favor and started stroking Ken, and his face took on an expression of pleasure Ken loved to see.

After a minute, Brad mumbled, "Oh, fuck, that is hot."

Ken smirked and asked, "So, who's the perv now?"

Laughing, they started kissing again and continued making out, and even though Brad was sweating, he pulled his mouth off Ken's and asked, "What happened to warming me up?"

<>

Twenty minutes later in a breathless pile, they collapsed on the couch. Ken didn't want to let go and stayed on top of Brad, his big arms holding them together.

The comfort of their warm, sweaty skin and accelerated heartbeats as they caught their breath was soothing, and after a while Ken started kissing and nibbling the back of Brad's neck and shoulders while continuing to enjoy the physical and emotional intimacy.

Each of them drifted in and out of sleep before the practical side of Brad exerted itself. With an effort, he said, "Alright, we need to get up, clean the couch and kitchen, and we both need a shower before bed."

He peeled their bodies apart, and they laughed at the sound their skin made as they separated from each other and the leather couch.

A loud, exaggerated grunt escaped Ken as he pushed himself up, saying, "B, you are such a buzzkill sometimes."

Totally relaxed, Ken did a massive full-bodied stretch making every muscle and vein in his body pop out for a few seconds, turning his face beet red. Even after the multiple rounds of sex they just had, the sight of Ken got Brad going again. He reached over and grabbed Ken's hand, pulling the big man to his feet.

"Alright stud, who wants couch cleanup and who wants dish duty?"

Ken said, "Go on back'n hop in the shower. I'll clean up out here and head back in a minute."

Brad looked at Ken like something was wrong with him, which got him a grin, and Ken said, "Seriously, it's the least I can do for the love of my life."

Ken gave him a quick peck on the cheek and leaned over, swiping a hand down and scooping up their shorts.

"Here, take these back 'ta the hamper."

Ken moved around the coffee table and into the kitchen, bare-assed naked, to start cleaning up.

Knowing Brad was staring, he hollered over his shoulder, "Starin' at my ass is not takin' a shower!"

Brad smiled and made his way to the bathroom, turning on the hot water. When it was ready, he stepped in and started soaping up, scrubbing the sweat and aftermath of their lovemaking off his body and enjoying the hot water running over him. His senses were still hyped, and he closed his eyes, focusing on the sensations.

Intense, debilitating cold struck him suddenly, so unexpected and violent it took his breath away, and he couldn't make a sound. His body jerked so hard he slipped and fell on the tiles, incapacitated for nearly a minute. Every bit of extra energy vanished, sucked out by the cold, and the memory of his isolation returned.

Oh, Fuck... no!

The cold faded as the hot water slowly warmed him back up. While Brad knew Ken was physically in the kitchen, in his mind Ken was gone forever, and the separation and loneliness were real and terrifying. The isolation faded with the cold, but the trauma left him drained and scared witless.

Brad pulled himself up and shut off the water. In a stupor, he dried off and brushed his teeth. He wanted to tell Ken what happened, but something in the back of his mind told him not to, whispering and convincing him that if he did something horrible would happen.

Brad crawled into bed and turned out the light, pretending to be asleep.

Ken wasn't trying to be quiet when he came down the hallway, fully expecting Brad to still be in the bathroom. When he realized Brad was already in bed, he let out a quiet, "Oh shit..." and stopped making any noise. A satisfied grin crossed his face, thinking he wore his lover out.

The light from the bathroom went dark as Ken quietly pulled the door shut, and Brad heard the shower start. He lay in bed, his mind racing, pondering his reaction, the overwhelming emotions, and where they could be coming from.

Ken turned out the light in the bathroom to let his eyes adjust before moving into the bedroom. With his enhanced vision, he had no trouble navigating to the bed and carefully crawled in, trying not to wake Brad. Ken loved falling asleep holding him and wanted to snuggle some more but didn't want to wake him, so he scooted close enough for their backs to touch, and the contact was enough to send him off into a comfortable, contented sleep.

The warmth of Ken's body usually put Brad out like a light, but the heat of his back caused more anxiety than comfort. His emotions twisted, uncontrolled, and he couldn't shake the feeling he was going to lose Ken forever. His mind fought back, applying logic and the awareness of Ken's touch, but some other force overpowered his intellect, wrenching his thoughts into a belief of what he would lose forever rather than what he had.

Ken woke in the middle of the night from the death grip of Brad's arms around his chest and ribs. Brad seemed to be having a nightmare, his body trembling and sweaty. None of them had gotten sick in the last nineteen years, so Ken wasn't worried about that, but he didn't like seeing Brad distraught. Extricating himself from Brad's arms, Ken put a hand on Brad's forehead. He didn't seem hot or cold but was soaked in sweat. Ken turned on the light on his nightstand and then put a hand on Brad's shoulder, gently shaking him.

He whispered, "Hey B, wake up. You're dreamin'."

Brad jerked awake, his eyes wide with fright, shaking violently and breathing heavy. Scrambling back, he pushed himself against the headboard and frantically kicked the sheets back like he was terrified of something.

"B! Hey, it's okay! It's okay!"

Brad seemed utterly panic-stricken, and Ken was at a loss.

In his panic, Brad was confused and disoriented. He thought he heard Ken's voice but couldn't see him, and he sounded far away.

"Brad! Snap out of it, man! Wake up!"

Breathing heavily, Brad slowly calmed down. Ken watched him intently, keeping a hand on his shoulder, not sure what to.

Brad slowly came back to himself, taking a minute before he seemed to relax and breathe normally.

Shaking his head, he rubbed his eyes with a confused look on his face and asked, "Ken? What's going on?"

"You tell me. That must've been a mother of a nightmare. What was it about?"

"I… I don't remember."

"Hang on a sec."

Ken hopped out of bed and came back a few minutes later with a warm washcloth and a towel. He handed the washcloth to Brad to wipe his face, and Ken used the towel to wipe the sweat off his body as best he could. Ken's strong hands rubbing him down helped to relax and bring him back to normal.

"Thanks, man. Sorry about the scare, I don't know where that came from."

Trying to lighten the mood, Ken tossed the towel at Brad and said, "I didn't do it for you. I don't wanna sleep next to a stinky pig."

Ken turned off the light and pulled Brad against him, wrapping an arm around Brad's chest. Kissing him on the shoulder, Ken whispered, "G'night, B."

As hard as he tried, Brad couldn't go back to sleep. Usually, he slept like a baby in Ken's arms, and Ken's shallow, warm breath on his shoulder always helped him relax. His love for Ken welled up inside of him, but instead of comfort, all he could think of was losing that love forever. His mind raced, and he couldn't let go of the thoughts. When the alarm went off at 0600, he was still wide awake.

<><><>

The next day Ken kept a close eye on Brad, but other than being tired he seemed fine, so Ken didn't bring it up to the doctor.

Sometimes a bad dream is just a bad dream.

Ken asked Brad about the nightmare later in the day, and he again said he didn't remember it. His answer bothered Ken because he knew Brad had perfect recall, but maybe dreams were different.

That night Ken took care of dinner and cleaned the kitchen so Brad could relax. Brad didn't even stay in the kitchen with him while he cleaned up, and it worried him even more. A few hours later Brad went to bed early, saying he was still tired.

A little after 0200, Ken woke up and realized Brad wasn't in bed with him. Getting up, he padded naked through the house and found Brad sitting on the couch in the dark.

"B? What're you doin'?"

Startled, Brad jerked slightly in surprise and said, "Sorry, Ken, I can't sleep, and I didn't want to keep you awake."

Sitting next to Brad, Ken held his hand, and it took every ounce of control to stop his trembling so Ken wouldn't feel it.

"B, is there somethin' goin' on we need 'ta talk about?"

Brad put an arm around Ken's shoulder and leaned in to give him a kiss on the cheek.

"No, I'm good. It's nothing. I'm just wired for some reason. Hell, I don't know, maybe Sally switched from decaf to regular at the office."

"Will you come back 'ta bed and try 'ta get some sleep?"

"I will if you make me a promise."

"What's that?"

"Don't go running to the doc about this. Seriously, I'm all right."

Ken pulled Brad to his feet and led him by his hand back to the bedroom.

When they were in bed, Ken pulled Brad against him as usual and whispered in his ear, "B?"

"Hmm?"

"I love you."

"I love you too, even if you are a douche."

Brad said it in a lighthearted tone to disarm Ken. It must have worked because Ken squeezed his hand gently in response and quickly fell back asleep. Brad stayed awake the rest of the night, his eyes open but not seeing anything while silent tears rolled down his cheeks.

God, Ken, I'm going to miss you so much.

Prelude to Chapter Four

Retired Four-Star General Theodore 'Ted' Burgess anxiously awaited Dr. Cromwell's arrival. After nearly twenty years he would finally have the information necessary to restart Project Glass Hand, except this time it would be under his direct command and not some panty waste doctor! He still had contacts at the Pentagon, and with the financial backing of his new benefactor he could recreate the Spec Ops team and use them however he wanted.

His new patron wouldn't meet in person, and so far communications were one-sided, but they shared a common goal and the General was practically willing to sell his soul to get revenge on Dr. Thomas for ruining his career. Little did the General realize his soul was precisely what his new patron wanted as payment.

Dr. Thomas covered his tracks so well that even after twenty years, the General was still unable to discern his whereabouts or the identities of any member of the Glass Hand Project. His new benefactor must have deep pockets and even deeper contacts because he not only managed to identify former Lt. Commander Bruce Dutcher, now Ken Habersham, he also located one other member of the team, a Lt. Alan Whetherson, now known as Brad Wilson.

Of the two, Dutcher was the one he wanted. If he managed to duplicate Dutcher's physical attributes and abilities, he could create an unstoppable team. Then he would discover who this so-called benefactor was and take him out so he could run things the way he wanted.

Grumbling to himself, he wished Cromwell would hurry up. It was blistering hot outside, and the air conditioner in his Escalade couldn't keep up with Georgia's summer heat.

A few minutes later another vehicle pulled up, and looking in his rear-view mirror, the General watched Cromwell's tall, thin form get out of the car. The General wanted to get their meeting over quickly; Cromwell reeked of pipe tobacco, which always made his nose itch.

Lowering the window as Cromwell approached, he gruffly asked, "Do you have it?"

"Yes, General, I think you will be most pleased with the results. My team is still deciphering data, but we have enough to move forward, perhaps as soon as next week."

Dr. Cromwell handed him a small flash drive.

The General's usual gruff demeanor didn't change, but internally he was elated. Finally, revenge on Dr. Thomas was within his grasp! Once his team was assembled, Dr. Thomas and the original Glass Hand operatives would be his first targets, then his new benefactor, and then... well, he had a list.

"Just keep the data coming Cromwell, and keep me apprised of your progress. I want to know as soon as we can start work on live subjects."

"Yes, General. I am sure it will not be long."

General Burgess couldn't wait to get home and look at the contents of the flash drive.

As soon as he arrived home, he hurried upstairs to his office and plugged the device into his PC. When the icon appeared a window to enter is encryption code followed, and as soon as he typed in his PIN the contents of the drive appeared. Excited, he clicked the summary file first.

Upon reading the header, his fist slammed so hard on his computer desk the keyboard popped up and nearly fell to the floor.

He couldn't believe it! It had to be a joke! What the hell was Cromwell thinking!?

The title across the top of the page read, "Calculating the air-speed velocity of an unladen swallow."

Undoubtedly there was some mistake! He yanked the flash drive out and looked at it. The number 42 was handwritten on the outer casing of the flash drive. In his haste to put it in, he must have missed it. Cromwell was an idiot, putting the encryption key on the outside for anyone to find.

He entered '42' instead of his standard PIN, and the screen blanked out. After a short delay, text started appearing a letter at a time in a large font, spelling out:

"So long, General Burgess, and thanks for all the fish!"

The General's eyes turned white, and his face went blank. He sat perfectly still as runes placed inside the casing of the thumb drive activated, erasing the memories Dr. Thomas wanted gone. General Burgess then got up, flushed the flash drive down the toilet, and went downstairs to polish his golf clubs, all thoughts and knowledge of Project Glass Hand erased from his mind.

Dr. Cromwell was now in charge of a team of top-secret scientists spending billions of taxpayer dollars to calculate the airspeed velocity of an unladen swallow, both the African and the European variety in case there was any doubt of the speed between the two.

Chapter Four

Brad was going downhill fast, and Ken didn't know what to do. That day, while on assignment with Kevin, Ken texted the doctor and asked to meet at the lab in the afternoon. It was a 711 message, and the doctor texted him back immediately, saying he would be available all day and to come as quickly as time allowed. Ken was on edge the rest of the afternoon, anxious to talk to the doctor.

When Ken and Kevin finished with their client and were walking to the car, Ken said, "Kev buddy, we need 'ta swing by the lab on the way 'ta the office."

"Ken, you've been distracted all day. Is there something going on you want to talk about?"

"Brad's been actin' weird the last few weeks, and it's gettin' worse. He's not sleepin' good, and he won't talk 'ta me about it. I want 'ta talk to the doc."

"Shit, man, I'm sorry. You know if there's anything Bill or I or any of the guys can do, all you have to do is say the word. I'm sure the doc will figure out what's up."

"Yeah, I hope so, Kev."

After a slight pause, Ken mumbled under his breath, "Fuck, I really hope so."

With a heavy sigh, Ken stared out the window as Kevin drove, worried about Brad and what could be wrong. His gut told him it was something serious.

◇◇

When Ken walked into the lab, he was surprised to see Lane and Bryan in the doctor's office with the door shut. As soon as the doctor saw Ken, he quickly brought things to a close.

Ken hadn't seen his buddies for a few days, and when they walked out of the office, Lane looked exhausted and his hair was disheveled. He nodded to Kevin and Ken, giving them a subdued "Hey, fellas" as he walked by, but his usual grin was absent. Bryan followed with a frustrated, helpless expression on his face and gave Kevin and Ken passing backslaps as he passed by.

Staring after his friends, Ken muttered, "Shit! Is everythin' goin' 'ta pot? What was that about?"

The doctor, standing at the door to his office, said, "Nothing you need to be concerned about Kenneth. They will be fine, and you will know more soon enough. Trust me, it is not a bad thing. Now, come in and have a seat."

Kevin told him, "Take your time, Ken. I've got plenty of paperwork to catch up on. Just let me know when you're ready to leave."

Ken went in, shut the door, and sat down with a sigh as the doctor asked, "Now, what is it you wish to discuss?"

Ken lowered his head to collect his thoughts, and taking a deep breath delved right in.

"Doc, it's Brad. Somethin's goin on with him. He keeps sayin' he's okay, but he's havin' nightmares and not sleepin' well. Every time I try 'ta talk to him, he says he doesn't remember what they're about.

"He's been havin' these cold spells where he shivers, and then other times his body just starts tremblin', but he's not cold. Sometimes I'll catch him standin' still starin' at nothin', and when I ask him what's goin' on, he tries 'ta hide it and act like everythin's okay."

Once Ken started talking, everything came out in a rush.

"Doc, he's pullin' away from me. I can feel it. I mean, I can literally *feel it*. It hurts like hell, and nothin' I do seems 'ta make a difference."

Ken rubbed a hand roughly over his face in frustration, his eyes red and bright with unshed tears.

There was a short pause as the doctor observed Ken's expression and body language.

"Kenneth, why did you wait to talk to me about this?"

"Brad made me promise not to. I've tried talkin' with him, but he insists everythin' is fine and said he didn't want 'ta bother you."

The doctor cocked an eyebrow, and Ken felt like a little kid in the principal's office being brought to task.

"Kenneth, I am sorry to ask, but it is pertinent. How are you and Bradford doing in bed since this started?"

"Well, at first everythin' was normal… hell, better than normal. With that new bondin' trick sex with Brad has been amazin'. But the last week has been… I dunno… strange? It's hard 'ta describe. On one hand, he seems 'ta be pullin' away emotionally, but when we're makin' love he almost seems desperate. The other night he was holdin' on 'ta me like his life depended on it, but when we aren't makin' love, it's like he's afraid for me 'ta touch him."

The doctor's voice was full of concern as he sat back and asked, "And how are you doing with all of this, Kenneth?"

"I'm holdin' myself together for now. I'm tryin' 'ta do everythin' I can to give him some alone time and sleep in since he's been so tired, but I'm pretty much doin' everythin' by myself. I'm scared for him, kinda pissed at him, and hurt. I don't understand what's happenin' or why he's actin' like he is. It hurts like hell that he's shuttin' me out and not lettin' me help him, and 'ta top it all off, after seein' Bry and Lane, I feel like I'm neglectin' the guys."

The doctor moved to the chair beside Ken, placing a hand on his shoulder and giving him a tight squeeze.

"I know it hurts, son, but based on what you have said, I do not think Bradford is himself right now."

Ken's brow furrowed, and he looked intently at the doc.

"Wait doc, do you know what's goin' on with him?"

"I am not entirely sure, no. I have some suspicions, and I was dreading something like this might happen. I have been waiting, and hoping my fears would prove fruitless."

"Spill it, doc!"

With a sigh, the doctor looked long and hard at Ken, staring into his eyes as if looking for something, and when he didn't find it, his suspicions were confirmed.

"Kenneth, how much do you remember of your abduction and what you experienced up to the night we rescued you?"

"Doc, we've gone over this, what does that have 'ta do with Brad?"

"Please, Kenneth, answer the question."

"Well... I haven't thought about it much 'ta be honest. I don't want 'ta remember. I... well...."

Ken frowned, looking confused. He didn't care to remember that horrible time, but now that he tried, he could barely recall any of it other than the fact it occurred. Everything seemed hazy and detached, mostly bits and pieces, and the worst parts were missing altogether, leaving gaps in his memories.

Ken's eyes went wide, and with a bewildered look on his face said, "Doc! I don't remember much at all!"

Nodding, the doctor replied, "I thought that might be the case."

"What's goin' on? Why can't I remember!?"

"There are many possibilities Kenneth, but two seem most prominent. one, you suffered severe mental and physical trauma, and to protect yourself, your unconscious mind has sealed off the experience and made the memories unavailable to you. It is a known type of self-induced amnesia, a defense mechanism many people employ for self-survival. The other possibility is the memories are no longer there, which leaves us the questions of where they are, who or what removed them, and how.

"I designed you to be resilient Kenneth, mentally and physically, but the type of torture you experienced, made possible because of your augmented physiology, was beyond imagining. I was terrified that by the time we rescued you, your mind would be broken beyond repair, yet here you sit, in full mental and physical health mere weeks after an experience that should have left you dead, or at the very least, insane.

"My boy, you and your brothers have exceeded my wildest expectations, but even your recovery is too much for me to take credit for. You are still human, even if you are the pinnacle of human potential. By all accounts, you should not be sitting here."

Ken wasn't sure how to react. What do you say when someone tells you that you should be dead?

Brad, what the fuck have you done?!

"While you were in an induced coma the second day following your rescue, we found Bradford in your room sleeping on top of you. He was also in a coma, yet he managed to disengage himself from my equipment, enter your room, and climb in bed with you. The next morning, the parts of your bodies that were touching seemed outwardly healed.

"I still do not know precisely what Bradford did, or how, but he should not have been able to move, let alone accomplish what he did. At first, I thought it might have been some physiological reaction between your body chemistry and his, but only you were affected. Whatever he managed to do took its toll on him, and for a time I was as worried about losing him as I was you.

"When your heart stopped briefly during the rescue, Bradford almost died as well when the connection between you severed. I believe he discovered a way to re-engage your bond but in a non-reciprocal manner. There is still much I do not know or understand about what happened that night, and I am guessing at much of this, but so far the results support my hypothesis."

"So, what are you sayin', doc? What did he do 'ta me?"

"I think he not only saved your life but your mind. The question is, at what cost to himself?"

Ken was shocked, leaning back in his chair with a stunned look on his face. What had Brad done to him? No, not to him... for him. It was so humbling... and infuriating! As a multitude of emotions boiled to the surface, Ken felt like he wanted to throw up. The only thing he could think of was he was going to lose Brad, and it was because of him.

The doctor had known Ken for nearly twenty years and understood his thought processes well.

"Doc…"

"No, Kenneth! You are NOT responsible for this! Do not go there, son. Bradford did this of his own volition. He did it because he loves you. You would do the same for him, so do not blame him either. Accept what he has done and let us find a way to help him."

Ken took a deep breath, trying to get himself under control. His only objective for the time being needed to be Brad and helping him.

"Alright, doc. What do we do for starters?"

"I need to examine him, but it will take time to prepare and recalibrate the equipment. You and Kevin return to the office, and then you and Bradford come back here after dinner. You can pick up food for me on your way back. It will be a long night. I will let everyone know you and Bradford are excused from work until further notice."

"Doc, can you wait 'ta tell everyone until after we get back here tonight?"

"Certainly."

"Doc, what do I tell Kev and the rest of the guys?"

"Nothing, yet. They must be told, but let me worry about that. You are not neglecting them Kenneth, and do not feel as though you are. You are one man, but as strong as your shoulders are, you cannot carry the weight of everything on your own."

After he finished with the doc, Ken found Kevin at his desk still doing paperwork. Kevin saw Ken was upset but knew his buddy would talk when he was ready. Kevin was Ken's oldest friend from the Navy, and they knew each other as well as any two men possibly could.

Ken asked him, "Ready 'ta go?"

"Yeah, man, let's head out."

Kevin put an arm around Ken's shoulders as they walked to the car. It was a gesture of comfort Ken appreciated, and it reminded him he wasn't alone in whatever he faced. His brothers would always be with him and have his back, just as he would always have theirs.

The drive back to the office was quiet. Kevin kept stealing glances at Ken with a worried expression on his face. Ken was his Captain and still their unofficial leader, aside from being one of his best friends. It unsettled him to see Ken so troubled, and he wasn't sure what he could do to help.

Bill was waiting at the door when Kevin dropped Ken off at the entrance to their building. Ken and Bill exchanged fist bumps as they passed, and Ken took the stairs from the lobby to the fifth floor. Sally was on the phone when he walked by, so he waved to her on his way back to the office he and Brad shared. The door was open, and when he walked in Brad sat at his desk facing the window.

Ken's greeting was subdued as he said, "Hey B, you ready 'ta head out?"

Brad spun his chair around slowly, and Ken noted the vacant, faraway look in his eyes like he was somewhere else. Brad blinked and focused on Ken, his expression changing immediately. It wasn't lust in his gaze… it was something Ken couldn't identify. If he didn't know better, he would say it was hunger.

Brad stood up aggressively, grabbing Ken by his tie and pushing him down into his chair. Kicking the door shut with his foot, he locked it with an audible 'click.'

"B, look man, it's been a long day, and I…"

Brad held his finger up to his lips.

"Shhhh…"

Brad knelt between Ken's thighs and started running his hands up and down Ken's legs and over his crotch.

"B, what the fuck? We don't have time for this."

Unzipping Ken's pants, Brad boldly stuck his hand through the opening to fondle him. Usually, Ken would be hard in seconds at Brad's touch, but after everything he learned his libido shut down. Brad tried desperately to get Ken hard for a few minutes, stroking and sucking, but Ken sat in the chair with a stony look on his face and remained soft. When Brad realized his efforts weren't getting any reaction, he seemed to become desperate and tried even harder.

Ken finally said, "Look, B, just give it up. I'm tired, and the magic ain't happenin'. I'm sorry."

Brad looked sad, and in a strained voice, he mumbled, "Not as sorry as I am."

Unlocking the door, Brad walked out. Ken stuffed himself back in his pants, zipped up, and walked to the lobby where Brad waited for him. An awkward silence hung between them as they walked to the car. Brad usually drove, but Ken quickened his pace and jumped in the driver's seat before Brad had a chance to get in.

Ken noticed the side glances Brad gave him as soon as he realized they weren't going home.

"Where are we going?"

"We need 'ta pick up some dinner for the doc and swing by the lab 'ta get a few things. I say we get somethin' for us too. I don't feel like cookin' tonight."

Brad turned away, looking out the window, and remained silent.

They swung through the Long John Silver's drive-in for the doctor, and Ken called in an order from their favorite Chinese takeout for himself and Brad.

Brad knew something was up, but Ken was being careful and kept an eye on him. He didn't have a chance to run, and besides, there was no way Brad could overpower or outrun him.

The doctor ate in his office, leaving Brad and Ken in the kitchen by themselves to eat their dinner. Instead of sitting at a table, they stood, leaning against the counter.

Brad kept glancing at him, but Ken's eyes remained downcast, intent on eating. Ken had removed his tie, undid the top few buttons of his shirt, and rolled up his sleeves. Brad looked at the open collar of Ken's shirt, at his muscular neck, and watched Ken's jaw and temples move as he chewed. He noted how the muscles in Ken's forearm danced under his skin as he used his chopsticks. The healthy glow of his darkly tanned skin, his five o'clock shadow, the hair on his forearms, his face in profile… to Brad, Ken never looked more handsome. He drank in the sight, wanting to remember the perfect features of the perfect man he loved more than anything.

Ken, remembering the expression on Brad's face at the office, couldn't make eye contact with him. He focused on his food, literally jabbing the chopsticks into his dinner.

Finally, Brad broke the silence saying, "If you aren't careful, you're going to poke a hole in that box and make a mess."

Ken remained silent, chewing angrily.

Brad continued staring, going over every detail of Ken's handsome face and body. He knew it was only a matter of time before his emotions would twist, and his eyes turned glassy.

"God, Ken, I'm going to miss you so much."

Too late, Brad realized he said his words aloud. They were barely a whisper, but perfectly clear to Ken's enhanced hearing and Ken froze, turning white as a sheet and his stomach clenched like he got punched in the gut.

With a steely glint in his eyes, Ken looked at Brad and said, "Look, B. I'm gonna say this once and only once. I don't know what the fuck you've done, but you aren't goin' anywhere, and neither am I!"

As he spoke, Ken moved in front of Brad, poking him hard in the chest with each word, pushing him back until Brad was nearly bent backward over the counter. As he finished, with a choked sob, Ken fell to his knees, grabbing Brad around the waist with his face pressed against Brad's stomach. He held on tight, sobbing helplessly, while Brad had a stunned, almost terrified look on his face.

His hands tentatively touched Ken, running his fingers through his short hair. It started as a comforting, loving gesture, but Brad's hands quickly started trembling, and he frantically tried to push Ken away like his touch was painful.

Brad started breathing heavily and could barely talk, but Ken heard him mumble, "Don't touch me! I... I can't handle it!"

Ken let go and slumped to the floor with his back against the cabinets, holding his head in his hands and sobbing quietly. The rejection in Brad's tone hurt more than anything, and he was confused over what was happening.

After hearing Ken's outburst, the doctor went to the door of his office and witnessed most of their exchange, his heart breaking for the two young men he loved as if they were his flesh and blood sons.

In a quiet but firm voice, he said, "Bradford, come with me. Kenneth, come in when you are ready, son."

The doctor led Brad into one of the exam rooms saying, "Strip down to your underwear and get on the bed."

Like a zombie, Brad did as he was told, his movements mechanical and lifeless. As he got on the bed, the doctor noted his eyes were bloodshot and bright with tears.

The doctor proceeded to give him a general physical. Brad's pupils were non-responsive, his blood pressure low, he showed evidence of mild hypoxia, and he was slightly hypothermic. The doctor drew blood, and as he was leaving to put the vials in the centrifuge, Ken walked in the room now wearing jeans and a t-shirt. His eyes were red and puffy, and he looked pale.

Brad shied away when Ken entered the room, so he stayed by the door. In a weak voice, Brad looked at Ken and said, "You need to leave."

His voice hoarse from crying, Ken responded, "I love you B, no matter what. Surely after all this time, you know that, right?"

Hanging his head, not knowing what else to do, Ken left the room to find the doctor.

"He told me 'ta leave, doc. He doesn't want me in the room."

"Kenneth, I know this is painful, and I am sorry for both of you. If you wish, you can observe on the monitor at your desk. Bradford does not know I have turned on the camera. I think you should watch if you can bring yourself to do it."

The doctor went back to the room where Brad was waiting.

"Now Bradford, while the tests are running you are going to tell me, from the beginning, what is going on. If I feel you are being dishonest with me in the slightest, I will resort to drastic and unpleasant means."

Brad seldom heard the doctor use such a serious tone and noted the steely look in his eyes that plainly said he was not joking.

"Just keep Ken out of the room, or I won't be able to do this."

"You know, Bradford, you are breaking his heart? How can you not see what you are doing to him?"

Brad sniffed loudly while he was talking, his eyes swimming with tears.

"At least he'll be alive. He's such a great man. He's my best friend. I didn't think it was possible to love someone so much until I met him."

"You say you love him, and yet you are doing this to him. Bradford, you are one of the brightest men I know, how can you say this when you know it does not make sense?"

"Are you familiar with Superman, doc? He gets his power from the yellow sun, and kryptonite is his weakness? Well, imagine Ken is both of those things to me right now. He's keeping me alive and killing me at the same time."

"Explain yourself."

"You see doc, when Ken and I were connected and I knew what they were doing to him, I was desperate to save him. You said there might be consequences from the bond between us staying up so long. You were right. I'm still not sure, but I think the connection left an imprint on my mind because it was active so long.

"When you suppressed that part of me... God, I never felt so alone! It was more than I could take. It sounds silly to talk about, but the intensity was soul-crushing. I think we love more intensely than ordinary people because of all the changes we've been through. I also think, because of that, we feel the opposite more too. When Ken's presence left me, I wanted to die. I couldn't imagine living without him. You know the human brain perceives time differently when it's asleep, and while I was unconscious for only a few minutes, it seemed like days to me, and I was on the verge of losing my mind.

"I've never been so desperate. So, my unconscious mind discovered a way to reconnect us. By the time I figured out how to do that, only shreds of Ken's mind were left and what I connected to was almost unrecognizable as the man I love. The last shred of his sanity was begging Kevin to kill him and stop the pain.

"I didn't know how else to save him, doc, so I took all his pain, all the broken pieces, his death wish, and pulled it into me. I know what a remarkable man Ken is, and I knew he would survive the physical torture if his body had a chance to do what you designed it to do. The problem now is that all of that is in me, and it wants out. It wants to get back to Ken and destroy him. It's relentlessly pushing, trying to find a way out through the connection I have with him. I'm holding it back, and it's killing me, but I'll be damned if I'm going to let it out! I'm going to die with it in me so Ken can live.

"When he touches me… this thing in me can feel it and starts clawing like a wild animal in my mind. That's why I can't have him around me right now. It feeds off my love of him, and I know how strong that love is, so I have to keep him away. But at the same time, the boost I get from Ken when we make love makes me stronger."

The doctor listened in silence as he took in Brad's words, his vast knowledge and intellect trying to formulate a solution. He was stunned at Brad's bravery and foolishness and by what he managed to accomplish. The part of him that created this circumstance was supposed to be dormant for years to come. With proper training, the current situation never would have happened. How could events advance so quickly and so coincidentally? First Ken discovering how to link their nervous systems, now Bradford, and Lane making his discovery... the doctor would have to consider everything carefully and devise a new strategy moving forward, assuming he could find a way to save Brad.

Ah, Albrecht, I miss you more than ever.

"Doc!"

Ken's shout from the other room shook the doctor out of his thoughts, and he reached over, squeezing Brad's arm, saying, "You were foolish to try and handle this alone, my boy. I am not saying I know what to do, but I would have had more time to work on a solution if you had confided in me earlier."

"In my defense doc, early on I wasn't in complete control, and it fought me tooth and nail to not let anyone know what was happening. I'm sorry."

"I understand. Rest and be still, and I will be right back."

With that, he went to find the reason for Ken's outburst.

"Did you hear?"

Ken choked up as he spoke, shaking badly.

"Yeah, doc, I heard everythin'! That stupid son of a bitch is killin' himself 'ta save me!"

"I need to check Bradford's test results. What were you yelling about?"

Ken lowered his head, blushing in embarrassment, holding something in his hand the doctor couldn't make out.

"Well… I heard what he said about the sun and kryptonite, and I had an idea. Uh… well, I figure I can give him what he needs without touchin' him."

Ken set a cup on the counter.

"Is that…?"

Ken blushed a deeper shade of red, nodding his head.

"Yeah."

It was a sample cup full of Ken's semen.

"Kenneth, that is brilliant."

"I was thinkin' you could start with this, but maybe make a serum or sumthin' that would make it stronger and last longer."

"Kenneth, that is also brilliant. Perhaps I should let you take over my duties? Such a simple solution. No pun intended, of course."

Ken gave the doc a sheepish grin and said, "Well, there's plenty more where that came from, so just let me know…"

The doctor reached over and picked up the biggest empty beaker within reach and shoved it into Ken's hands.

"Get to work, my boy. Remember to drink plenty of liquids so you don't dehydrate yourself."

The doctor filled a syringe with the contents of the cup and hurried back to Brad's bedside.

"Bradford, this is a bit unorthodox, but I see no reason why it will not work. Please turn over."

Brad saw the syringe and practically shouted, "No! Your suppression serum won't work on this, and I can't take any sedatives. Weren't you listening?!"

"Calm down; this is neither. If anything, I would consider it a stimulant."

He jabbed the needle into Brad's butt, and when he pressed the plunger Brad's eyes widened in surprise.

"Doc, what the hell was that?"

"Is it helping?"

"Yes! The pressure is letting up!"

"You can thank Kenneth. This was entirely his idea."

The glazed look in Brad's eyes faded, and he sighed in relief, his body visibly relaxing as he absorbed Ken's DNA and received a boost to his strength and resolve. With the temporary reprieve from fighting the creature, Brad lay back on the bed, closed his eyes, and fell asleep in seconds.

When Brad woke the next morning, the first thing he saw was a tired looking Ken sitting by his bedside, watching him. Exhausted, his eyes were red, his hair disheveled with a cowlick on top, and he needed to shave, but to Brad he looked as handsome as ever. It was his Ken, the Ken he saw every morning when they woke up together, and he smiled, but his thoughts woke the beast and immediately he tried to move away. He was exhausted and groggy himself, and before he moved too much Ken held up a hand.

"B... It's okay. The doc gave you a shot an hour ago. You didn't even wake up."

Brad stared at his feet, afraid to make eye contact lest the creature fight him even harder.

Ken spent all night thinking about everything Brad explained to the doctor. He still didn't know what to say but knew he had to say something, determined to fight for Brad and their relationship.

"B... Before I say anythin' else, I wanna tell you again how much you mean ta' me. You don't have 'ta look at me, but I'm gonna have my say, and you aren't budgin' from that bed 'til I'm done."

Fighting his emotions, Ken held back tears, struggling to tell Brad what he needed to say.

"First off, I can't imagine bein' in this world without you. I want you 'ta know I understand what you did, and why. I wish I could stay mad, but I know I would've made the same decision. That doesn't mean it doesn't hurt like hell when you won't look at me and I know my touch causes you pain, but we're in this together, and with the doc's help we'll figure a way out."

Brad still couldn't bring himself to look at Ken, and the pain in his voice took all Brad's willpower to stay on the bed and not rush over and grab Ken and hold him tight. While Ken spoke, Brad sat up, pulling his knees to his chest as tears rolled down his cheeks.

Ken watched Brad curl up on the bed, and the effort not to take Brad into his arms was almost more than he could bear. The strength of his emotions had Ken breathing hard, and his body trembled.

"God, B, bein' apart like this is killin' us. Don't you know there isn't anythin' we can't handle if we're together? I can't stand sittin' here watchin' you suffer 'cause 'a me."

Brad's shoulders slumped, and he quietly said, "I wish I were as strong as you, Ken. I've never been as strong as you."

His words were a shock, and Ken blurted out, "What the fuck are you talkin' about? You're the strongest person I know! My God, man, how can you say that? You have no idea, do you? For someone so smart you can sure be a dumbass sometimes!"

There was a silent pause while each of them thought about what the other said.

Taking a gamble, it was Ken who broke the silence first.

"Okay, Brad, here's the way I see it. The reason we've made it all these years is we complement each other. For instance, someone has to be the handsome one, so that's obviously me…"

Brad's head snapped up, and he instinctively replied, "Oh fuck, no! No way! Not with those Dumbo ears of yours!"

Brad stopped when he realized he fell for Ken's ploy, and the brief grin on his face faded as he mumbled, "Douche" under his breath.

Ken had a hint of a smile on his face, but his heart leapt in his chest at Brad's smile, as brief as it was. It was the sign he needed that the situation wasn't lost, and Brad had more in him than he realized.

"Okay, B, seriously. We do complement each other, and we've always been there for each other through good times and bad. This time isn't any different. It's probably the worst fuckin' situation we've ever been in, hands down, but still. We've learned 'ta lean on each other, and right now you need 'ta lean on me. I don't care how fuckin' hard you have 'ta lean on me, you keep pushin' until I say uncle or you break my back. I know I can't touch you, but I can deal with that as long as I know you're fightin' for us. If you don't give up, we can figure out a way 'ta win this. Do you hear me?"

A glimmer of hope sparked in Brad. Being so close to Ken was hard as hell as the beast clawed and pushed, trying to break out and destroy Ken, but his renewed hope gave Brad the strength to drive it down.

Brad looked up, looking directly into Ken's eyes, and quietly said, "Okay."

"You promise?"

"Yeah, I promise."

"Damn! That means I'm gonna have 'ta run 'ta the drugstore."

"Why?"

"I need 'ta stock up on lube. Do you know how many times I'm gonna have to jack off 'ta keep you goin'?"

"You know you love it or you wouldn't be bragging about it."

"Hey, B?

"Yeah?"

"Isn't this better than both of us cryin' like babies?"

The hint of a smile returned, and he said, "Yeah. Hey, Ken?"

"Yeah?"

"Come here."

Ken moved over, and Brad shifted to the edge of the bed, wrapping his legs around Ken's waist. Leaning forward, he lowered his forehead until it rested against Ken's chest.

Taking a deep breath he smelled his partner, the scent he was so familiar with and loved, and muttered, "Fuck, this is going to hurt."

Reaching up, Brad took Ken's face in his hands, feeling his strength, and brought their lips together. The kiss was short but intense, and they were both breathing hard when Brad pulled back. Reaching around Ken, he pulled them together in a tight hug, squeezing as hard as he could. Ken's arms surrounded him, holding Brad's head more firmly against him, and he felt Brad's warm breath through his t-shirt.

They both said, "I love you" at the same time, which brought a smile to their faces.

Their bodies were reacting to the physical touch, and when Ken leaned down to kiss the top of Brad's head he saw the strain on his face and realized how much the display of affection cost him, so he pulled away.

"B, I'm sorry, but I need 'ta cool off, or I'm gonna rip your clothes off."

"Yeah, I love you, but that hurt. I'm not sure I can do that again anytime soon."

"You hungry?"

"Yeah, I'm starving."

"Alright, I'll be back in a bit."

Brad watched Ken as he turned to leave, his blue jeans and t-shirt hugging his big frame.

I promise I'll hold out as long as I can, Ken. I'll give everything I have for you. For us.

However, deep down, Brad already had an idea of what was happening to his body and didn't know how much time he had left.

<>

When Ken got to his Explorer he started shaking, and instead of getting in he collapsed on the ground with his back against the front tire. Events of the previous night and the morning repeated in his mind, and the front he put on for Brad shattered. Crossing his arms over his knees, he put his head down and fell apart. He had to get the worst of his emotions out of his system, and he couldn't do that in front of Brad. He had to stay strong and be the rock. He knew Brad wasn't out of the woods by a long shot, but at least now he felt like they had a fighting chance.

A car pulled up, and Ken heard Bryan and Lane get out.

It took Lane a second to realize Ken's condition, and he said, "Hey Ken... fuck bro! What's wrong?"

Ken was a wreck, his face wet with tears, his cheeks unshaven, and his eyes bloodshot. Lane and Bryan both rushed over, their faces masked with concern. Ken had to clear his throat a few times before he could talk, and his voice sounded rough.

"Hey, guys... sorry, I wasn't expectin' anybody 'ta pull up. I was just gettin' some shit outta my system. Brad's not doin' so good."

As soon as he started vocalizing what was happening, his throat closed up and the tears started again. Bryan pulled Ken into a tight hug, whispering, "Take as long as you need, Ken. We're here."

Lane joined the hug from the other side, and the two big men sandwiched Ken between them, holding him until he stopped crying. Ken's arms went around them almost desperately, needing their support and comfort.

Once Ken calmed down enough to talk, Lane said, "Okay Ken, we know something's up. The doc's been tight-lipped, but it's obvious to all of us there's some leftover shit going on."

Bryan held up a hand, interrupting Lane and asking, "Where were you going?"

"I was headin' out 'ta get some food for me'n Brad and the doc."

"Get your ass in the car and tell us what you can on the way. We want to know everything you can tell us so we can help."

On the drive, Ken filled his buddies in, leaving nothing out. He wasn't sure the doctor wanted anyone else knowing what was going on, but Ken badly needed to talk to someone who could relate to what he was going through or at least understand how he felt.

When he finished, Ken noticed a look pass between Bryan and Lane, and he asked, "Is somethin' else goin' on? Fuck, I don't know how much more I can take!"

Lane piped in quickly, "No, Ken! It's nothing like that. Look, the doc didn't want us talking about this quite yet either but with everything you just told us… Well, I don't know, I think you should know too."

"Know what?"

"Well, me and Bry, we tried that bonding trick you and Brad figured out, and it's as awesome as you said."

Bryan's grin expressed just how awesome it was.

Lane continued, "But in the last few weeks something else happened. I started having this dream after me and Bry finish making out. You know how much into music I am, right? Well, in my dream I'm working on a song, but when I wake up, I can't remember the words or the music, but here's where it gets weird. While I'm working on the song, I'm sitting on a big rock outside in the sun. I don't know where it is, but it's beautiful and peaceful. There's this big river flowing by, and Brad's on the other side looking like he wants to cross but can't. Bry's there too and all the guys except you and the doc. It's like we're camping. Everyone's talking, but no one except me sees Brad. I'm feeling frustrated with the words to the song when all of the sudden, I hear this horrible scream from the woods across the water that sounds like you. That's when I wake up every time.

"We were on our way to talk to the doc more about this when we ran into you."

"So, what does he think?"

"He thinks it's another ability manifesting; some kind of precognition. The thing is, outside the dream I feel the need to finish that song, and it's driving me nuts."

In between their conversation, they picked up food for them and hit Long John Silver's for the doc on the way back. As they got out of the car, Ken gave both his buddies another heartfelt hug.

"Thanks, guys. I feel better talkin' about all this with someone who can relate. I love the doc, but sometimes I'm not sure he gets everythin' on the emotional side."

Lane put an arm around Ken's shoulder and squeezed hard.

"Look, Ken, you and Brad are family, and you know you don't have to go through any of this shit by yourself. I know you want to be all macho and studly like you don't need anybody's help, but that's bullshit. Lean on us as much as you need to. We mean that. That goes for Brad too, that dumb fucker. If you don't, we'll have to kick both your sorry, ugly asses. You got that?"

Ken laughed and shook his head at the irony of Lane's words.

Lane asked him, "What's so funny?"

"That's pretty much what I said to Brad before we left."

Lane laughed, saying, "See!? You need to listen to your own bullshit!"

Bryan and Lane spoke with the doctor, but Ken wasn't privy to their conversation. Before they left, they stopped to see Brad and soundly berated him for being a dumbass while giving him a big hug. Brad got the same speech as Ken, and they made Ken and Brad promise, again, to let them know how they could help, no matter what it might be.

Moving forward, Brad and Ken were able to spend more time together. They had to maintain a physical distance, but the emotional tension was gone. The doctor increased the potency of Brad's injections, so Ken didn't have to jerk off as frequently. Ken could always tell when Brad needed another shot and joked that Brad was hooked, and Ken was now his 'dealer.'

The next day the doctor called Ken to his office. As he shut the door, Ken noted the look on his face and braced himself for bad news.

"Kenneth, I have enough data to form a prognosis. I will continue to run tests in case there are any changes, but right now it looks as if Bradford's organs are shutting down. Whatever this thing inside of him is, it is slowly killing his body."

"Doc, how can that be? It's not even real."

"There, my boy, I think you are wrong. We have stepped beyond science here. What Bradford accomplished he should not be able to do, at least not yet. It was not only the memories of the pain he took from you; he took the part of your soul that was damaged into himself. The creature is a part of you, and it is real and very much alive. It has intellect, of that I am now certain, and it is killing Bradford because it wishes to return to you. It believes we will not allow Bradford to sacrifice himself, and in essence, it is holding him hostage."

Ken's stomach knotted as he listened, and he struggled to keep his voice even as he asked, "How long?"

"It is not exact, perhaps another few weeks. I can partially counter the effects and slow it down, but at this point the end result is inevitable. I am sorry."

"I don't wanna tell him, doc. He has enough on his plate and doesn't need this."

"As you wish. I think Bradford already suspects, but I will not bring it up if he does not. Know, Kenneth, I am not giving up, and there are other forces at play that are still unknown. Again, I am faced with what appears to be a coincidence, and I feel that Lane, Bryan, and perhaps the others still have a role to play I cannot yet see."

Brad was beyond tired, his soul exhausted from the constant battle to keep the beast caged within him. He wished Ken was with him, but at the same time was glad he wasn't; kryptonite and yellow sun.

Unable to stay awake, Brad drifted off to sleep…

… and found himself on the bank of the River. It was a beautiful place, peaceful and serene, a place filled with wonderful memories from his childhood. It was one of the few memories he cared to remember from the time before his mother died.

The bubbling sound of the water soothed and refreshed him.

Within seconds of his arrival the beast screamed, and Brad walked down the narrow path from the beach to its prison. Its cage was an old fort Brad and a friend built when they were kids. The rickety structure rattled as the beast fought to free itself, and some of the boards were starting to come loose, but it held. The strength and happiness of his memory were still too strong for it, keeping it confined.

Using a few dead branches on the ground nearby, he shored up the little fort as best he could. As he worked, bloody fingers poked through knotholes in some of the boards. Attempting to get a better look at the creature through a knothole, a piercing green eye appeared, startling him. Jumping back in surprise, he lost his balance and almost fell over.

In his dream, as the creature grew stronger, Brad became weaker in the Physical Realm. It was changing, evolving, and taking on more aspects of Ken from the night of his rescue. It had all the broken bones, the flayed and burned skin, and dark, wet, blood covering its tortured body. Brad knew it wasn't Ken, not his Ken, but a part of Ken he needed to keep trapped. If Brad died before it escaped, it would die with him and Ken would be safe.

On his way back to the beach Brad heard music. It was faint but sounded like someone playing a guitar. When he reached the shore, he looked around and saw a man sitting on a large rock across the river with a guitar in his lap. The song was hauntingly beautiful, and Brad stopped to listen. Strangely, the music tugged at his mind, making him stronger.

As is often the case in dreams, Brad's perception shifted, and a group of men were now on the far bank camping. His blood ran cold when Ken walked out from the tree line and stopped at the water's edge. Brad didn't understand why he didn't recognize the others at first, but as soon as Ken stepped out, their identities became clear. All the guys were present now; Kevin and Bill, Pat and Darren, Ricky and Loy, Bryan and Lane, and Ken. It was important everyone was there. He didn't know or understand how he knew that, but he did.

It was Lane on the rock playing his guitar. He was a great musician and always played and sang for them at their get-togethers. Bryan occasionally played the bongos and even sang if he had time to practice beforehand; his deep baritone harmonized with Lane's tenor beautifully.

Lane seemed to be the only one aware of him and raised an arm in acknowledgment. When the music stopped, Brad snapped back to himself and rushed to the edge of the water, frantically yelling at them. Ken had to get away from the River, or all his efforts would be for nothing and Ken would die!

The creature screamed again, a long howl filled with rage and frustration. It sensed Ken and wanted to break free and devour him. Brad turned to run back to the fort...

<>

... and jerked awake. He sat up in bed trembling and sweating, unsure of the time, but the lights were out. Ken slept in a chair by the door but woke immediately, sensing Brad's panic and sudden motion.

Even though he had been asleep, Ken sounded alert when he asked, "Hey B... you alright? Another nightmare?"

Ken was shocked at how rough Brad looked. Earlier he looked tired, but just then he looked like death warmed over.

His voice tinged with concern, Ken asked, "You need me 'ta get the doc?"

The creature hit Brad hard, and his eyes widened in panic, his chest heaving.

"Ken! Hurry! I need a shot now! No time to get the doc!"

Desperate and exhausted, his body shook violently with the effort of holding the creature back. Sensing his weakness, it clawed at his mind, pushing relentlessly against his will trying to break free.

Brad was already on his side with his shorts pulled down, and Ken grabbed a syringe from the small glass refrigerator next to the door, jabbing the needle into Brad's butt cheek and pushing down the plunger. Ken backed away and after a few seconds, Brad's breathing slowed and his trembling subsided.

"Better?" Ken asked tentatively.

The strain in Brad's voice was painful to hear as he weakly responded, "Yeah."

Brad reached over and turned on the bed lamp, then fell back on the pillows with his eyes closed, completely drained. He didn't see the tears or the look of desperation on Ken's face.

<><>

Ken woke before Brad. The lamp was still on, and he moved to Brad's bedside, looking closely at his lover. He looked tired but not as bad as a few hours ago. The nightmare took its toll, but after the last shot he seemed a little better.

Ken heard the lab door open and quietly left the room to find Kevin and Bill arriving with breakfast. Ken knew he looked rough and probably smelled but didn't care.

As soon as Kevin laid eyes on Ken, he said, "Come here, buddy," pulling him into a tight hug.

Bill said, "Bry and Lane called everyone together at the office last night and filled us in. We all knew something was up but didn't realize how serious it was. Fuck, man, we're sorry. How's Brad this morning?"

"He's asleep right now. We had a close call in the middle of the night, and if I hadn't been sleepin' in the chair, things might've gone south quick. I'm gonna talk 'ta the doc when he wakes up, but I don't think we can leave him alone anymore."

Bill moved behind Ken, pushing him down onto one of the lab stools and started rubbing his tense shoulders.

"I'm sorry to break the news to you, but you look like shit. You need to take better care of yourself if you're going to be of any use to Brad."

No one noticed the doctor until he said, "You are quite right, William, and I agree Kenneth, Bradford should no longer be left unattended. I will prepare a schedule and email everyone. Lane and Bryan are on their way to take you home for a few hours. No argument, my boy. Kevin, you and William can start now and stay with Bradford through lunch."

Ken didn't want to leave, but the doctor was adamant, and it wasn't long before Lane and Bryan showed up and drove Ken back to his house. Ken was quiet and moody on the drive, and Lane stopped trying to keep a conversation going. When they walked into the house, he was in a stupor and stood in the den looking around, tense and sweaty, his eyes glassy.

Bryan came up behind him and ruffled his hair, saying, "Get some clothes together, you're coming to our place."

Ken sniffed, holding back tears, and said, "Thanks, Bry. This place is too empty without Brad."

Bryan and Lane didn't live far away, and fifteen minutes later they pulled into their driveway. Bryan was quite the gardener; his flower beds were in full bloom, and his vegetable and herb garden looked incredible. Ken didn't notice the looks of concern between his buddies over his behavior. He stood, staring into the backyard through the sliding glass doors with tears slowly falling down his face.

Memories of how happy he and Brad had been the last twenty years filled his mind. He thought about his buddies and their lives together, and even after everything they had gone through, he never imagined something like what was happening. All of the sudden everything was uncertain, and the thought of a life without Brad scared the hell out of him. In a matter of days Brad would be dead unless they could figure something out, and the doc was fresh out of ideas.

Lane watched Ken standing at the back door staring into the yard. Ken was a strong, resilient man, but the situation was taking its toll on him, and his friends saw how drained he was. Lane motioned for Bryan to follow him out to the garage so they could have a private conversation. He whispered his idea to Bryan, who didn't hesitate to nod 'yes.' Bryan leaned down and kissed Lane on the lips and then popped him on his ass as he turned to go back into the house.

In the den, Lane took Ken's hand, pulling him down the hallway to the bathroom. He started the hot water running in the huge bathtub and squirted something into the bathwater. Untucking Ken's shirt, Lane lifted it over his head and tossed it on the floor.

He started unbuckling Ken's belt but hesitated, saying, "Ken, I don't know how to say this other than to be blunt."

Ken looked at his friend, his brow creased in curiosity.

"I know you're a stud, and you've been jerking off like a zillion times for Brad, but that's not what you're used to. How long has it been since you and Brad made out?"

"Honestly, I don't remember. Weeks, I think."

Lane put his hands on Ken's thick shoulders, kneading them. His body was like a rock, the tension clearly visible.

"I'm not pushing this, but I know how highly sexed you are, just like Bry and the other fat asses. Your needs aren't getting taken care of like you're used to. So, I'm offering that to you if you want me to help you out. Bry is totally cool with it before you ask."

Ken sniffed and teared up again, this time out of love for his buddies and what they were willing to do for him.

"Thanks, Lane. You don't know how much I appreciate that. Fuck! I want to, but I can't. It's not you, bro. You're one seriously good lookin' man, and I couldn't ask for a better friend, but if Brad's goin' without, then I am too. It sounds weird, but it's another way I'm tyrin' 'ta support the sacrifice he's makin' for me."

"Okay, I respect that."

Lane grinned and added, "Honestly, I was hoping you'd say yes because I've had the hots for you for a long time. The offer stands until Brad's better, but after that it's back to both of us being off-limits."

Ken laughed and said, "Okay. I doubt I'll change my mind. Just don't parade around naked in front of me, or we both might be in trouble."

"You got it. Alright, now that's out of the way, I'm taking over Brad's other duties. Strip and get into the tub."

Ken took off the rest of his clothes and stepped into the hot water, now full of soapy bubbles.

"A bubble bath? Really?"

"Don't be dissin' Mister Bubble, he takes care of business."

Ken sank into the hot water and moaned as the heat surrounded and washed over his body.

Lane took off his shirt so he wouldn't get it wet or soapy, grabbed a washcloth, and started washing Ken. Lane was very thorough, and Ken enjoyed the sensation of someone else taking care of him. Closing his eyes, Ken relaxed in the care of his friend, soothed even more by a song Lane hummed under his breath. He was sure he hadn't heard it before, but at the same time it seemed oddly familiar.

With Lane's empathy, the same as with Brad, his concern and care for Ken bled through with his touch, and the emotional comfort added to the physical ministrations as Lane took care of him. Once Ken was clean, Lane rolled up a towel and laid it down as a headrest.

"Lean back, put your head on the towel, and relax."

Lane knelt at the edge of the tub leaning over him, so when Ken opened his eyes he was staring upside down at Lane's muscled chest, admiring his body.

Lane saw him looking and grinned.

"Quit peeping. Close your eyes and relax. You're getting the full service."

Lane giggled and added, "Except for the happy ending!"

Doing as he was told, Ken closed his eyes, enjoying Lane's ministrations. The next thing he knew, Lane smoothed hot shaving cream over his face and neck. Ken hadn't had a hot shave in years, and it felt amazing. He had Ken lean forward to get the back of his neck, and when he was finished, Lane wiped off any remaining lather and wrapped a steaming hot towel over his face for a minute.

"Ok, now for part two. You have some serious bedhead going on, and you're way overdue for a haircut."

Lane was a great barber and had Ken looking like his old self in no time.

"Alright, let's get you dried off and come with me. You can keep a towel on if you want, but I'm sure Bry would enjoy the show if you want to leave it here."

Lane chuckled and said, "He's already jealous I've been handling the goods."

Lane took Ken to their bedroom, which had the same massage chair Ken and Brad had in theirs. Again, Lane was very thorough and spent a good hour going over Ken's body, working the stress out of his muscles. Lane hummed the same tune as he worked, and with his calming voice and strong hands, Ken was so relaxed he fell asleep shortly into the massage.

By the time Lane finished, he was dripping sweat. He was also horny. Careful not to wake Ken, he padded down the hallway to get Bryan.

"Hey, Bry, he passed out in the chair. Can you get him to bed?"

Bryan got off the couch where he had been reading the new issue of *Organic Gardening* on his tablet and headed down the hall to their bedroom.

Bryan saw Ken on the massage chair and leaned over, whispering in his ear, "Relax, Ken. You're exhausted and need to take a nap, so I'm putting you in our bed."

Ken was like putty in Bryan's arms, so exhausted he was like a little kid that never really wakes up when they are taken out of their car seat and put into bed. Bryan moved Ken to their bed, lifting his head gently onto a pillow and pulling their comforter over to cover him up. He quietly shut the door to let him sleep.

When Bryan got back to the living room, a big grin crossed his face. A very sweaty, very handsome Lane stood by the couch, wearing only a towel tented out at full mast. Their eyes flashed white as Bryan stripped off his shirt and pulled Lane's towel off. They tried hard to be quiet over the next few hours and not wake Ken up.

◇◇

Ken's stomach woke him out of a deep sleep with a loud rumble, and it took him a second to remember where he was. It was dark outside, and his clothes, washed and folded, sat on the dresser. Bryan and Lane let him sleep himself out, and he felt like a new man.

Bryan and Lane were in the kitchen, and before Ken's feet hit the floor, he heard the clanking of plates and silverware being put on the table. The source of his rumbling stomach became obvious as the smell of Bryan's famous lasagna hit him. Taking a deep breath, he also identified garlic bread, Greek salad, and that craft beer Lane liked so well. Bryan's deep voice greeted him as soon as Ken emerged from the hallway.

"How'd you sleep?"

"Like a fuckin' rock. You guys shouldnt'a let me sleep so long."

"Everything's fine, and you needed the shut-eye. I talked to the doc a little while ago; Ricky and Loy are with Brad, and he's doing fine. We're supposed to take some lasagna in for them. Don't worry, I made two pans. Grab a plate and dig in."

Ken eyed the food, and another wave of hunger hit him from the smells.

"Shit guys, this looks fantastic."

Lane opened the fridge and asked, "What do you want to drink? We have red wine, beer, sweet tea, Coke, Dr. Pepper, milk, water, apple juice, grape juice, and orange juice."

Ken chuckled, saying, "What a menu! Beer sounds great."

"Beer it is. There's plenty in the fridge if you want more. In fact, there's plenty of everything, so eat and drink your fill. I'm going to take a look at that fine stomach of yours after dinner, and all I want to see is bloat, no abs."

Ken knew what Bryan and Lane were doing and loved them for it. After events over the last few weeks, Ken relished the normalcy of a good dinner with two of his best friends, joining the constant banter between his buddies, just like it was with him and Brad. Ken didn't realize how badly he needed what they gave him and felt a twinge of guilt that Brad wasn't with them.

As they finished eating and were clearing the plates, Ken pondered the situation with Brad. The doctor always said the human mind was a funny thing, and in the time Ken spent with his two friends, he arrived at a conscious decision he realized he had already made but hadn't admitted to himself. He would stand with Brad, and they would defeat the creature together or die trying.

Ken helped clean the kitchen and get the extra food packed to take back to the lab. His disposition shifted slightly when they pulled into the parking lot, but his friends had done wonders for him and he didn't let his mood get the best of him. Now that he had made his decision, a tremendous weight was off his shoulders.

Bryan and Lane dropped Ken off with the food, and he received a long supportive hug from them before they left.

When they got back to the house, Lane pulled out his guitar to work on the song from his dream, frustrated because the words and music seemed just out of reach.

Since Lane and Bryan spent all afternoon making out, they only had one round of sex before bed and Lane fell asleep with his head on Bryan's chest, listening to his heartbeat and letting it lull him into a deep relaxing sleep.

<>

At 0300 sharp, Lane shot out of bed and ran to the den.

Startled, Bryan growled, "What the fuck?" and took off after him.

He found Lane on the couch, naked, guitar in hand and strumming a song.

Bryan stopped and stared, unsure of what was happening. In the darkness of the room, to Bryan's enhanced vision, Lane's dark brown eyes were almost white. Looking directly into Bryan's eyes,

Lane exclaimed, "Fuck yeah, Bry! I got this son of a bitch!"

A satisfied smirk crossed Bryan's face. He was very proud of Lane and his abilities and was confident Lane would figure everything out.

"Play it for me, Little Buddy. I want to hear what all this fuss has been about."

Lane started playing, and the song was both beautiful and haunting at the same time. Before the end of the first stanza, Bryan's green eyes flashed white, and his mouth opened in surprise. The music tugged at his mind, and warm sunshine covered his face while a gentle breeze flowed over his naked body.

As soon as Ken got back to the lab, he found Brad asleep. At Brad's bedside, studying the man he loved, Ken saw the gray tinge to his skin and haggard lines on his face. The desire to reach out and touch him was strong, but he knew it was a bad idea, so instead, he sat in a chair by the door and stayed with Brad through the night, sleeping lightly in case he needed anything.

In the middle of the night, Brad woke to go to the bathroom and saw Ken sitting nearby. As Brad moved towards the door, he smelled Ken and instinctively inhaled deeper. Even in the dim light, he noticed Ken was clean-shaven and had gotten a haircut, most likely from Lane. As soon as he inhaled the clean, fresh smell, the distinct smell of Ken, he stumbled. Ken's scent was like crack to the creature, and it went wild, ripping and clawing at his mind. Stumbling, he reached out to try and regain his balance, grabbing Ken's shoulder.

As soon as he touched Ken, Brad had a full-body seizure. Losing control, his back arched and he would have fallen if Ken hadn't caught him. Ken was prepared, ready, and waiting with a syringe, expecting something like that to happen. Pulling Brad to his chest with one arm, he jabbed the needle into Brad's butt with the other and set Brad on the bed as quickly as he could before moving away. It took longer than usual for Brad to recover, and he was breathing hard, exhausted by the ordeal.

As soon as he could talk, he mumbled a weak, "Thanks."

"Do you need me 'ta get the doc?"

"No, I can manage."

Brad got back out of bed, but it took him several minutes to make it to the bathroom, his movements slow and deliberate, grabbing onto things as he got close to help stabilize him.

It was hard to watch, but this time Ken's tears weren't from sadness, they were from anger.

Hold on, Brad, just one more day. Tomorrow night we're gonna' end this one way or another.

By the time Brad got back from the bathroom, he was white as a sheet and fell asleep immediately. Ken left the room and watched Brad on the monitor at his desk, keeping some distance so Brad could rest more comfortably.

Ken didn't sleep the rest of the night but was still sharp and wide awake the next morning, waiting for the doctor.

A couple of the guys dropped off food for Brad, Ken, and the doctor, and once he finished, the doctor went to his office, motioning for Ken to follow. He shut the door and sat down, astutely looking at his young charge.

"You have something to say."

It was a statement, not a question.

"Yes, sir."

"You have made a decision?"

"Yes, sir, but I don't want Brad 'ta know what's goin' on."

"That is wise."

"Doc, I can't take watchin' him slowly die in front of me like this. Tonight, I wanna have everyone over for a cookout. I'll tell Brad it's for him, 'ta get him out of here for a night and be with the guys. That's not a lie; spendin' time with Bry and Lane last night did wonders for me.

"Doc... This is my decision, and I take full responsibility for both of us. Brad's gonna die anyway if we don't do anythin', and I can't envision a life without him. I'm gonna force a showdown with the creature tonight. I think we can beat it if we stand together. If we can't, then we'll both still be together, just not here, and that thing'll be gone either way."

The doctor looked at Ken long and hard, his eyes bright when he finally spoke.

"No matter what happens, Kenneth, I want you to know how much I love you and Bradford. You are like sons to me, and I am proud of all you have become. I respect your decision, and frankly, I have no alternatives. The only issue, and I beg your forgiveness, is that I cannot be there."

Ken didn't expect that and asked him, "Why not?"

"I am not permitted to be present. I wish that were not so, but it is, and I can say no more at this time."

"Alright, doc. If Brad and I make it through this, we're gonna sit down over a beer, and you can explain to me exactly what you meant by that."

Ken got in touch with everyone, and the guys said they would be at his place that night come hell or high water. He asked them to arrive early so he could explain his intentions and asked Kevin and Bill to pick up Brad after the meeting.

When he went to Brad's room, even though his eyes were closed, Ken knew he was awake. His breathing was shallow, and his skin yellow from jaundice.

"Hey B, how ya doin'?"

There was a long pause, and Brad's voice was weak and thready when he finally responded.

"Tired. I'm sorry, Ken. I'm still fighting, but I don't know how much longer I can hold on."

Ken hung his head and sighed, saying, "I know B. I know."

Taking a deep breath, he continued, trying to sound upbeat, "Hey, I had an idea. Last night Bry and Lane took me to their place. Just bein' out of this stuffy lab for a few hours did wonders for me. What say we have a little gatherin' tonight at our place? All the guys wanna see you. I'll have some shots there if you need 'em, and I'll give you plenty of space to make it easy on you. The doc said it was okay if you feel up to it."

After a minute Brad replied, "I'd like that. I wasn't sure how to bring it up because I don't want you to think I'm giving up, but I'd like to see all the guys. It might be my last chance to say goodbye."

Ken lowered his head again, his throat tight with emotion.

"Yeah, there's that. I'll c'ya tonight. Kevin and Bill will be by around 1900 'ta pick you up. I love you, B."

If Ken's hearing wasn't enhanced, he wouldn't have heard Brad's reply.

"I love you, too, Ken. More than you can possibly know."

Ken left before he lost it again. Seeing Brad in such a condition and hearing his words tore him up, but it also strengthened his resolve to win this fight and save them both.

Ken picked up groceries on his way home, going against protocol by traveling alone. Seething over events, he dared anyone to mess with him, even wishing someone would show up and claim responsibility for everything so he could beat the shit out of them. It took most of the day, but shortly before everyone was due to arrive he had the house in order and the food prepared.

As he stepped out of the shower, as an afterthought he put on Brad's favorite cologne, knowing it would piss off the creature. He just finished changing clothes when everyone started showing up.

Ken noticed Lane brought two guitars, one acoustic, and one electric, and Bryan had his bongo drums under one arm and Lane's amplifier under the other. Ken and Brad loved to listen to their buddies play, and he was grateful they planned to.

The den seemed full with all the big men packed into the room. The four couples sat together either on the couch, the floor, or in chairs. Ken noticed, maybe because Brad wasn't there, that everyone was touching, either holding hands, an arm around the other's shoulder, or leaning against each other.

They were all openly affectionate with one another, but that night especially he realized why; the idea of losing any one of them drove home how much they meant to one another. Instinctively they sought the comfort of touch to remind themselves they were together, and it made Ken wish Brad was there with him all the more.

Their usual banter was minimal given the seriousness of the situation. Most of the guys had a beer or a glass of wine in hand, looking at Ken expectantly. He was their Captain, and they waited to hear what he had to say.

"Thanks, guys, for bein' here. It means the world 'ta me, and I know it will 'ta Brad too. You all know the basics of what's goin' on. Brad's in a bad way. He made a decision 'ta save me, and that decision is costin' him his life. I can't stand seein' him suffer like he is 'cause of me, and I can't stand the thought of livin' without him."

As Ken spoke his throat tightened, and he had to clear his throat a few times to keep talking. Looking at his buddies, he saw the brightness of their eyes.

"As the sayin' goes, desperate times call for desperate measures. I'm gonna end this tonight one way or another. Either I save us both, or me and Brad die, tonight, along with that thing inside him."

Whispered 'oh shits' and 'fuck me's' were heard around the room in reaction to his statement.

Kevin asked, "Where's the doc? Even if you win this fight, you might be in bad shape."

"The doc can't be here tonight."

Confused looks crossed all their faces at Ken's remark.

"It's cool, guys. I talked with him this mornin', and there's a reason he can't be here. He won't be far away and can be here quickly if he's needed.

"Brad doesn't know any of this, and I couldn't tell him because the thing inside him would know too, and I don't wanna lose the element of surprise. Honestly, I don't know how any of this is gonna go down, and I'm not sure what'll happen when this starts or what you'll see or hear.

"I want you all 'ta know how much you mean to Brad and me. If tonight goes south, well, this is goodbye. Brad thinks tonight is about sayin' goodbye, but if we're gonna have any chance of success, I need every ounce of strength he has in him. I think together we can beat this thing."

Raising his hand to get Ken's attention, Lane said, "Ken, I'm not sure how this is going to play out, but I finished the song last night, and I know it's somehow connected to what's happening to Brad. I think it will help; I just don't know how. I only know I need to play it tonight."

Trying to lighten the mood, Ken smiled and said, "I don't know how anythin' that's been brewin' in that wacky brain of yours can help Lanester, but beggars can't be choosers. I'll happily take whatever you got.

"Okay, ladies, time to use the Kleenex and shut off the waterworks. Remember, tonight is about Brad. The better he feels, the stronger he'll be. Everyone be your usual fuck-up selves and make him happy."

Rick, Loy, Pat, and Darren covered the majority of the security jobs the last week and were the most out of the loop, so while Kevin and Bill left to pick up Brad, Ken did his best to fill them in on more details of what was happening. While they talked, Lane set up his amp, and Bryan fired up the grill.

Even with their genetic enhancements and abilities, what was happening was uncharted territory, and everyone remained quiet and pensive. The thing in Brad wasn't an enemy they could shoot or fight with their hands, but every one of them reiterated to Ken they were there for him and Brad in any capacity and would do whatever was needed or required. After everyone had a chance to express their support, Lane pulled Ken aside to talk privately.

"Ken, I'm going with my gut on this. After dinner, me and Bry will play some songs as usual. Just give me the sign when you're ready, and I'll start… and hold on to your hat when I do."

"What do 'ya think's gonna happen? Should I be worried?"

"Hell yeah, you should be worried. I don't have a fucking clue how this works, but the doc said to trust and have faith in myself. He also said he thinks all this is more than coincidence, which is scary as hell, so I'm trying not to think too hard about that."

It wasn't long before Ken heard Kevin and Bill pull into the driveway with Brad, so he made himself scarce.

Brad was weak and moved slowly, but insisted on making his own way, and as soon as he entered the kitchen he was greeted loudly and happily by all his brothers. The guys covered their emotions well, but they were shocked at Brad's appearance. He had lost weight, his skin was yellow, his face haggard, and his eyes dark and bruised.

He received a tight hug and back slap from each of them, expressing their love and support through the strength of their arms, ruffling his hair, or kissing a cheek. As soon as their arms wrapped around him it was apparent how weak he was, but they acted like it was just another summer get-together, one of many with many more to come. He wasn't sure who, but someone shoved a beer in his hand.

Brad kept glancing around looking for Ken but didn't see him, and smiled sadly as he headed to the backyard where Bryan manned the grill. Their house was the primary gathering place for most of the get-togethers, so he and Ken invested in a large patio grill. Bryan had steaks on one side, and ears of corn wrapped in foil, baked potatoes, and fresh asparagus coated in butter on the other. Brad smelled bread baking in the kitchen and hoped it was Bryan's famous yeast rolls. He hadn't had much of an appetite for days, but his stomach rumbled from all the smells.

Unexpectedly, a pang of sorrow hit him at the sound; he was going to miss the cavernous rumbles of Ken's stomach when he was hungry.

Someone started the fire pit, and he sat close to soak up the warmth, reclining against the short brick retaining wall that made up part of their flower garden. He hadn't felt warm in days and missed the warmth of Ken's body more than ever. Even with his melancholy thoughts, Brad felt better. The heat of the fire and the sound of his buddies around him was nice. Ken was right; getting out and seeing everyone was good for him, but it just prolonged the inevitable.

Once the steaks were ready, Rick brought him a lap tray filled with more food than he could possibly eat even when he was completely healthy. Brad did his best to make a dent but was full after only a few bites.

Everyone moved to the backyard and found a place near him, wanting time with him to catch up on things. Of course Brad didn't have much to offer, but he listened to what had been going on with them at the office. They had new funny stories about clients and talked about Sally's latest boyfriend troubles, and Brad found himself laughing more and more as the night went on.

While Brad stayed put, everyone chipped in on clearing the plates and getting them into the kitchen. An odd feeling of contentment washed over him from the heat of the fire, the clean, fresh air, and the voices of his friends. The only thing missing was Ken.

Leaning his head back, he closed his eyes. He was tired, but for the first time in what felt like forever it was a normal tired, and he felt like he could drift off to sleep, wrapped in the comfort of his friends. He knew what they were doing and loved them all the more for it. They put on a good front, but he knew them well and saw the cracks in their demeanors when they thought he wasn't looking.

Lane broke out his electric guitar and started playing, taking requests if anyone wanted to hear something specific. Bryan sang with him if he knew the words, and it was clear he had been practicing.

Brad drifted in and out of sleep for a while but woke when Ken's hand gripped his shoulder. He smelled Ken even before he opened his eyes.

"Hey B, scoot up a little."

Ken practically picked Brad up and moved him forward, putting his back to the wall and then pulling Brad back against his chest. A needle stuck in his arm, and then Ken's strong arms wrapped around him.

For a brief second he relaxed against Ken, thinking everything was normal, but his mind snapped back to the present and he started to panic.

"Ken…"

"Relax, B. I know what I'm doin'."

Ken looked at Lane, indicating it was time. Lane put down his electric guitar and picked up his acoustic one.

Brad noted the look between them, and the usual infectious grin Lane often wore appeared, and he winked, saying, "Here goes nothing!"

Absolute silence fell in the backyard as all eyes turned to Lane. His eyes closed briefly before his fingers started moving across the strings, and a beautiful, haunting melody came out of his instrument. Before the end of the first stanza, Lane's eyes turned white. Bryan started on the drums, and his eyes turned white as well as their mind's opened, transcended by the music.

Nature, Nurture, Heaven and Home,

Sum of all and by them driven,

With all ten of them present there was a tangible difference, and this time Lane's soul lifted out of his body, taking Bryan with him. Lane had never experienced anything like it in his life, and it was beautiful. In his mind the music was visible in the air around him, emanating from his guitar and through his body, igniting something in him, in all of them, that could never be extinguished.

Each of them felt the music. It wasn't just a song; it had some deeper meaning that tugged at their minds, unlocking something within them, a gateway to a place that could never close. Ken felt it and knew it was time to start his plan.

<>

None of them yet had the perception to see or hear the giant robed form of a man crouched by the hedges. Even kneeling, his head nearly reached the roofline of the house. A cowl covered his face as he watched intently, and as soon as Lane started playing, the man stood and looked skyward. His massive head nodded once, and he went on bended knee in homage to the humans who were unaware of his presence. After a moment he stood and vanished back across the veil.

<>

Ken leaned forward and kissed Brad's cheek, hugging him tighter.

"I love you, Brad. I can't stand this anymore, so we're endin' this tonight one way or another. Don't fight me, B... Help me kill this thing."

Ken squeezed his eyes shut and buried his head against Brad's shoulder.

Brad panicked, trying to move away, but Ken's grip was too firm.

"Fuck! You idiot, you don't understand..."

To conquer every mountain shown

But I've never crossed the River...

Brad's voice faded as he lost consciousness, his eyes white. He slumped against Ken while the song carried them out of their bodies and to the River.

<><>

Ken no longer felt the bricks against his back. He opened his eyes, surprised to see he was sitting by a huge bonfire on a beach next to a river. The moon, full and bright, illuminated the cove.

Ken realized Brad wasn't with him but heard him yelling some distance away. It took him a few seconds, but by the light of the full moon he saw Brad on the far shore waving his arms frantically.

Fuck! We were supposed to be together!

Chapter Five

Brad knew where he was right away. At the River, out of his body and within his mind, he was healthy and whole. The bubbling sound of the water and the cool evening breeze enveloped him. He expected Ken to be at his side, but when he opened his eyes he was by himself.

Frantically looking around, Brad went numb with fear when he saw Ken on the far bank, in the cove leading to the fort. Splashing into the water, he rushed forward but slammed into an invisible barrier. He knew he faced the will of the creature, now strong enough to orchestrate their separation and prevent him from reaching Ken.

No! He was on the wrong side!

He desperately started pounding his fists against it, yelling, "Ken, you idiot, gct out of there! You don't understand! It's too strong! Kennnnnnnnn!"

He knew Ken didn't stand a chance.

<>◇<>

A horrific scream cut through the woods, sending a chill down Ken's spine. It was his voice, and he knew it was the creature. In that place, it was on the edge of his awareness, and he sensed its need and desire to return home, to him.

Cupping his hands to his mouth, Ken yelled as loud as he could, "Alright, you bastard, come and find me!"

The creature, recognizing Ken's voice and knowing he was near, screamed in rage and hunger. A loud crash followed by the sound of splintering wood told Ken it finally broke free of the prison Brad kept it trapped in.

Fuck, B, I wish you were beside me. I know together we could kick this thing's ass.

Ken pulled a large log out of the bonfire, the end glowing bright orange, with flames licking along its length past the tip at least a foot high. Swinging it a few times to make sure it was sturdy, he moved to the water's edge facing the woods and knelt down to wait, wanting to draw it into the clearing and away from the cover of the trees.

Crashing noises through the underbrush grew louder, and suddenly it emerged from the woods and stopped, knowing he was there. Their eyes met and Ken stared into his own green eyes, stunned by its appearance and the rage and insanity staring back at him.

Fuck, is that how I looked when they found me?

The creature's muscles gleamed in the firelight, covered in slick, wet blood. Its arms and legs were broken, with splinters of bone penetrating through the skin at various points. Burns covered its body, and large patches of skin were missing, exposing muscles and tendons. Its face was swollen and bruised... but it had his eyes. As damaged as the creature appeared to be, it moved blindingly fast.

Even prepared, the creature surprised him as it lunged, moving across the cove from the edge of the woods with incredible speed. Ken dodged, barely avoiding a blood-covered fist. Spinning around, he swung the log with both arms as hard as he could, cracking it across the creature's back. The wood split from the strength of his blow, and the creature stumbled forward as sparks flew from the end that was still on fire. It let out another blood-curdling scream, but Ken wasn't sure if it was from pain or annoyance.

It whirled around, and before Ken could react it was on him. He never saw the blow that sent him reeling through the air. Sand softened his landing, but it stunned him long enough for the creature to jump on him while he was on the ground recovering. He had never been struck so hard.

Fuck! Maybe this wasn't such a good idea!

Rolling, he scrambled away as the creature swiped at him, ripping his shirt and scoring deep cuts across his back. Ken cried out in pain, arching his back as he twisted away, but the creature was on him again, not giving him any time to recover, relentless in its aggression and hatred. It straddled his waist, striking back to back blows across his face, stunning him. Ken's head snapped back and forth, and he saw stars, unable to focus.

It paused briefly, watching Ken's eyes glaze over. Reaching down, it grabbed the front of Ken's t-shirt, ripping it off and throwing it aside. Their muscular bodies were clearly defined by the sharp shadows cast by the bonfire, one wet with sweat and the other blood.

The creature placed one hand high on Ken's chest above his collarbone, splaying its bloody fingers out until they wrapped around the base of his neck, cutting off his oxygen supply. Looking at its other hand with a blissful smile, it slowly brought its palm down onto the center of Ken's chest.

Ken's eyes went wide, and his mouth flew open in a silent scream as pain ripped through his mind and body. Every muscle, vein, and cord stood out in reaction to the sudden and unexpected agony as the memories and experience of his torture started returning to him. His combat instincts took over, and in a gut reaction to the pain coupled with the adrenaline in his system, he struck the creature so hard it flew ten feet into the air, landing in the fire and sending a mass of sparks high into the night sky.

Ken knew if the creature touched him like that again, he was done for.

Shit that hurt!

Brad watched the fight, beating his fists against the invisible barrier. As strong as Ken was, Brad knew the creature was stronger. It wasn't just driven by rage and insanity; *it was rage and insanity*. The only intelligence it had was the drive to return to Ken and devour his mind. It was a creature of thought and malice, given physical form in that constructed place within Brad's mind, but its strength came from the pain and torture that destroyed Ken's mind the first time.

At that moment, Brad was sure he and Ken were going to die, but damned if he was going to let Ken die alone! At least he could lessen Ken's pain. With no thought as to what it would do to his body or his mind, Brad opened the place within him he had been desperately holding shut to protect Ken.

Pain hit him hard, and he fell to the ground clutching his head as Ken's torment and suffering tore through his mind.

You son of a bitch, give me all you got! The more you give me, the less you have for him!

◇◇

Ken became aware the moment Brad opened himself to the creature.

No, B! No! Fuck!

Ken knew Brad was trying to save him, but he also knew the creature was too strong, and now that it was free, they were both going to die. He didn't understand how it could be so strong.

How had Brad kept it trapped?

The memory of his conversation with Brad came back to him: *"What the fuck are you talkin' about bro? You're the strongest person I know! Oh my God, man, how can you say that? You have no idea, do you? For someone so smart, you can sure be a dumbass sometimes!"*

The creature screamed again, sensing Brad's interference. It spun, clotheslining Ken and knocking him down onto the sand, moving so fast it was unstoppable. Even Ken, as strong and fast as he was with all his combat training, skills, and genetic enhancements, was a little boy fighting a grown man and had no chance.

The creature dropped onto Ken again, plunging its hand into his chest. There was no blood, its hand simply disappeared into his body, and it sighed in pleasure as it fulfilled its purpose.

As Ken's sanity slipped away, through the blinding fire of pain and agony, two unrelated thoughts came to his mind. The first was how much he loved Brad and wanted nothing more than to be in his arms when he died. The second was an epiphany about the Project, the doctor, and his work, the Vitruvian Man. The man in a circle and square by Leonardo da Vinci the doctor used as a symbol for the project. It was also referred to as the Proportions of Man; The body, mind, and spirit.

The pairing of Ken and Brad and the others became clear. Ken was the body, Brad was the mind, and their spirits, their souls, were one. How could science do that? There was more to the doc than they ever realized.

You clever, clever, man, doc.

Ken's epiphany gave him the strength to face his end with grace, and he stopped fighting, welcoming the missing part of him back home.

Ken lay still, his breath shallow, the blank stare on his face reflecting the fact his mind was gone. The creature faded as the essence giving it form returned where it belonged.

Across the River Brad lay on the ground, barely conscious, his breath coming in ragged gasps. He wanted to let go and stop the pain. If he let go it would all stop, but something pulled at his mind, refusing to let him rest. A song... getting louder. It sounded familiar. It was beautiful... *and powerful,* and he knew as long as it continued, he couldn't let go and be at peace or find Ken in Heaven.

The tempo of the song was slow, and it was nearly five minutes before it came to a close. Ken and Brad were unconscious, breathing shallow, but Ken's arms were still wrapped tightly around Brad. Bill knelt beside them, holding Ken's wrist to feel his pulse, which was slow and sporadic.

In a subdued voice, he said, "Guys, this doesn't look good. Maybe we should call the doc."

The silence after the song was deafening. The music still resonated within them, and they knew something profound was happening. Each of them felt the icy calm that always accompanied a difficult mission.

Bill started when Ken's arms fell to his sides, and his head rolled back as Brad's body slumped further down his chest. Their faces relaxed in peaceful expressions, and they stopped breathing.

Bill lowered his head with a choked sob, cupping a hand on Ken's shoulder. All their eyes were bright, and tears unabashedly fell down their faces

Most of them jumped, startled, when Lane's voice cut through the silence, yelling, "Fuck this shit! This isn't how it was supposed to go down! I know it! I can feel it! We're missing something! There's no fucking way they're dead!"

Bryan's deep, gravelly voice pushed through the sadness threatening to overwhelm them, saying, "Guys, we're idiots. The words are telling us what to do. The lyrics said, *'the hands of the many must join as one.'* Lane, start playing Little Buddy; I don't think we have much time!"

Lane started the song again, forcing his hands to remain steady, but his face expressed the desperation they all felt. As soon as he began singing, the words fell into place in their minds. Kneeling around Ken and Brad, they formed a circle, gripping their hands tightly together.

The hands of the many must join as one

And together we'll cross the River

Bill was on one end of the circle touching Ken, and Darren was on the other touching Brad. Lane had to play, so their hands were on his shoulders. As the first chord rang out their eyes flashed white, and the music carried them back to the place in them that was waking up. Faintly, they heard the bubbling sounds of the River.

The eight men focused as one on helping Ken and Brad, willing them to breathe, and sending them strength to fight a battle none of them understood.

Even the slightest movement was excruciating, but Brad knew he had something else to do before the music would let him go. It stirred something in him, and even through the pain it gave him a strange sense of well-being and belonging and something else he couldn't quite figure out. The pain didn't lessen, but the music helped him to punch through it.

Lane's voice resonated in his mind, and along with it, the love and support of his brothers. Their presence was overpowering, wrapping around him and bolstering his soul. Whatever stirred inside him, his friends were somehow taking part in it, making it stronger, and they carried him across the River.

Opening his eyes, he was now with Ken on the beach.

His voice was barely a whisper, "Ken?"

How did I get here?

He felt no sense of movement, but he was now across the River, beside Ken.

Is this what it's like to die?

Brad had just enough strength to crawl to Ken. He rolled over, resting his head on Ken's chest, wanting the last thing he felt to be Ken's warm body and heartbeat. Beneath his closed eyelids, as Brad lost consciousness, his eyes flashed white as the music and presence of his friends filled him.

<><>

Something was different. It took a moment, but Brad's brain finally registered the pain was gone and he felt warm and safe. As his senses asserted themselves, he realized he was naked, with Ken's warm arms wrapped around his stomach and chest, holding him as he rested against Ken's torso. Ken was naked too and seemed to be asleep, his chest rising and falling in a slow, steady rhythm. Ken's chin rested in its usual spot in the crook of Brad's neck and shoulder, and his thighs were spread wide to make room for Brad to recline against him with his calves and feet wrapped around Brad's lower body. Brad was acutely aware of Ken's solid body and steady heartbeat against his back, and the warmth and softness of his manhood pressed against him.

His brain also registered that not only did he feel Ken, he *felt* him, not just his body but his presence. Along with his arms, Ken's presence encapsulated Brad, inciting an intimate physical and emotional reaction.

Brad wondered where they were. He assumed they were dead and in some transitionary stage to wherever it was they went after. To Brad, it was enough like Heaven to be in Ken's arms with their bodies touching, neither of them in pain but whole and healthy.

Yeah, I could spend eternity like this.

Brad put his hands over Ken's, squeezing gently, and Ken's arms tightened in response.

His chin lifted and sounding sleepy and relaxed, Ken's deep voice whispered in his ear, "About time you woke up, fucker. I thought you were gonna sleep forever."

Ken kissed Brad's neck and rubbed their stubble covered cheeks together in the way that drove them both crazy. Moving one arm up, he cupped Brad's chin, bringing his face around to press their lips together in a tender kiss. Smiling, Ken kissed him a few more times and then pulled back far enough so they could stare into each other's eyes.

Brad not only saw Ken's love for him, *he felt it*, and his face drew back in surprise.

Ken grinned at his reaction and said, "Yeah, I feel it too. I always knew you were one hot fucker on the outside, but the inside is a thousand times better."

"Ken? What's happening? Where are we?"

"You tell me, B. I'm pretty sure you're the one who brought us here."

"I'm not sure where *here* is. Lane's song... I think it was a key of some kind. I felt the guys inside me, *in me*... they got me to your body, and I knew you were dying. All I wanted was to die with you, but the music held me back... and now we're here."

Ken eased his grip and stood up, pulling Brad to his feet. There seemed to be a floor, and they could see each other clearly, but everything around them was dark.

Brad looked around, his forehead furrowed in concentration, and said, "I remember this place. I had a dream, or thought it was a dream. I saw you on a table, tortured and broken. I couldn't reach you at first. Some kind of barrier kept us apart."

Ken's eyes widened in surprise, and he said, "I remember that! I mean I didn't, 'til just now. I was at the end of my rope, and you told me 'ta hang on, that you knew where I was and how 'ta find me. It gave me enough hope 'ta keep goin'."

There was a short pause, and then Ken continued, "But 'ya know B, I think by hangin' on it fucked things up worse."

Brad felt the truth of Ken's statement, and his words cut like a knife into his heart. The hurt in Brad was palpable to Ken, and he felt like a jerk.

Brad spun around to face Ken and asked, "What was I supposed to do? Let you die?!"

"It was selfish, B, but you know I would've done the same thing. We can't lie to each other about it. Not here, in this place."

Brad paused as Ken's statement sank in.

"What do you mean?"

"Because I can't lie to myself. Believe me, B, I tried. I lie 'ta myself all the time in little ways. Hell, everybody does. I think it's part of bein' human. Somethin' about this place rejects that, or doesn't permit it. I'm not sure which."

"How did you figure that out?"

"Because while that creature was flayin' my mind away a piece at a time, the pain was more than I could take and I wanted so badly 'ta die and put an end to it all, I tried 'ta blame you. I tried 'ta blame you for everythin' B. For makin' me hang on beyond my strength, and creatin' this impossible situation because you were too selfish, or too weak, 'ta let me go."

A cold sliver of fear crept down Brad's spine at Ken's words. It was overpowering, and his chest tightened to the point he could hardly breathe. He fell to his knees, his shoulders slumped, and tears filled his eyes. The harsh truth of Ken's words cut him, not just the words but the truth behind them.

Ken sat beside him, pulling his knees up to his chest. He rested his chin on one of his forearms, and his other hand reached out to grip Brad's shoulder.

"I'm sorry, B, I know that hurt, and I know you're mad at me. I'm not tryin' 'ta be a bastard. This place is harsh, but it's also kinda' beautiful."

Ken had been awake in that place longer than Brad. He wasn't sure how time moved where they were, or if it moved at all, but Ken seemed to have been there hours before Brad woke up. Ken's senses were much more acute than a normal human, but in the place they were in, it was like his senses and perceptions were on steroids. Brad's emotional pain was so tangible Ken could *see* it. When he looked deep and sifted through the emotions running through his best friend, he saw anger along with everything else.

"I know you're pissed at me, B; I can see it."

It took Brad a minute to get himself under control.

"So, tell me, B, what're you mad about?"

"What am I mad about!?"

As soon as Brad allowed his anger to surface, it quickly boiled over. It had been building for over a month, needing an outlet, and everything that was happening, especially Ken's words, pushed him over the edge.

He stood up suddenly and faced Ken, practically screaming, "You stupid shit! What am I mad about!? Because this is all your fault, that's fucking why! You're the one who had to switch jobs with Kevin that night. You're the one who got lazy and let his guard down and got himself captured! Then you sit here and blame me?! God! You are so fucking conceited I can't even begin to tell you how pissed that makes me! I love you more than anything you fuck-head, even my own life, and I was willing to sacrifice myself to save your sorry ass, and then you turn this around and say it's my fault!"

Brad's body was taut from anger, and he yelled so hard spit flew from his mouth. His face and upper body flushed, and veins started showing on his neck, and across his chest, shoulders, and arms.

Ken stared, taking in Brad's beautiful, naked, muscular form, not only seeing Brad's physical beauty but everything he loved about him.

Almost wistfully, Ken mumbled, "God B, you are one sexy fucker when you get fired up."

Brad stopped abruptly, surprised by Ken's comment, but his anger quickly returned, and he continued, "You always do that! When things get too hot for you, you always crack a joke and try to change the subject! You…"

Ken held up his hands in surrender and started to chuckle, "Damn Brad, chill out a minute."

Putting his hands on his hips, Brad paused his tirade but continued to glare, breathing hard and sweating from the tension, anger, and other emotions coursing through him. He had a bad temper and usually kept it in check, rarely letting it lose, but when he did let it go, he always had a hard time putting a lid back on it.

"To think only a few minutes ago, I sat there in your arms thinking I could spend eternity with you?! What the fuck was I thinking?! I'm an idiot! I want to spend eternity with a total dick! How fucking idiotic is that?!"

Ken couldn't hold it in anymore and started laughing while Brad glared at him.

"Oh man B, if you could see your face!"

Ken was about to cry from laughing so hard, but he finally got himself under control. Moving behind Brad, Ken put his hands on Brad's shoulders, kneading them.

"I'm not laughin' at you, B, I'm laughin' at us. You know I love you more than anythin' in the world man, even my own life. How couldn't I, after what you did for me? After everythin' we've been through together? You're my life."

Ken turned Brad around by his shoulders to face him. Ken's warm hands, coupled with the emotional intensity soaking into him through the physical contact, affected him. He couldn't help himself and became erect. Ken's hands always affected him that way, but the emotions bleeding through his touch were impossible to resist.

Ken whispered in his ear, "Come here, B."

Pulling Brad into the tight, full-bodied hug they both loved, Ken started a kiss. Their eyes flashed white, and they lost track of how long they stayed together. The changes in them that had been building over the last months, their new and more powerful connection, were more potent in the place they were in, and they lost themselves in the embrace, unaware of the passage of time.

At some point, Ken lowered them to the floor, their bodies still pressed together, arms and legs wrapped around each other as they held each other tight. The heightened emotional sensitivity caused the same reaction in Ken, and when he activated their physical bond, this time Brad's empathic abilities blended too, and it sent them into a shared emotional orgasm so intense it took their breath away. It was extreme, unexpected, and more potent than anything they ever experienced. There was another unintended effect; all the pent-up emotions of the last month, the tensions and stress left them, expelled with their discharge. They continued grinding against one another, their movements slowing, leaving them content and peaceful until they were still, with Ken resting on top of his lover. They were sweaty, and Ken loved the feeling of Brad's warm breath on his neck, and with the bond Brad felt it too, along with the emotion it incited in Ken.

Minutes went by, and eventually Ken lifted his head to stare into Brad's eyes, and with a cocky grin he asked, "Now, are you sure you wouldn't want to spend eternity with this dick?"

Seeing Ken's handsome face, inches from his own, with the little kid grin he adored, Brad couldn't help but smile.

Laughing, he hugged Ken tighter and replied, "You are such a fucking douche."

After another short time of holding each other, Brad said, "I don't know about eternity, but it looks like we might not have a choice unless we can figure out where we are and how to get out of here."

Ken slid off Brad and onto his side, propping his head up on one hand. Brad did the same, so they faced one another. It was one of their favorite positions after sex, so they could continue to touch each other and talk about whatever came to mind. It was always an intimate emotional time to match the physical intimacy shared moments before.

They were both quiet as their hands roamed, tenderly touching and caressing each other.

Ken broke the silence with another grin, "Yeah, about that…"

Chuckling, Brad said, "You, shit. I knew you were holding out on me."

"Well, B, I'm not sure, but I think I figured somethin' out about us, and it might help get us outta here, or at least explain some things."

"Well, I'm not going anywhere so you better start talking or I'm going to take matters into my own hands."

Brad reached down and fondled Ken playfully when he said that.

"Have you ever wondered, B, how the doc knows so much? How he knows so much more than anyone else on the planet about genetics, and computers, and almost every other field of science out there?"

"I think we all have at one time or another."

"Well, he said somethin' today that didn't make sense. When I told him what I planned 'ta do, he said he couldn't be with us tonight. When I questioned him, he said he wasn't permitted to be with us or to say more than he did."

Brad's eyebrows rose in surprise, and he exclaimed, "Holy shit!"

"Yeah, as far as any of us know he doesn't work for anyone, so there's obviously more to him than meets the eye. I mean even more than we thought. That and a lot of other things clicked into place, and I had an epiphany as I was dyin'.

"Whoa big fella, don't use words you don't understand."

Ken gave Brad a light punch to his chest as he laughed, retorting, "Shut the fuck up and listen, I'm trying to enlighten your sorry ass.

"So, as I was sayin'... you know the symbol the doc uses for the project, right? The Vitruvian Man by da Vinci? He's also referred to it as the Proportions of Man, representin' the three parts of man that make him whole; the body, mind, and spirit. I could be crazy, but I think the doc fashioned the project with da Vinci's idea as the drivin' concept. When he changed us, I think it was for some higher purpose, and he hasn't gotten around to tellin' us what that is yet. I think he somehow bound our souls together, knowin' we'd love one another."

"How could he have possibly done that?"

"I don't know, I'm still thinkin' this through, but it makes sense. I know I'm physically stronger than you, but you're stronger than me in every other way. You're smarter, more compassionate, and more emotionally mature than I am. Take that creature; as tough as I am that fucker kicked my ass like I was a baby, but you kept it trapped for weeks. You even created the place to trap it in."

"I don't like what you're saying, Ken. Yes, you're physically stronger than I am, but don't make me out to be more than I am. You make me a better man. I want to be a better person because of you. You deserve as much credit for those characteristics in me as I do."

"Okay, B, maybe that's true, or maybe not. But don't you see? I still think it's all by design. We complement each other like two sides of a coin, and we're bound together because we share our souls."

"Alright. I'm not saying I agree with you, but I see where you're going."

"Well, for one thing, I don't think we're dead. I think you brought us here, wherever here is. I think time is movin' slowly because all this is in our heads. It's like we're in a dream inside the dream world where the creature was. I think our bodies are dyin' in the backyard.

"The problem is I'm not sure what'll happen if we do get outta here. That creature shredded my mind, and you, you dumb shit, probably don't have much of a noodle left either after you tried 'ta help save me; again! I think what you and I are, here, are our souls. When our bodies finally stop breathin', I'm not sure what'll happen 'ta us here. I think, though, that if we have any chance of gettin' outta here, it lies with you, B."

Brad chuckled at Ken's comments and said, "Yeah, no pressure though."

Ken stopped talking to give Brad time to think, process, and focus on what he said, and they were both quiet for a long while. Ken seemed calm, almost serene, having every confidence in his lover, as he continued intimately touching and caressing Brad the entire time in ways he knew Brad liked.

Ken gave him his space but could tell Brad was becoming frustrated, and after a while Brad got up and started pacing. After letting Brad pace for a while, Ken motioned for Brad to come back over to him.

"Hey B, come back over here."

"We don't have time to cuddle. I need to figure this shit out."

"B, shut 'yer trap and get your ass over here."

Brad moved over and stood looking down at Ken, who sat up and spread his thighs.

Ken patted the space between his legs, saying, "Turn around and sit down."

Brad sat down with a heavy sigh of impatience.

"What you need 'ta do, Mr. Wilson, is relax. That's one thing I learned in sniper school back in the day; you need 'ta relax so you can focus on your mission."

Ken started rubbing Brad's shoulders and upper back. It took a minute, but Brad finally leaned his head forward and let Ken's warm, strong hands work their magic. Out of the blue, Brad had a thought that made him laugh.

"You know, for someone who doesn't have a body you sure give a good backrub."

"Yeah, B, well for someone who doesn't have a body you sure have nice hard muscles I can't keep my hands off of."

Ken started their normal banter, knowing it would distract Brad and slow his thoughts. Ken's hands wandered, pushing every button he knew, not to turn things sexual, but to relax and soothe his lover. Once again, he rested his chin on Brad's shoulder from behind, while his hands rubbed up and down Brad's arms, or snaking around to hold him or rub his chest. He continued talking, making Brad laugh or smile, and besides that being one of his favorite things to do, he achieved his goal.

Brad lay in Ken's arms, the place he never wanted to leave. Ken's hard chest against his back, and Ken's hands touching his body calmed him, allowing him to release the worry, anxiety, and pressure of figuring things out.

Brad knew what Ken did and why. While he rested in Ken's arms, Brad continued processing their discussion, every word and detail, everything they said, everything they were… body, mind, and soul. Ken was the body, Brad was the mind, and they shared their souls.

If I'm the mind, I need to stop thinking in physical terms.

The words from Lane's song echoed in the back of his mind, instructing him.

Open your Heart and Hands, my son...

Making a fist, Brad held his hand up and took a deep breath. As he slowly exhaled, he opened his hand, envisioning his mind and heart opening with it, like a flower in bloom. In his mind, he bound the images together metaphorically, and as his hand opened, Brad felt a slight sensation of falling outside himself.

Son of a bitch! I can feel it!

Locking onto the feeling, he repeated it, each time with more confidence. It was like learning to control a new muscle, by isolating it from everything else. His mind opened, expanding out of his body, and he went still to let himself acclimate for a moment. He still sensed Ken, and if he concentrated, felt their bodies touching.

Brad's mind and body were now separate, yet one, and with concentration he could move his body, but he quickly adapted to what was happening. Reaching for Ken's hands, he intertwined their fingers and pulled Ken's arms around his waist.

The paradox of Ken and Brad having physical bodies while the place they were in was some sort of mental or spiritual construct was not lost on him. He assumed their minds were translating their interaction into terms they could grasp and understand.

Okay, here goes nothing.

The part of Brad outside himself dove into Ken. It was a strange sensation, like swimming through thick air, and once inside Ken's mind, Brad sensed his surprise.

Brad?

Yeah ... this is amazing!

What the hell did you do?

I'm inside you! Hold on to your hat. I know what I want to do, but I'm not sure how to do it.

Brad brought their minds completely together. With everything new to him he acted on instinct, and rather than being gentle, the merge was more like a high-speed head-on collision. Their blending wasn't physically painful, just startling and highly uncomfortable emotionally. Neither of them was prepared for the brutal honesty between them, and the lack of barriers and self-protection mechanisms was overwhelming and frightening.

Even though humans are born innocent, early in life they learn deceit, often lying to get what they want. Children discover how to manipulate parents and siblings, and kids can be devastatingly cruel, lashing out because of self-centered needs or wants, or insecurities and emotional wounds, and those habits and behavioral patterns become ingrained in them as adults at various levels of their consciousness. Even good, honest men like Ken and Brad are potentially full of self-deception, petty jealousies, and lies. With their minds open and bare to one another, all their buffers, lies, and self-protection mechanisms were absent, leaving them genuinely naked to one another for the first time in their lives.

On every level imaginable, the awareness each of them had of the other caused a torrent of emotions - fear, resentment, embarrassment, anxiety, shame, guilt, and more – and it was overwhelming to the point that coherent thought eluded them. Brad was shocked at some of Ken's insecurities regarding their relationship, and everything Ken wanted to say to him but never found the courage, all the things he wanted to try in bed but was afraid to ask, even how terrified he was the first time they made love. Ken discovered the same types of things in Brad and was just as shocked that deep down, Brad felt inferior to him and didn't believe he was worthy or deserving of Ken's love.

The reality of the myriad discoveries was traumatic, causing a significant amount of hurt and grief, but at the same time their underlying love for each other softened the harshness. They thought they were in love, and they were, but only as much as they were able to love one another in their bodies with their minds closed off from one another.

With everything about the other exposed and raw, they realized that to some degree, they were total strangers. Yet through the same exposure, they began to connect on a level neither of them could ever have imagined, delighting in discoveries and realizations about each other. They found themselves forgiving and asking for forgiveness for trespasses and transgressions neither realized they made and apologizing for any hurt they ever caused one another over inconsiderate actions, usually done unaware but sometimes made out of jealousy or anger.

The longer they stayed together, and the deeper they went into one another, the more their love grew, and the connection they built was beyond anything they believed possible. They saw each other as they were, emotionally naked with all their faults, and loved each other more than ever, with no judgment between them. They established true intimacy in the freedom to be themselves and be loved and accepted for who they were, as they were, unconditionally.

The merge happened at the speed of thought, and what seemed like hours, or even days, occurred in the blink of an eye. With no secrets between them, Ken knew what Brad planned to try. It would never have been possible without the connection they now shared and the knowledge they gleaned and put together of the doctor's intent.

Brad had to force them apart, and as uncomfortable as their connection was at first, the thought of being separate was now worse.

Their eyes opened at the same time, with Brad still reclining against Ken, one hand holding Ken's forearm and the other held before him where he opened his hand and mind. Tears ran down their cheeks, and their breath caught in their chests as their bodies reacted to the emotional intimacy between them.

They were silent for a second before blurting out a quiet "Fuck me!" at the same time, causing them to laugh. Ken's other arm wrapped around Brad and pulled them together, burying his face in the crux of Brad's neck and shoulder. The hug was intimate, even desperate, expressing everything physically that just happened emotionally.

Ken's throat was tight, but he managed to say, "My God, Brad, you're so fuckin' beautiful. I always thought you were amazin' on the outside, but damn, what the hell did I ever do to deserve such an incredible man in my life."

Brad smiled in response, saying, "We deserve each other, Ken, and now you know beyond any doubt I feel the same. There can't be any secrets between us after this. Assuming we live, we can be together like that as often and as long as we want."

Ken laughed and said, "I'm gettin' a mental hard-on, just thinkin' about that."

"Well, technically, everything up to now has been mental, which leads us to the next part of getting out of here."

"Yeah. I understand what you're gonna try. I hope it works. I can't imagine us comin' this far and then crappin' out at the last second."

"I'm still not sure what I'm going to do. I'll have to improvise when I get back to the River. All these different levels are confusing. Whatever we are here, I'm pretty sure our minds are at the next level up where you fought the creature, and our bodies are still in the backyard with the guys. Who knows how much time has passed since all this started."

Brad wasn't sure if his plan would work, but he concentrated, sensing the part of him on the beach with Ken. Taking a deep breath, he leaned against Ken to relax and opened his mind, rising out of his body and hovering for a moment.

His focus was on getting back to the beach. If he was going to have any chance of saving Ken, he had to get back to the River. He envisioned the beach and the night sky in his mind's eye and imagined the heat from the bonfire on his skin and the cracks and pops of the burning wood.

Brad went slack in his arms, and Ken remained still, enjoying the sensation of their naked bodies touching. Ken closed his eyes, took a deep breath, and suddenly Brad was gone, the weight of his body vanished. He hoped that was a good sign.

Looking up into the darkness he said, "Good luck, B. If anyone can do this, it's you."

Ken crossed his legs to wait, already missing the other half of his soul.

<><>

There was no sense of movement, but the connection to his body strengthened, and suddenly Brad was on the beach hovering over their bodies, looking down on them with his new perceptions. The hurt and brokenness were tangible to him now, and while the damage to his own mind was significant, at first glance Ken's seemed far worse.

Brad dove into his body, briefly fighting to maintain control and prevent himself from merging back where he belonged, and once settled, he pondered his next move.

Alright, I got here by visualizing where I wanted to be. Maybe that will work to fix what's wrong, too.

Brad studied the damage in detail for a few moments, creating a visual image of what he needed to accomplish. The damage was mental, not physical, and he looked at the energy patterns of his psyche with an inherent sense of how his mind should be healthy and whole.

Satisfied he had a basic understanding of what needed to happen, Brad began knitting the tatters of his mind back together, starting with the less damaged areas. The task was slow and arduous, but his efforts seemed to work. He didn't know the ratio of time between where Ken was and the constructed reality within his mind, or even the backyard where their bodies were. He had no choice but to keep working, and it seemed to take hours. Periodic exhaustion forced him to rest and refocus his efforts, and if he had been in his body, he was sure his chest would be heaving from exertion.

Staying focused, he lost himself in the pattern of finding and reuniting connections until finally, there was nothing left to fix. Exhausted, Brad merged back into his body, and his perceptions abruptly changed. The construct, even though it existed in his mind, seemed to operate like a physical place, and the pain and stiffness in his body returned. He was still draped across Ken, and the warmth of his solid body drove home a sense of urgency. He wanted Ken back more than anything so they could be together.

Opening his eyes, he rolled off Ken, and when he sat up, fresh tears filled his eyes at the vacant expression on Ken's face. Repairing the damage to his own mind took its toll, and he realized the worst was yet to come. It took quite an effort because of his fatigue and the weight of Ken's body, but Brad managed to lift Ken's head and shoulders onto his lap. While he caught his breath, he stared at Ken's face, caressing his forehead and brushing his hair back lovingly, drawing strength from the simple act of touching his soulmate.

It struck Brad how much he already missed the newfound bond he and Ken shared, literally feeling like half of him was missing.

Taking a deep breath to brace himself, he said, "Well, Ken, let's get this show on the road."

Brad placed his hands on either side of Ken's head, holding him firmly, and with a furrow of concentration creasing his brow, Brad entered Ken's mind.

Immediately he bounced back, recoiling in horror.

Fuck! How could it be so much worse!?

The damage wasn't anything like what he repaired in his own mind!

Fear gripped him, fear that there was no way he could fix the devastation he witnessed. He started to cry, holding Ken's head in his lap and rocking slowly as his tears dripped onto Ken's forehead. His prevailing thought was he should have taken more. If he had only taken more… but then they would both be gone. The earlier truth of Ken's words hit him, and he realized Ken might have been right all along.

How is this possible!?

Steadying himself, Brad plunged back into the desolation of what remained of Ken's mind.

The connections were so shattered and disconnected, it was like finding ten thousand needles in a thousand haystacks, hunting and shifting through every shred until he found a match to repair. In only a short time Brad was about to pass out from exhaustion, and he had barely scratched the surface.

As the song came to an end, the backyard fell silent again.

Kevin broke the quiet, asking, "Now what?"

Lane replied, "Now we wait. Whatever we did helped, I just hope it was enough."

Bill, monitoring both Brad and Ken, said, "Guys, they're breathing again; their pulses are weak but steady. If they get worse, we'll call the doc."

After a long, tense five minutes, Brad's pulse started racing and Bill said, "Something's happening."

Brad broke out into a heavy sweat, his breathing labored and raspy like he was exerting himself. His face flushed, and veins in his forehead, temples, and neck stood out as tears leaked from his eyes.

While Brad exhibited signs of extreme exertion, Ken's pulse weakened to the point where it was barely discernible.

Desperation was taking hold. Exhausted from his efforts, Brad was barely making any progress, and he instinctively felt time was running out. A groan of frustration escaped him when he had to stop and rest again, about ready to collapse.

Okay, Brad. This isn't working. Think, dumbass! Think!

A thought tugged at the back of his mind, but whatever it was kept eluding him. His thoughts racing out of control, he was beginning to panic. Just a short time ago Ken helped him relax, forcing him to stop and slow down, allowing him to focus.

Ken always knows what's best for me.

Brad repeated the phrase like a mantra and used his perfect recall to remember Ken's hands and their effect on him. Immersing himself in the memory calmed him, and when his thoughts slowed, he heard it… the haunting, beautiful song Lane sang. The one from his dream. The one he wrote at the River!

Fuck! Lane's been here! Maybe he can help!

After a short rest and encouraged by the thought of help, he focused and tried to contact Lane. Visualizing Lane in the backyard with everyone, he formed the picture, holding it firmly in his mind and mentally shouted as loud as he could.

Lane and Bill huddled on either side of Ken and Brad. After Lane finished his song, he set his guitar down and moved closer, holding one of Brad's hands and keeping his other hand on Brad's chest, feeling his heartbeat. Bryan stayed at Lane's side with his hands on Lane's shoulders.

Out of the blue, Brad's voice shouted in Lane's mind.

Lane!

Lane's head snapped up in surprise, and he would have fallen over if Bryan wasn't supporting him. His eyes widened, and everyone saw them turn white.

Brad!?

Lane! Thank God, you can hear me. Fuck, man, I need your help. I can't do this by myself!

Brad, you and Ken aren't looking so good. We can tell something's happening, but we don't know what to do. How the fuck are we talking in our heads?

Lane, I don't have time to explain. This might hurt, and I'm sorry, but...

Lane groaned and grabbed his head, unprepared for the searing pain as Brad pushed the information into his mind to show him how to help.

Through their mental communication, Lane was keenly aware of Brad's regret at causing him such discomfort. Instinctively, Brad knew he needed to keep their communication as much on the surface as possible. Merging like he did with Ken would have been too much, too soon.

As Lane's mind assimilated the information, the realization Ken and Brad had about the project and what the doctor did to them became clear, and he let out a mental: *Oh shit!*

Damn, that hurt like a son of a bitch!

I know, and I'm sorry. This is all new to me, too, and I'm learning as I go. Do you think you can help? Please, Lane, I don't think Ken has much time.

Not only yes, but hell yes. You know you don't have to ask, you dumbfuck. Gimme a sec, I need to talk to these ladies before they pee their pants.

<><>

Bryan's fingers digging into his shoulders brought Lane's perceptions back to his body.

"Lane! Talk to me! What's wrong?"

"I'm all right, Bry. Help me up."

Bryan stood up and brought Lane up with him.

"Guys, we don't have much time. I know it's weird, but Brad's talking to me in my head and needs our help. Ken's in bad shape, and Brad's not much better. Bill, Darren, and Loy come over here. Bry, Kev, Ricky, and Pat, if Brad or Ken stop breathing again do whatever you need to do to keep them alive and give us as much time as you can."

Turning back to Bill, Darren, and Loy, he continued, "Guys, we should sit down for this. I don't want you knuckleheads falling like sissies and splitting your skulls open. Face me and hold hands."

Between the strangeness of Lane's song and the effect it had on them, coupled with Ken and

Brad's condition and Lane talking to Brad in his head, they were unnerved. Adrenaline coursed through them, and they were tense and sweating, but Lane's instruction triggered their military discipline, and the act of following orders gave them something to focus on in the middle of the chaos and uncertainty.

<><>

Brad?

Yeah, I'm here.

I'm bringing company, buddy. Hold tight!

Understanding how Brad was able to leave his body, Lane didn't have time to be gentle and yanked Bill, Darren, and Loy out of theirs. He figured they were wired for it, just as he and Brad were, and he didn't want to give them time to overthink the situation, letting their instincts kick in. The doc told him to have faith in himself and go with his gut…

Lane grinned and couldn't help but think to himself: *Fuck, yeah! I could get used to this shit!*

<><>

Bill, Darren, and Loy felt like they got hit with a two by four on the back of their heads.

Alright guys, take a breath and settle down.

No longer in the backyard of Ken and Brad's house, they found themselves standing on a beach under a clear night sky beside a roaring bonfire. Brad sat on the ground with Ken's head in his lap and seemed unaware of them, his legs and shorts covered in blood from the gashes in Ken's back.

Alright, Brad, I'm here with Bill, Dar, and Loy. We're with you and Ken on the beach. Guys, I know this is all new and sudden, but you're going to have to learn how to do this on the fly if Ken has a chance of making it out of this. Ken's mind was shredded, and Brad's trying to piece it back together before their bodies give out in the backyard. All this Professor X bullshit is taking its toll, and we have to give Brad whatever he needs to finish the job.

Shit Lane, you brought the cavalry. Thanks, guys. I don't know if this is going to hurt or not. Hell, I'm not sure it won't kill some of us, so if anyone wants to back out, there's no hard feelings.

Through the mental link, the raw emotion behind Brad's words was clear; his desperation to save Ken, his gratitude at their presence, and his sincerity about giving them a chance to back out.

They wondered briefly at the strange transition between their minds and bodies, but their military discipline coupled with their love and support of Ken and Brad overrode any concerns, and they pushed all other thoughts and questions aside so they could face their brother's need.

Their voices were loud and clear in his mind, and Brad heard their words along with the intent behind them.

Loy: *I'm in.*

Bill: *Take whatever you need, Brad.*

Darren: *No way these sissies are outdoing me. You know I'm in.*

The selfless support and care they offered deeply affected him, filling Brad with warmth in the middle of his worry and anxiety over Ken, and even though they weren't touching, he felt their hands on his shoulders and back supporting him.

Lane moved behind Brad, placing his hands on Brad's head. He wasn't sure if it mattered, but it couldn't hurt.

Guys, get behind me and put your hands on my shoulders.

Bill: *Take your shirt off, Lane. The doc's always talking about the importance of skin contact. Your hands are touching Brad, and he's touching Ken. It might not matter, but why take a chance?*

Grinning, Lane stripped off his t-shirt, thinking: *I'm sure you just want to cop a feel, but whatever.*

Even in the direst situations in all their years running missions in Syria, Lane always managed to lighten the mood. With their newly awakened perceptions, all of them sank into the camaraderie between them, letting it wrap around them; their bonds ran deep, forged in their time in the military as SEALS running covert Special Operations and depending on each other for survival. They were brothers and would do anything for one another with no questions asked.

Loy, Bill, and Darren each placed a hand on Lane's back, and their other hand gripped the hand or shoulder of the man next to him. Brad held Ken's head in both his hands and Lane did the same to him.

Operating on pure instinct and intuition, Lane was going with his gut and following the doctor's advice. Even though what was happening was new to all of them, it seemed natural. The part of them that had been dormant for years after their initial changes was waking up; they were, as Lane put it, wired for what was happening.

Lane: *Alright, guys, I'll be the conduit. I'm going to channel all of us together and feed Brad what he needs.*

With the comfort of his brothers around him, feeding him their strength, Brad plunged back into Ken's mind. To his awareness, they were pillars of light, and he was unprepared for the amount of power that hit him.

Lane: *Sorry! I'll dial it back a little.*

No! It just was more than I expected. You guys are badass! I'll need it all before we're finished.

Bolstered by the support of his friends, Brad dove back into Ken, and with their backing he moved much faster. Because the damage in Ken's mind was unlike his own and far more extensive, it took longer, and near the halfway point they started to falter. None of them were used to the new type of exertion and didn't know how to conserve their strength or maximize their efforts, and they were breathing hard and sweating, pushing full throttle with everything they had in them.

With jaws clenched, their faces showed the intensity of their efforts.

Brad: *Guys, how are you holding up?*

Brad heard the mental equivalent of them gritting their teeth, but each of them said they were fine. They couldn't lie mind to mind, so he knew the truth of their words. They were tiring but would not give up, not when Ken needed them.

Lane, can you manage to talk to Bryan and see how Ken's doing topside?

With the time variance Lane was silent for a short time while he spoke to Bryan, and when he finally replied, he sounded worried.

Brad, they just started CPR on you and Ken. Your hearts have stopped, and Kev is calling the doc.

Damn! Okay, guys, don't panic. There's a significant time differential, so we're alright for a bit. I know you're tired, but if we can hold out just a little longer...

With the news of what was happening the power flowing into Brad surged, but he had no idea how long they could keep it up. He worked as quickly as he could, becoming more adept at finding and repairing connections, and the overall damage lessened as he learned how Ken's mind worked, enabling him to see patterns where Ken's unconscious mind tried to protect itself. Despite their efforts Brad had an intuitive sense something more profound was happening, but he didn't have any idea what to do about it, so he continued as best he could, hoping and praying it would be enough.

Brad realized they weren't going to finish in time and focused on making as many essential connections as possible and left the rest incomplete. He hoped if there was an initial connection, Ken's mind could attempt to build off those links and heal itself.

Within seconds of one another, his friends dropped out of the link. Darren passed out first, then Loy, and then Bill. Lane was still with him but hardly had anything left to give, and Brad was holding on by a thread himself.

Lane, I still need to get Ken back to his body. I have to save what strength I have left for that, or all this won't mean anything.

What do you mean get him? Where is he?

It's hard to explain. We were together, somewhere, and I came back here to do this.

Can I help?

No Lane, you've done more than enough. You've all done more than Ken and I have a right to ask.

That's bullshit, and you know it. Alright man, I'm going to bounce. I think I'm going to sleep for a week!

See you topside.

<><>

Taking a deep breath, Brad set the image of Ken in his mind and willed himself back to his lover. The blackness seemed colder and longer returning to Ken as if he were much further away, and as he appeared Brad barely squeaked out, "Hey, man," before collapsing.

"Brad!"

Ken moved fast enough to catch him before he hit the ground, picking him up and cradling him against his chest. Brad didn't have the strength to form words, so he merged their minds again.

Immediately, Ken was aware of everything Brad and his buddies did up to that point. Stunned at how much danger they put themselves in for him he was angry at Brad for asking and allowing them to do what they did, but at the same time their love and intent were evident. His anger turned to acceptance, even pride at their efforts, and he was humbled by what they were willing to sacrifice for him.

With tears in his eyes from the emotional intensity of everything he learned, Ken thought: *So, what now, B?*

Ken, I'm not sure what we did was enough. I tried so hard, we all did, but the damage was so much worse than I imagined.

Ken tightened his arms, kissing the top of Brad's head and wrapping his presence around him.

I know you did your best. All of you did. How could I ask for more than you've already done?

When Ken picked him up, with the touch of their skin, Brad started feeling better, but he was still near the end of his endurance. With the intimacy of their merge, both men were very aware of being naked and touching, taking comfort from both aspects of their connection. Ken set Brad down, and they assumed their signature hug with their chins resting on each other's shoulders and their arms wrapped around each other tightly. The physical touch soothed them even more with their minds blended, and with Time barely moving they held their embrace, not wanting to let go.

Realizing they were putting off the inevitable, Ken eventually broke the silence.

B, you gotta promise me if we make it back and it didn't work... Well, I don't wanna live broken. Promise me you won't try 'ta keep me around if I'm too far gone.

It tore Brad's heart out, but he reluctantly agreed.

First things first, we need to make it back to the beach, then I need to get us back to our bodies. Let's go.

Brad expected it to be more difficult, but there was no strain; their souls wanted to return to the part of them still at the River. It took longer than expected and he almost panicked, thinking they would be lost in the darkness forever, and a sigh of relief escaped him when they appeared on the beach.

Separating their minds, Brad gently pushed Ken into his body and then went back into his own.

Opening his eyes, he gazed down at Ken, noting the now peaceful expression on his face as if he were asleep. His eyes were closed, but the chilling, vacant expression from earlier was gone, and Brad took encouragement from that.

God, I hope it was enough, Ken. You have to be alright.

"Okay, step one completed. I don't know what to expect when we get back to our bodies. No matter what, I love you."

He leaned over and kissed Ken's forehead, putting all his love into the gesture.

Closing his eyes, Brad gathered the last of his strength and willed them out of that place and back to their physical bodies in the backyard. The River was a construct within Brad's mind, a place he needed to hold the creature prisoner, and with the construct no longer needed it shattered into non-existence as Brad and Ken left it for the final time.

Bryan and Rick monitored Ken while Kevin and Patrick watched Brad, keeping tabs on their vital signs. While watching over Brad and Ken, they kept stealing nervous glances at their partners to make sure they were alright. The events of the night were unlike anything they had ever experienced even with their enhancements and abilities, and there was an edge of nervousness they were unaccustomed to. Together, particularly as a team, they had yet to encounter anything they couldn't overcome.

Bryan's deep voice tensed as he said, "Ricky! Ken stopped breathing!"

They immediately started CPR with Bryan blowing air into Ken's mouth while Rick performed chest compressions, maintaining oxygen perfusion to Ken's brain and heart.

Seconds later Brad stopped breathing, and Kevin and Patrick started CPR on him. Rick set his phone down and hit the doctor's number on speed dial, putting it on speaker. The call went straight to voicemail, and Rick hit the key to bypass the greeting message, yelling towards the phone, "Doc! We have multiple 911s here! We need you now!"

Rick kept shifting his eyes to Lane and the others, watching for some sign of what was happening. He had no way to signal and let them know what was going on with Ken and Brad.

It wasn't long before Lane, Loy, Bill, and Darren started breathing heavy and sweating, outwardly exhibiting the strain of what was occurring in their minds. A minute later Darren fell over unconscious, followed by Loy, then Bill, and finally Lane, all within the space of a few seconds.

When Darren collapsed Pat let out a frustrated, "FUCK!" and rushed over to check on him, but it was quickly apparent Darren and the others were alright and breathing normally.

Pat said, "I think they passed out. They seem fine, just exhausted."

He leaped back over and resumed chest compressions on Brad.

Kevin was about ready to call it when Brad's eyes popped open. He jerked upright, sucking air into his lungs, and looked around briefly with a confused expression before promptly passing out.

A split-second later Ken's body jerked and went still, but he started breathing on his own.

Rick's phone dinged with a text message from the doctor.

"The doc says he's aware of everything and to get everybody to the lab, ASAP!"

It took a few trips to get the six unconscious men loaded into their Explorers without the neighbors seeing anything, and then they took off for the lab.

An agitated doctor waited for them at the door, adding to the strangeness of the night's events. In all their years of working with him, the doctor never panicked even when someone was hurt, and seeing him upset was unnerving.

Kevin, Bryan, Rick, and Pat quickly and efficiently got everyone inside, stripped, and into a bed, helping the doctor with the ECG leads, catheters, and other equipment.

Bryan was normally stoic and reserved, but Kevin noticed how calm he seemed even with Lane unconscious. Wondering if something else was going on, he asked Bryan if everything was alright.

"It's hard to describe Kev, but I just know Lane's okay. We've been using that trick Ken and Brad discovered, and ever since that first night we've been more in tune with one another. Then Lane started having these dreams, which were all a part of this. I'm not sure what's happening to us, and I know it looks like a disaster tonight, but I can't help feeling that everything's fine. I just wish the doc would tell us more."

Kevin looked thoughtful but didn't reply, and not long after their exchange the doctor called everyone together.

"William, Loy, Darren, and Lane are stable. None of them are familiar with exerting themselves in this new manner, and they exhausted themselves. If you think of the mind as a muscle, they will need to exercise their new abilities over time to gain strength and endurance. What they did was remarkable, and you should be very proud of them."

Bryan asked, "What about Brad and Ken?"

"I am not sure. I believe Bradford will fully recover, but we must wait until Kenneth wakes to assess his condition."

Later that night, the doctor stood between the beds where Brad and Ken lay recovering. With a heavy sigh he recited an ancient prayer for his young charges, wondering how events could have gotten out of control so quickly. The timing of

Ken's abduction just as he, Brad, and now Lane, experienced their first awakening... He sensed outside influences amidst events, but whose?

Ken showed no outward sign of any injuries, but the Doctor wasn't sure what state his mind might be in when he regained consciousness. The temptation to find out was almost unbearable, but in all the years of his penance he had not broken his oath, and for the sake of the other young men in his care, he refrained.

Brad and the others were heroic in their efforts to save Ken, even at significant risk to themselves, and would recover with rest, but the doctor had an uneasy feeling about Ken.

As he went back to his office, it dawned on him how quiet the lab was. Looking around, he saw Bryan, Rick, Pat, and Kevin fast asleep. He thought it odd, but with the stress of the evening they were most likely exhausted. The only sounds in the lab were the occasional chirps and beeps of equipment.

In the middle of the night, while monitoring Ken's brain activity from his office, there was a sudden massive spike on the monitor. Rushing to the room where Brad and Ken were still asleep, he saw no outward sign of what happened. He turned on the small reading lamp at the head of Ken's bed to see better, and as he reached for Ken's wrist to check his pulse, he noticed a rolled-up parchment sitting on the nightstand.

The doctor's heart nearly faltered at the sight of the wax seal binding the apparent missive. His hands trembling, he picked it up, examining it more closely. Yes! It had been nearly a century since he last saw it, but he would recognize it anywhere; two quills crossed, each with a drop of ink at its tip. His heart raced as he looked around the lab, almost frantic for any sign of the man he knew left the note.

Not seeing anyone, he thought: *Disappointing, but not unexpected.*

Quickly checking Brad and Ken to reaffirm they were alright, the doctor left the room and returned to his office. Once at his desk, his hands shaking, he broke the seal and unrolled the parchment. It was written in an elegant flowing script, in a language few in the world could now read.

<>

Aaron, my love,

How I yearn to see you again after the long years that have separated us. I begged Charisa to bring this message so I could at least be near you, even for the briefest of seconds.

It seems you are doing well. I have had news of your mission, and the Elders are pleased. Pleased enough to right a grievous wrong of which you are most likely unaware. It seems one of our brethren betrayed The Order to The Enemy, and he is the one ultimately responsible for the deception and kidnapping of Kenneth Habersham, orchestrating the entire affair through a former colleague of yours, General Burgess.

I am sure you found it curious that two of your charges, and now possibly others, have experienced their first awakening. This is no coincidence. Nephilim have shown themselves recently, but we are unsure what their presence means, and there are ripples everywhere.

Because of the direct interference of The Enemy, I was allowed to act and restore Kenneth Habersham. As brave and heroic an effort as Brad Wilson and the others made, their efforts were not enough. The damage to young Habersham's mind was not natural, and even with full training and at the height of their abilities, it might not have been possible. Fortunately for us, the zeal of our Enemy was their undoing. Their transgression against the balance allowed us an opening to correct this wrong. Sent by Charissa with a Blessing from The Mantle, I finished what Brad Wilson and the others started.

In the morning, Ken Habersham will awake healed and whole and can continue his path of discovering his awakened talents along with your other charges.

Aaron, after reading Ken and the others, I believe we were right all along! The Elders must see it even if they are too stubborn to admit it. These young men will be our salvation!

It is my fervent prayer that you and I will be united once again before too many years come to pass. Until then, my love, I wish you well and safe journey and continued success in your mission.

With all my love,

Albrecht

<>

Knowing Albrecht had been in the lab, so close yet unable to communicate in person, was heartbreaking. Even in the joy and relief of knowing Ken would fully recover, in a rare show of vulnerability, the doctor wept silently in the quiet of the lab, holding the scroll in his hands and trying to envision the face of the man who wrote it.

He decided not to tell his young charges what happened, at least not immediately. They needed time to recover and grow into themselves. He was so proud of each and every one of them and realized over the years if he gave them space, they grew better and stronger without being pushed.

It was late, so the doctor checked on his charges one more time and then went to his bed to dream about Albrecht, the love of his life and the other half of his soul.

<><>

Early the next morning, everyone except Ken was up and moving by 0600. None of them were in the mood to do PT, so a few of the guys ventured out to get breakfast for everyone. The doctor, not an early riser, didn't come out of his room until nearly 0930.

When he finally emerged from his room, nine impatient men awaited him. Shuffling over to get some coffee, which they politely left for him, he sat down to eat his breakfast, deliberately eating slow. Knowing the men would fidget, he had a hard time not smiling at their impatience. He enjoyed teasing them but knew their anxiety over Ken was very real, so he didn't prolong his joke.

Once finished, pushing his plate back and wiping his mouth with a napkin, he turned to them and asked, "I take it you are all feeling better?"

Everyone nodded their confirmation.

"And you, Bradford, are you sure you feel well?"

"Just a little tired, doc. Other than that, I feel better than I have in over a month. With that thing out of me, I'm as good as new."

"I am pleased to hear that; however, I wish to run some tests to be sure. We must be absolutely certain your body suffers no lasting damage."

Brad asked impatiently, "Doc, Ken's still asleep. Do you know if he's going to be okay?"

"Well, I have some good news and some bad news as far as Kenneth is concerned. Which would you like to hear first?"

All of them needed some good news, especially Brad, who was about to burst, and he blurted out, "Good first!"

"Well, my boy, the good news is that Kenneth is going to make a full recovery."

He didn't get any further before Brad let out a "WHOOP!" and jumped into the air. His eyes immediately reddened, and his chest tightened with emotion as relief took hold of him.

Everyone let out cries of 'alright!' and 'I knew it,' and there were hugs and high fives all around. Each of them pulled Brad into a firm embrace, expressing their own relief and happiness at the news. The smiles and tears in their eyes stated how much the news meant to them. It took a minute for everyone to settle down, and even then none of them could wipe the grins off their faces.

Brad felt as if the weight of the world lifted from his shoulders, and with a slight tremble in his voice, he said, "Okay, doc. Let's get the bad news out of the way."

"The bad news is that you will have to contain yourself for a few more days. I have Kenneth in an induced coma to give his mind time to finish mending. I am assisting his recovery as much as I am safely able to do, but it will still take a few days. The mind is very complex, and the damage severe, but you all did an exceptional job and should be extremely proud of yourselves."

The doctor disliked bending the truth, but the time wasn't right to reveal what happened.

Brad picked the doctor up in a bear hug and whispered with a choked voice in his ear, "Thank you so much, doc. I don't know what I would have done if I lost him."

One of his rare smiles crossed the doctor's face, and he patted Brad on his back, saying, "Me too, my boy, me too."

Another round of exuberant hoots and hollers followed, and the smiles and tears of relief continued. They were going to get their friend, their brother, their Captain back!

With the assurance Ken was going to be alright, everyone but Brad left the lab. Before they left, the doctor reiterated the rule of no one traveling alone, whether it was work, shopping, running errands, or whatever. It would make life more difficult, but everyone would cope, and after Ken's abduction, the necessity from a tactical and safety perspective was more evident than ever.

Each couple asked Brad if he wanted them to stay and be with him while he waited, and he was touched by their offers but declined, knowing they needed their own rest and recuperation after all the stress. They hugged him long and tight or cupped his neck or shoulders with firm squeezes of comfort before they left, making sure he knew how important he was to them, as well as Ken. Brad soaked it all in, and their support and affections, along with knowing Ken was going to be alright, gave him a sense of inner peace and strength to wait patiently. He promised to let all of them know as soon as Ken woke up.

The doctor used the last of the prepared syringes on Brad to ensure his body's full recovery. His organs did exhibit signs of minor distress, but by the following morning, with the increased potency of the serum, his body completely regenerated.

The doctor started returning to his house in the evenings, and Brad pulled another bed into Ken's room so he could sleep beside him. Even though Ken was going to be alright Brad hardly left his side, holding his hand while watching TV, reading, or while he slept.

Without being asked, the guys took turns dropping by over the next few days to visit and make sure Brad and the doctor were well fed.

The doctor didn't tell Brad he scheduled the induced coma to stop the morning of the third day.

Brad had a strange sense of being watched, and it woke him up out of a deep sleep. Slowly opening his eyes, he saw Ken stretched out on his side with his head propped up on one hand. The sight of him, awake and healthy, even though Brad knew he was going to be alright, hit him hard. Brad's eyes raked over all of him, from his feet to his handsome face, drinking in the sight, and finally their eyes met.

With a grin, Ken said, "Hey, handsome. What's a fella gotta do around here 'ta get some food? I'm starvin'!"

Even knowing Ken was going to recover, when Brad saw him awake and heard his voice he was overcome with emotion. He threw himself on Ken, wrapping his arms around him and burrowing his face against Ken's neck, bawling like a baby, sobbing so hard his throat closed and he couldn't talk. Ken cried too while he held Brad and let him cry, one hand cupping the back of his head and the other rubbing his back.

Brad finally managed to say, "Fuck, Ken, I love you so much. I don't know what I would have done if you hadn't made it."

Ken's throat was tight too, but he managed to whisper, "Shhhh B, it's okay. I love you too! I'm right here, and I'm not goin' anywhere."

After a slight pause Ken chuckled, hugging Brad even tighter and said, "I was about 'ta say more than you'll ever know, but that's not true anymore, is it?"

Brad pulled back enough to look into Ken's eyes, and Ken cupped Brad's face in his hands, wiping away the tears with his thumbs. Ken was right, and now that he was awake, they were aware of the connection between them.

Brad sniffed and said, "This is going to take some getting used to. We won't even have to talk if we don't want to."

Brad put his comment into action, pulling their minds together, and their awareness of each other deepened to an intimately painful state with their thoughts and emotions open and bare to one another.

The relief Brad experienced when he saw Ken awake was there, and also excitement at seeing his naked, muscular body. There was no embarrassment over that, and Ken's reaction was the same. Their bodies wanted to connect just as their minds did, and their breath caught in their chests as their eyes watered in response to what was happening.

Brad lifted up his t-shirt, slowly peeling it off, and Ken drank in the sight of his lover, grinning when he saw the tent in Brad's jeans.

B, you better get those jeans off fast unless you want me 'ta rip them off.

Ken somehow managed to produce a small bottle of lube, handing it to Brad, and he realized Ken planned what was happening.

With a grin, Brad thought: *You douche.*

Ken grinned back and thought: *You're just jealous 'cause I'm one step ahead of 'ya. You slept too long.*

Unable to quit smiling, Brad was naked in seconds. It had been weeks since they had been together in the physical realm, and their need for one another was apparent. Ken started their physical bond, and with the additional element of their minds blended, their lust and love elevated to an entirely new level.

When Ken entered Brad, both of them thought: *Oh, fuck, that's amazing,* at the same time, making them laugh, but the shared intimacy of their minds and bodies quickly consumed them.

Neither one of them had ever been more turned on or attracted to the other. As much as Ken wanted to take things slow and reacquaint themselves with one another, their urgency was too much to put off, and their coupling became a fast and frantic need to get off. In only a few minutes, they were both sweating and breathing heavily, while Ken continued a running dialogue in Brad's mind of how hot he was, how much he loved him, and what a great lover he was. Brad was never as verbal, but his emotions were clear, which turned Ken on even more.

The moment seemed to take forever, and it might have as deeply as they were in each other. Their orgasms built quickly and hit them hard, but neither of them went soft. Strength flooded into Brad as their DNA reacted, and Ken was able to rest his full weight on his lover. It was the first time they made physical love while merged, and the entire experience was different. Each knew what the other wanted without having to be told; where or how to touch, or lick, or caress. With one orgasm behind them they lasted longer, exploring each other and relishing their new connection.

Once they both came again, they continued to kiss and cuddle, pressed together while looking into each other's eyes. No words were spoken or thought, they simply rested in one another, content to be together in mind and body.

As their breath finally returned to normal, Ken's stomach let out the loudest rumble of hunger Brad had ever heard. Their eyes went wide in surprise, and they both busted out laughing. Brad put his hands on Ken's chest to push himself up, getting in one last squeeze of Ken's rock-solid body.

Brad said, "Okay, let's get you something to eat. I need to feed you."

Ken sat on the edge of the bed and wrapped his arms around Brad before he could move away, pulling Brad back against him for one more hug and kissed his back. With his face pressed against Brad's back his voice was slightly muffled as he said, "Yeah, B, seriously, I can't believe you put your selfish need 'ta get off before my well-bein'. I'm gonna have 'ta talk 'ta the doc about the hired help."

Brad laughed and replied, "Alright mister, get your ass off that bed. We need to throw these sheets in the wash and grab a quick shower. I want to take you someplace nice, and while I have the utmost appreciation for how you smell right now, I'm not sure the general public does."

◇◇

Neither of them stated the obvious because now they could feel it, but they were relieved to have all the nastiness behind them and to be back to normal. Well, mostly normal. The fact they heard and felt each other's thoughts wasn't exactly normal and would take some getting used to. It was nice to relax with each other and be themselves, with no barriers between them.

They thought they were perfect together before, but living with their minds open and bare to one another was both liberating and frightening. It was also beautiful, and neither of them would change it for all the world. To know each other so intimately was something neither of them had ever dreamed possible.

They knew the doctor wanted to talk to them, but for the time being he gave them space and time to themselves. There were significant adjustments ahead of them, and Brad had a lot to learn about controlling his new abilities.

Here ends Book One of **The Order: Vitruvian Man**

The story of Brad and Ken and their brothers continues in:

Book Two of **The Order: Heritage**

Book Three of **The Order: Nephilim Rising**

Book Four of **The Order: Revelation**

Book Five of **The Order: Sacrifice**

Book Six of **The Order: Redemption**

Email:
bookofloagaeth@gmail.com

Twitter:
BATownsend_Author
@BookofLoagaeth

Appendix for Book one of The Order: Vitruvian Man

The team

Rank/Birth Name	Current Name
LCDR Bruce Dutcher	(Capt.) Ken Habersham
LT Alan Whetherson	Bradford (Brad) Wilson
LT Don Elenburg	Bryan (Bry) Gunter
LT Jim Barton	Lane Weaver
LT James Schrader	Patrick (Pat) Manning
LT Dan Shogren	Darren (Dar) Wilcox
LT Keith Abrams	Kevin (Kev) Ayers
LT Fred Martin	Willian (Bill) Brennan
LT Paul Tibedeaux	Richard (Rick(y)) Crawford
LT Gary Bolin	Loy Barton

The Couples

Brad/Ken

Lane/Bryan (Bry)

Darren (Dar)/Patrick (Pat)

Bill/Kevin (Kev)

Loy/Rick (Ricky)

Their Mentor

Dr. Aaron Thomas

The bodies (Ken, Bryan, Pat, Kevin, Ricky)

At the inception of the program Ken, Bryan, Pat, Kevin, and Ricky (under their original names of Bruce, Don, James, Keith, and Paul) had their physical bodies changed by Dr. Aaron Thomas, altering their genetic code into a 'perfect state.' They are the pinnacle of human physical potential, immune to viruses and diseases, their skin smooth and blemish-free. As a result of the genetic alterations, the men stopped aging, and while they can be killed, they are effectively immortal.

Their muscle and bone density is nearly four times that of a fit, adult, human male, vastly increasing their strength and weight. When pushed, they can bench press nearly one thousand pounds. To compensate for the increased density, their bodies contain a significantly higher level of oxygen, which helps with buoyancy and fuels their muscles. Numerous other changes exist, many of which are still dormant.

Their body fat percentage is fixed at 8%, making them lean and vascular. While they are large and muscular, they are not grotesquely so (more like an off-season bodybuilder).

Their body temperature is five degrees higher than a normal human and coupled with their natural charisma, it makes them very comforting to be around. They radiate health and strength.

Their senses are also greatly enhanced along with their balance, agility, and dexterity.

The minds (Brad, Lane, Darren, Bill, Loy)

At the inception of the program Brad, Lane, Darren, Bill, and Loy (under their original names of Alan, Jim, Dan, Fred, and Gary) had their physical bodies and minds changed by Dr. Aaron Thomas into a 'perfect state' just as their counterparts, the bodies. They are also the pinnacle of human potential, immune to viruses and diseases, and their skin is smooth and blemish-free. They stopped aging, the same as the bodies, and are also immortal.

Their bodies were altered somewhat but not to the extent of their partners. They do not have the bone or muscle density of the bodies, rather their minds were altered, and they now have perfect recall and photographic memories. Their intelligence is extremely high, with their IQ's approaching 200. They keep in exceptional physical shape, mainly to perform the physical exams on their partners to keep their bodies in alignment. Numerous other changes exist, many of which are still dormant.

The most powerful aspect of their initial change is their empathic ability, allowing them to read and project emotions. Their empathic ability can be used at range, but is much stronger through touch.

Physical Characteristics and Upbringing (current names are used to avoid confusion)

Ken Habersham:

Ken is 5'10", weighs 420 lbs., and has dark brown hair and green eyes. Ken is one of those men who has a perpetual five o'clock shadow. He is physically the most muscular of the group, although Kevin has more mass. Ken has a light dusting of hair on his chest, arms, legs, and under his arms.

Ken has no knowledge of any living relatives. He was placed in foster care as an infant, and then transferred to an orphanage at age twelve when his foster mother died, and the father could not handle an extra child in the house. Ken stayed in an orphanage until he graduated high school. He left, got a job, and entered a community college, managing on scholarships and financial aid. He was able to transfer to a four-year university and attained a degree in Criminal Justice before joining the Navy. Ken met Kevin in the Navy, and they went through BUDS together. They are the only two men that knew each other prior to the program.

Brad Wilson:

Brad is 6'2" and weighs 245 lbs. He has light blond hair, almost golden, and light blue eyes. Brad has a hairy chest, arms, and legs, but no hair on his shoulders or back. He does occasionally trim his body hair but rarely shaves smooth.

Brad has no knowledge of any living relatives. He never knew his father, and his mother passed away when he was eleven. He was passed between three separate foster homes until he graduated high school. Brad went straight to college, attaining a degree in Mathematics before joining the Navy.

Bryan Gunter:

Bryan is 6'0" and weighs 425 lbs. He has light brown hair and green eyes. He has minimal body hair and does not trim or shave.

Bryan was raised in a foster home from the time he was an infant. His foster family died in a car accident, and the State of Georgia managed to track down his natural grandparents in Savannah, GA. He lived with them through high school, but they passed away from old age and infirmity just after he graduated. Not knowing what path in life he wanted to take, Bryan worked for a few years before joining the Navy. As a result of not having a college degree, Bryan was forced to pass additional tests before being accepted into the BUDS program and becoming a SEAL.

Lane Weaver:

Lane is 5'11" and weighs 235 lbs. He has dark brown hair and eyes. Lane has some hair on his chest, arms, and legs, but is otherwise smooth.

Lane's mother died giving birth to him, and when he was four his father abandoned him. He was fostered temporarily and passed between a number of families until he graduated high school. While in high school, he was notified of his birth father's death by a rare and aggressive form of cancer. Lane attended a community college and achieved a two-year degree before transferring to a major university and finishing a dual degree program in Music and Fine Arts. Unsure what to do with his degrees, Lane joined the Navy hoping to travel the world.

Patrick Manning:

Pat is 6'0" and weighs 430 lbs. He has light brown hair and brown eyes. Pat has thick, dark brown hair on his chest, stomach, arms, and legs, but his shoulders and back are smooth. He occasionally trims his body hair.

When he was six years old Pat was the only survivor of a tragic and fiery car accident, where his entire family was killed. He almost died himself and was in a coma for weeks before waking up. He remained catatonic for days, and it took him almost a year to start speaking again. He had troubles through school and was passed from family to family until he graduated high school. Pat went to a four-year college and attained a degree in History before joining the Navy.

Darren Wilcox:

Darren is 5'9" and weighs 240lbs. He has dark brown hair and green eyes. Darren has very little body hair and doesn't trim or shave.

When Darren was three years old, he was the only survivor of a house fire and became a ward of the state. He was fostered through three different families until he graduated high school. Darren went to a local university and attained   a   degree   in   Business Administration before joining the Navy.

Kevin Ayers:

Kevin is 6'2" and weighs 450 lbs. He has jet black hair and dark brown eyes. Kevin is very hairy but keeps himself trimmed, shaving his shoulders and back (with Bill's help).

Kevin has no knowledge of any living relatives. His mother gave him up for adoption at birth, and any knowledge of her was kept from him. He lived in an orphanage until he was five when he joined a foster family. There was trouble with other fostered children in his home, and he was passed to another few families as a teenager until he graduated high school. Kevin stayed out of school for two years before going to college and getting a two-year degree in English before joining the Navy.

Bill Brennan:

Bill is 6'4" and weighs 265 lbs. He has medium brown hair and blue eyes. Bill is naturally smooth.

Bill was literally left on the doorstep of an orphanage and has no knowledge of his parents or any living relatives. He was fostered as an infant up through grade school, where his foster family had to turn him back over to the state for financial reasons. As a teenager Bill found out they were killed in a plane crash. Bill stayed with another foster family temporarily but was eventually put back in an orphanage where he stayed until he graduated high school. Bill went to a major university where he attained a degree in Computer Science before joining the Navy.

Rick Crawford:

Rick is 5'10" and weighs 425 lbs. Rick has brown hair and blue eyes. Rick has a moderate amount of body hair which he keeps trimmed.

Rick's father was in the Army and died in a training accident when Rick was nine years old. After his father's death, his mother went into a deep depression and a year later committed suicide, leaving Rick on his own. He was fostered, but troubled, and his foster family put him back in an orphanage until he graduated high school. He had a few run-ins with the law and ended up in the Juvenile Justice System, where a guard took him under his wing and kept him out of any serious trouble. The guard was former Navy and convinced Rick to go to college and join the service. While Rick was in College the guard was killed in a prison fight, and to honor his memory Rick continued the path he promised and became a SEAL.

Loy Barton:

Loy is 6'1 and weighs 245 lbs. He has dark brown hair and eyes. Loy is very hairy but trimmed, keeping his shoulders and back smooth.

Loy was born to a single mother and never knew his father. His mother was killed in a robbery when he was seven, witnessing her getting shot in front of him. He was troubled and often ran away from his foster families. Eventually, he ran away and managed to live on his own. He dropped out of school but got his GED before going to a community college and getting a Vet Tech degree. He was never able to settle and wanted to travel, so he joined the Navy in hopes of seeing more of the world.

www.ingramcontent.com/pod-product-compliance
Lightning Source LLC
Chambersburg PA
CBHW030914050726
47498CB00003BA/741